CASCADE

SATURN'S LEGACY BOOK 2

JOSHUA JAMES

Copyright © 2022 by Joshua James

———

Cover Artwork by J Caleb Design
Edited by Scarlett R. Algee

———

GET FREE BOOKS!

Building a relationship with readers is my favorite thing about writing.

My regular newsletter, *The Reader Crew,* is the best way to stay up-to-date on new releases, special offers, and all kinds of cool stuff about science fiction past and present.

Just for joining the fun, I'll send you 3 free books.

Join The Reader Crew (it's free) today!

—Joshua James

SATURN'S LEGACY SERIES

All books available in Kindle Unlimited

Artifact

Cascade

Lineage

Awakened

PROLOGUE

Presidential Emergency Operations Center, Washington, D.C.

A DOZEN MEN and women sat around the table, watching the screen in silence. They had viewed the same video half a dozen times: first, the recording of Lt. Larry Munroe threatening the general of the Tiān Zhuānjiā ship; then the video of Space Corpsman Frank Grady, denouncing the behavior of his former commander.

As the video ended, frozen on an unflattering still of Frank Grady's face, the assembled officials let out a collective sigh.

"Bottom line," said Vice-President Perez. "Was he acting on anyone's authority when he fired on that German ship?"

General Reeves shook her head emphatically as Defense Secretary Owens said, "Absolutely not, sir."

Perez slumped against the table, letting out a disgruntled sigh. "So what are our options?"

"Honestly?" Reeves drummed her fingers against the table. "They're few and far between. From what we can tell, the Russians have a crew deployed out there, and the Tiān Zhuānjiā too, obviously. Our next closest ship is stationed near Titan, but it's mostly researchers."

"What about the research station on Enceladus?" asked the press secretary.

Everyone turned their heads slowly to examine him. Secretary Kelley was new to the job, and despite his posting, he never actually seemed to read the briefs.

"They're dead," said Perez flatly. "Enceladus is being contested."

"If we don't have people in the area, what's the point?" asked Kelley, leaning back in his rolling chair.

"The point," said Perez bitterly, "is that at the heart of that sad little moon lies one of the greatest weapons known to man, *allegedly*, and we don't want it falling into the hands of the enemy."

Kelley pursed his lips. "Look, I understand the image issue here—it's not going to look good if word gets out that we're sitting on a state secret of this magnitude, and the fact that an American fires the first shot in the incident is a major problem. Now, I can spin that, but let me tell you something." He jabbed his pen at the screen. "If the Tiān Zhuānjiā forces had actually gotten their hands on a weapon that remarkable, that would *not* be the message they'd put out. They'd be making a public statement, undermining our authority, taking what they wanted. It would be all over the internet. They wouldn't be playing games."

Perez studied Kelley. No wonder he'd been promoted to the position.

"You think there's still time to get someone else out there," said the defense secretary thoughtfully. "Enceladus isn't a lost cause?"

Kelley waved a dismissive hand at the screen. "Trust me, these folks know how to run a mean PR campaign, and this doesn't add up."

That certainly put a new spin on things. Perez leaned forward, drumming his fingers on the glass-topped table. "All right, then let's play it this way. Reeves, I want your best men out there *yesterday*. And somebody get me an astrophysicist who knows what the hell they're talking about. Someone who can keep their mouth shut. And Kelley..."

Kelley folded his hands, sitting up straight as if he was a fifth-grader hoping to get a gold star for participation.

"Kelley, figure out how to spin this. We need to get ahead of this story."

"Yes, sir," said Kelley.

"What exactly is my team supposed to do?" asked General Reeves.

Perez got up from his chair and pulled on his jacket, straightening the sleeves as he answered. "They're going out to what's left of Enceladus, and God willing, they're going to get that weapon before our enemies do. Does anyone know what happened to the artifacts that Munroe took up there? The ones that got us into this mess?"

"Impossible to say, sir," said the Director of National Intelligence. "Best guess, based on Operation Cascade mission parameters, is they are lost on Enceladus."

Perez rubbed his temples. "All right. Understood." It was a

shame, given how many man-hours had gone into retrieving the things, never mind the budget. It was too bad that Munroe had blown the whole scenario, too.

Oh, well. At least if they were lost, that meant *no one* had them. It was comforting to know that the other heads of state were sweating bullets, too.

Ur-An, Iraq

LANCE CORPORAL WILLIAM COLLINS stared down at the coffins and sighed.

"Is it just me," he asked, "or does it feel like we're always on cleanup duty?"

"It's not just you." His buddy, Michael Vasko, fired up his vape. "But here's one for *you*—is it just *me*, or does this have Munroe's stink all over it?"

There were plenty of similarities between what had happened here not so long ago and what had happened on Mars, now that Collins thought about it. He unwrapped another stick of gum and leaned back against the dig house, watching the men move around them. He composed a private list of everything that seemed familiar: the sand, the archaeological site, the dead researchers killed under mysterious circumstances. Munroe wasn't the only jackass with a commission in the Space Corps, but this was mighty familiar.

Vasko gagged. "Don't know how you can chew that shit. Rots

your teeth."

"Says the man smoking a cancer stick," Collins retorted. "Settle down, Vasko. We're on the same side."

Vasko sat down on one of the coffins and smacked his hand against the cheap wooden lid. "That's what these poor saps probably thought, too."

"Gentlemen!" called a voice from across the hills, and both men looked toward the woman who was striding down the hill toward them. Collins straightened his spine and saluted, tucking his gum into his cheek. Vasko saluted lazily. He didn't bother trying to hide the vape, but he did stand up from the coffin.

Collins didn't recognize the woman who came striding down the hill towards them. She wore a Space Corps uniform, and the two silver bars on her chest marked her as a captain. Her nametag said *Sanz*.

"Collins?" she asked. When her eyes flicked toward Vasko, she wrinkled her nose. "May I ask what the two of you are doing?"

"Following orders, ma'am," said Vasko, lifting the vape to his lips with a smug smile. The guy hated authority.

Collins and Vasko had been in the first batch of recruits to go through the Space Corps. Back then, Space Corpsman had largely been picked for their size and hardiness—Vasko certainly hadn't been selected for his *brains*—but apparently there'd been a shift in that trend. Captain Sanz was small but sturdy, with thick black hair pulled back into a tidy bun that nestled just beneath the band of her hat. Judging by her build and the way she surveyed the terrain, Collins would have put his money on her training as a sharpshooter. He also suspected that she didn't miss a thing.

"You're being reassigned," she said. "Grab your things. I want you at the helicopter in ten minutes."

"Everyone?" asked Collins.

Sanz shook her head. "Just the two of you. We're forming a task force. Didn't you get the memo?"

"No service out here," Vasko drawled.

Sanz took a step back, the hint of a smile tugging at her lips, as if she knew something they didn't. "Get used to it," she said. "The service at our next posting will be worse."

"We're going offworld," Collins said flatly. He and Vasko had been shuffled around ever since the events on Mars, and they hadn't spent much time in space. He'd missed the novelty of it, but after everything that had gone down, he wasn't sure how he felt about shipping back out.

"Told you this had something to do with Munroe," Vasko muttered.

Sanz's smile disappeared. "Lieutenant Munroe is dead. Nine minutes, men. The clock is ticking."

Collins' eyebrows shot up as Sanz stalked back toward the helicopter.

"Dead," Vasko said. "Well, what do you think of that? Didn't see that one coming, that's for sure." He tucked his vape away, then headed for the tents, leaving Collins to stand guard over the dead.

He should get moving, he knew, but Collins was stuck in his own head. He was certain now that there was a connection, and if he and Vasko were being reassigned, it was because someone up the chain of command thought that they had particular value. The only thing that came to mind was their experience on Mars, which meant that whatever was going on now was related to that mess.

He couldn't help wondering what their old friend Carpenter Lowell would have to say about all of this.

CASCADE

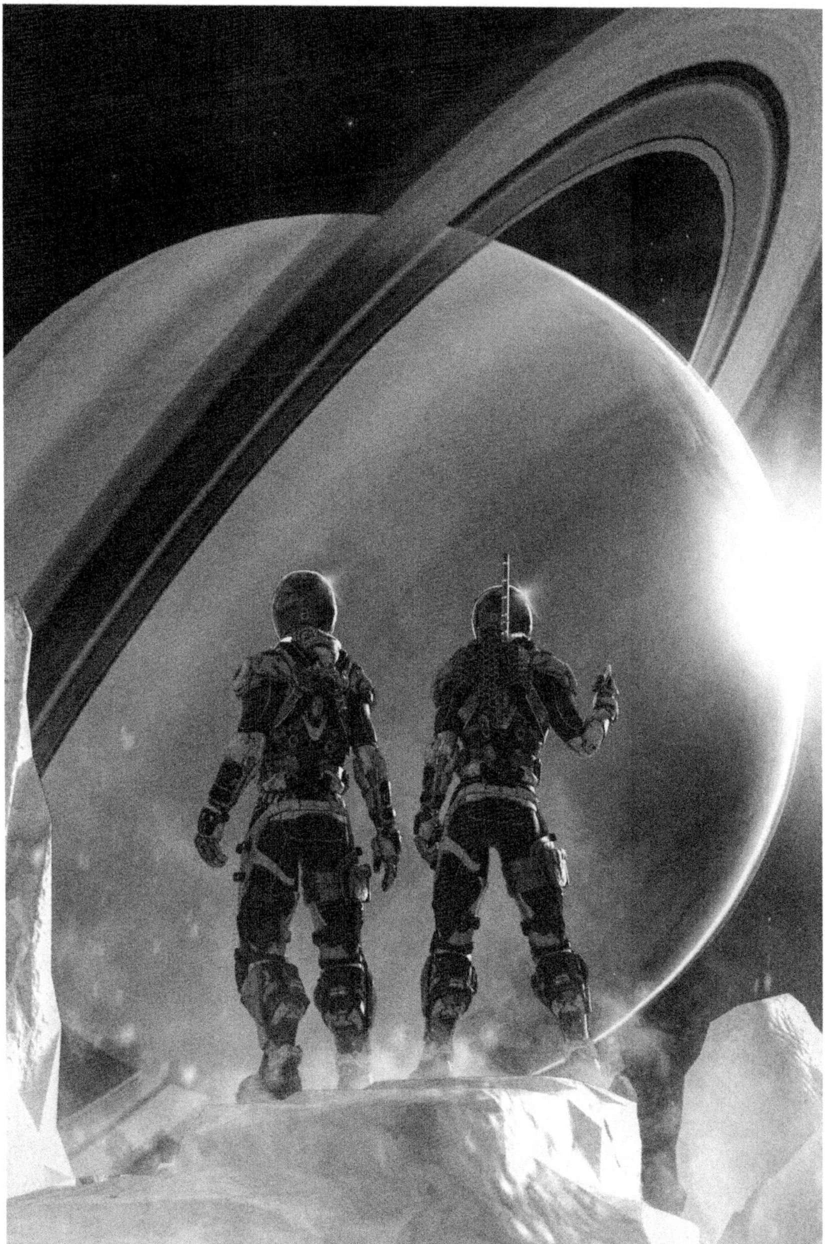

1

CARPENTER LOWELL HAD NEVER FELT MORE like a third wheel in his life. Somehow, in the four days since they'd been picked up by the aliens, Peter had become fluent enough in ancient Akkadian to communicate with them. It was irritating, if not downright insulting.

"How are you feeling today?" chirped Peter, leaning over the side of the tub in which Lowell lay.

He'd taken to thinking of it as a tub, in spite of the fact that it wasn't filled with water. The viscous liquid reminded him of the Jell-O cups he'd been fed at the hospital when he'd broken his arm as a boy. It was thick enough that it was nearly opaque. It was also warm and oddly pleasant to the touch, and left his skin smooth and rehydrated. Lowell couldn't be sure, but he was also fairly confident that it was responsible for his rapid recovery from the various beatings he'd taken over the last few days.

On the downside, it was grey. Every time he lifted his hand and the sludge dripped from his fingers, Lowell had to stifle a gag.

"I feel great," he admitted, squelching a handful of the slime between his fingers. "These aliens of yours offer better healthcare than the Space Corps, but that doesn't mean I have to like it."

"You could at least *try* to get along with them," Peter insisted.

"How? We can't talk." Lowell sank lower into his unappetizing bath, careful not to let his lips touch the grey substance.

"You could learn."

Lowell snorted. Did Peter really want him to learn some dead language just to talk with the tall, aloof creatures holding them prisoner? Peter seemed bound and determined to defend their hosts. It was a sentiment that made no sense to Lowell. Sure, the aliens had scooped them up out of the sky, and that was nice and all…but they'd only done it because they wanted something.

"Have you asked them about the moon?" he asked. "All those fish and whatnot swimming around under the ice? How about the weapon?"

Peter held a finger to his lips, glancing around nervously. "I may not have let on everything I know. I wanted to wait until you're better."

"Thanks," Lowell said, leaning back against the side of what he was coming to think of as the sludge tank. At least the kid hadn't gotten *totally* sucked into the narrative the aliens were selling. He might go starry-eyed every time he saw them, but he wasn't entirely gormless. And he hadn't handed over the stellar key, the one thing the aliens had specifically mentioned when they picked them up. Then again if the aliens had them they had the key. *No need to rush.*

A moment later, the automatic door hissed open, and one of the aliens stepped through. Lowell immediately turned his head away. He couldn't stand to look at them, not head-on. They made his head hurt, because they shouldn't be *real*.

Besides, their eyes were creepy. Lowell preferred to look away.

The alien spoke in the same lilting cadence that she always used. Lowell was pretty sure that she was female—it was hard to tell, they all looked the same to him, but the way Peter's eyes lit up when he saw her was awfully suspicious. Canny or not, the kid was a weirdo, and Lowell wouldn't put it past him to have a crush on one of these things.

"I'll be back later," Peter said. "Maybe you can come to dinner with us today."

Lowell watched them depart in silence, then lay back in the tank, his arms folded over his chest. He sometimes got a crick in his neck from leaning his head against the side of the tank, but the idea of falling asleep and waking up fully submerged was too horrible to contemplate. He wasn't sure which was more horrifying: the idea of choking on the thick, almost mucous-y substance, or having to taste it and live. Sometimes he hooked his arms over the side of the tank and slept with his head lolling to the side. It left him with a headache.

His discomfort was all for the best, Lowell reckoned. Peter was getting too chummy with these things. If an uncomfortable position kept Lowell awake and keen, so much the better.

He had no intention of letting his guard down.

2

"HOW HAVE YOU BEEN?" Peter asked.

Muul looked down at him, her large dark eyes fixed on his face. "It has only been ten hours since the last time we spoke. I am much the same as I was."

On the first day aboard the alien ship, Peter and Muul had engaged in a clumsy conversation about who they were and what they did. It had taken Peter ages to understand that Muul held a position that he had long coveted: she was an exobiologist. She studied alien lifeforms. Peter had trotted after Muul, eager to keep pace. More than once, he'd slipped on the slightly damp floor, and now he was careful to move a little more slowly. He still hadn't quite gotten used to the higher humidity levels aboard the alien vessel, and the relatively dim lighting sometimes made it harder to see. A few years ago, his stepfather Kevin had taken him hiking through the Hoh River Valley in Washington State, and the mossy substance growing over the UFO's walls—which Peter had at first mistaken for vividly green shag carpeting—

reminded him of the lichen that had dripped from the trees up there.

Early on, Peter had tried to ask Muul about how her species managed to maintain the dim, damp atmosphere in deep space without damaging the ship's wiring and internal mechanisms, but she'd looked at him as if he was very simple and said, *The usual way.* He'd stopped asking questions along these lines, as her answers were never very satisfying.

Which, in this case, meant that she was studying *him*.

Muul's office, for lack of a better word, was on the same floor as the medical bay. Peter still hadn't gotten used to what passed for chairs among Muul's people. They folded up out of the floor into an upright, slatted wall about a foot wide. According to Muul, one was supposed to stand behind them and slowly lean forward; the slatted segments bent forward until one could lie on them chest-down, looking over the top at the person leaning across from you.

Peter had made a valiant effort to use the chairs properly during the first few days, but found it wildly uncomfortable to lie on his stomach for so long. The fact that they were designed for someone significantly taller than him didn't help. He found it slightly easier to use it 'backward,' standing with his heels against the base of the contraption and leaning back. It was surprisingly comfortable, so long as his feet didn't slip out from under him. He'd cracked his head against the damp floor more than once that way.

With her arms reaching around either side of the inclined 'chair' and her chin resting on the top, Muul reached out toward the hemisphere that stood on a pillar in front of her. Peter still hadn't figured out quite how it worked, but from what he could work out, the single object served as both a monitor and a keyboard, of sorts. It was angled to face her, and supposedly contained her notes, although Peter hadn't managed to get a look at them—not that he would have been able to read them, even if he had. Muul might be fluent in Akkadian, but she took notes in her own language, and Peter didn't know a single word of it. He still hadn't figured out whether it was a syllabary or not.

Which was both humbling and frustrating. He'd have loved to know what she was saying about him.

"Are you fully rested?" she asked. "Ready to continue?"

"Actually, I have a question first." Peter cleared his throat. "I'm wondering if we could get in touch with someone at home? We were part of this big battle, the one I was telling you about, and I'm afraid that my family may be in danger. We need to warn people on Earth…"

"My commander has heard your request," Muul said gently. "I understand your intentions, Peter, but at the moment we are monitoring the situation on Enceladus—or what is left of it. We will not let things get out of hand. We have been watching over your people for a very long time, and the extent to which we can get involved is carefully calculated. After all, if we swept in and involved ourselves in every altercation, it would have vastly impacted the course of your species' history."

"I understand," Peter told her. "But surely if only Lowell and I were the ones to—"

"My commander has heard your request," Muul repeated. "Is that all, or shall we proceed?"

Peter let out an annoyed puff of breath. What was the point of making contact with extraterrestrial life if it didn't help him solve the problems Munroe had created?

Maybe he was too passive. Maybe Lowell could help him

make his case—but that would only work if Lowell and the aliens were able to communicate. "One other thing. My friend, ah... he's not so great at languages. I was thinking that you might be willing to learn English to help him? I know it's a big request, but it would open up another whole field of study for you."

Muul tilted her head to one side, glancing up at the dim lights. When they were talking normally, Peter did his best not to stare at her, but once her attention wandered, he couldn't help himself.

The sleek dome of her head was as grey as the rest of her, but her skin wasn't uniform by any means. Instead, it was a dappled monochrome; other animals used that sort of patterning as camouflage. The more he stared, the more questions he had. *What was your world like? Where did you evolve?*

Are we neighbors, or did you put us here?

But whenever he asked probing questions like that, she changed the subject.

"It might be worthwhile to learn his language," Muul admitted. "I don't think anyone else has made a particular study of modern human tongues, and the Akkadian is a bit archaic. It's more useful for reading texts, but it might be a viable field of study. Yes, I think I might be interested."

"You can always practice with me," Peter pointed out, aware that he sounded borderline desperate, but unable to contain his curiosity.

He wished that his father could meet her. Dr. Chang would have known exactly what to say.

"In the meantime," said Muul, "let us continue where we left off. I wish to know more about your homeworld. What can you tell me about its biology? The diversity of its species?"

This wasn't Peter's wheelhouse, but just as he had for the last few days, he did his best to answer the questions.

So far, his limited interactions with the aliens made it seem as though they lived in a sort of self-made utopia. He and Lowell had been greeted with kindness, cared for, fed, and nourished. But any time he'd tried to address the urgency of what had occurred on Enceladus, Muul put him off. He was beginning to feel less like a guest and more like a specimen.

The most important concern niggling at the back of his mind was one he was afraid to ask: not only because he might not like the answer, but because he didn't want to tip his hand and reveal how much he knew.

Why had they hidden a weapon of war inside the heart of Enceladus?

3

HE MING HAD EXPECTED that when she and General Wu arrived on the surface of the dead moon, they would find exactly what they were looking for. Instead, they were greeted with inert stone.

Major General Yevgeniy Ilin had joined their landing party, and the Russian forces were helping them search the area for any sign of the weapon they had all been sent to retrieve.

"We were not adequately briefed," Ilin complained. The three of them shared a small surface transport vehicle, along with two soldiers: one Russian, one Chinese, just to make sure that the situation didn't escalate. "We have had four days to retrieve the weapon, and there's no sign of it."

"Surely you didn't expect it to be lying around on the surface of the moon?" asked General Wu mildly. "You saw the changes that Enceladus underwent—its atmosphere is altered entirely."

Sure enough, the icy mantle that had been the frozen moon's defining feature was long gone, and the ocean had gone with it. All that remained was bare stone, which maintained the complex structure of the original moon, absent any sign of life.

Unlike Ilin, He Ming hadn't expected the moon to yield its secrets so readily. This was not some small-scale project, as simple as exchanging a package or gathering intelligence. The reward they had all been promised existed on a grand scale, so it stood to reason that it would not be the work of an afternoon to retrieve.

The landing party was fairly small compared to the amount of ground they had to cover, but He Ming had deployed the drones as well. Over the last four days, they had mapped a large portion of the moon's surface.

He Ming was looking out the window, wondering if they even really knew what they were looking for, when the watch at her wrist beeped. She lifted it, examining its face.

"The drones have spotted something." She leaned between the seats, past the two soldiers piloting their little vessel, and punched in a set of coordinates. "Take us there," she said.

The soldiers obeyed, and Ilin rubbed his hands together in excitement. "Do you think they've found it?"

"The weapon?" she asked. "Doubtful. But I expect that what they *have* found may be a step in the right direction."

The current face of Enceladus wasn't entirely smooth. It was still pockmarked by craters, cut through with canyons, and—most noteworthy of all—marred by the deep gouge of what had once been a sub-aquatic trench.

He Ming's coordinates took them to the edge of this trench, and then down into its declivity. If the ocean had still existed, it would have been a lightless rift, enough to inspire claustrophobia in even the most stalwart of soldiers. Now, it was just another valley on the surface of the moon.

To her right, Ilin was becoming increasingly agitated; to her left, General Wu was perfectly still, his hands braced against his thighs, breathing shallowly. Each time they thought they'd found something, both men seemed on the verge of launching into a flurry of action, and each time they had been disappointed.

He Ming was patient. This would take time. It could, in fact, take years. After all, Munroe had spent nearly half a decade tracking down the key and the map.

Truthfully, He Ming was skeptical that there was anything down here at all.

At the base of the rift, her watch pinged again. Their pilots pulled up short, and one of them punched in the command sequence that would open the door of the hovercraft. Ming, General Wu, and Ilin all stepped out, and Ming led the way.

They were only a few dozen paces from the drone that had flagged her, and when she saw what it was examining, Ming's eyes widened.

A skeleton nearly the size of their warship lay in the stone, fossilized into the moon's crust. It was recognizably piscine, with an enormous armored head that could easily have swallowed the five of them whole.

"What is that?" asked Ilin, his blue eyes widening behind his helmet's visor. His blunt, unsubtle features betrayed something akin to terror—he wouldn't like the fact that Ming could see it, if he realized. He might complain about their situation, but he was also a man who prided himself on his casual demeanor. He wouldn't appreciate the realization that he had tipped his hand so completely.

"I think it was one of the creatures that lived here, under the moon's surface—an echo of Earthly life in an alien landscape."

General Wu knelt before the massive mouth, examining it curiously. "I think that you may be right, Major General."

"How's that?" asked Ilin.

"We were not adequately briefed." Wu stood up, then turned to Ming. "Is this all that your drones have to show us?"

"Yes, sir, that's all so far." It was irritating not to have more answers, but the general only nodded before heading back to their pod.

"There has to be a way inside this moon," Ilin grumbled.

I'm sure there is, thought Ming, *and the moment one of us figures it out will be the moment our alliance ends.*

4

FAI STOOD in front of the classroom, adjusting his glasses as he gestured to the screen behind him.

"For thousands of years, people have looked at the night sky and wondered...what are those celestial bodies? What exists in worlds beyond our own? We limit ourselves to the idea that extraterrestrials will look like us, but with subtle differences—that they'll walk on two legs and build spaceships and contact us through the technology we currently possess. What we forget is that even on our own planet, we've evolved alongside millions of other species who have thrived at one time or another. Furthermore, we haven't finished evolving. The technology that we possess today was unthinkable two hundred years ago."

Fai stared out at the sea of faces, most of which were slack and bored. Some twerp in the third row was clearly watching a movie with those new digital contacts. On one hand, he was making Fai's point, but on the other, if he was going to spend the whole period dicking around, he could have at least had the decency to skip class.

Well, never mind him. It was a Gen Ed course, after all, and a summer session at that. At least a cluster of students in the front row was listening with obvious admiration.

Pushing his glasses back up his nose, Fai thumped his index finger on the desk for emphasis. "The point is, we already *know* that extraterrestrial life exists in the form of microbes. We *know* that there is life on other worlds. When we assume that it will look like us, and think like us, and talk like us, we assume that our scale and our intellect is ubiquitous."

The kids in the front row quickly scribbled notes, all of them dreamy-eyed. This was the only reason Fai even taught classes anymore: once in a while, when he got lucky, he got to teach the odd student who actually cared about the subject.

At the end of class, a handful of students hung back to ask him questions. One of the girls even shyly requested that he sign a copy of one of his books.

"I'm so glad there was an open slot," she said, clasping her hands in front of her. "The class is always full."

"It's a blow-off Gen Ed," Fai told her, chuckling. "I'm well aware of the reputation, but I hope you learn something this summer. See you in class."

She waved excitedly as she ran toward the door, chatting with her friends as they all spilled out into the hall. Fai smiled fondly after them. His college students seemed more like children every year—or maybe he was just getting old.

The guy in the third row was still sitting there, and Fai shot him a nasty look. *Guess his movie didn't end with the lecture,* he thought.

He slung the strap of his bag over his shoulder, ready to leave, when the young man spoke up.

"Doctor Chang," the man said. "Might I have a word?"

Fai frowned up at the young man. "My office hours are on the syllabus."

"I'd prefer to talk in private."

Fai's eyes swept over the man again, and he snorted. He hadn't looked that closely before, but now a wave of recognition swept over him. "No thanks," he said drily. "I don't talk to suits." He stomped heavily up the stairs, hunching his shoulders toward his ears. He'd gotten a slap on the wrist from some folks in Area 51 a few years ago, but Fai preferred not to interact with the military if he could help it.

"Dr. Chang," the man called.

"I already have a job," Fai replied. "And I'm not for sale."

"It's about your son."

That was enough to stop Fai dead in his tracks.

"Peter Chang. Graduate student. Doing a semester abroad at a dig in Ur-An, under a professor by the name of Keating?"

Fai closed his eyes, then turned slowly on the spot. "Ten minutes," he said.

The young man pursed his lips. "Off campus."

Fai nodded despite the sinking feeling in his stomach. "Follow me," he said. "I know a place."

THERE WAS a coffee shop two blocks from campus that Fai frequented. He'd toyed with the idea of going to a park, but the notion of sitting outside made his skin crawl. He'd spend the whole conversation watching the trees to see if they had snipers in position.

And yes, maybe he was being paranoid. But as a Chinese expat whose loyalty to any government was tenuous at best, Fai didn't believe that it was possible to be too careful. There were only 'appropriately careful,' and dead.

Fai ordered a small coffee, black, while the suit ordered a complicated beverage with steamed milk, two pumps of butterscotch, and a shot of espresso. The casual way that he carried himself made Fai nervous, perhaps because—despite all of his years of study and multiple awards—he had never felt entirely confident in his own right.

They took a seat at the back corner table, far away from prying eyes. Fai kept his back to the wall, just in case.

"I'm sorry to be the one to tell you this," the young man said. Now that Fai was looking, he actually didn't seem all that young. He was a chameleon, almost, the sort of man who always looked like he belonged, no matter where he was.

"Tell me what?" asked Fai.

The man reached for his tote bag, and Fai flinched, but all the man took out was a slim folder, which he handed across the table to Fai. Cautiously, he flipped the folder open to reveal a stack of pictures.

"My God," Fai breathed, looking at the top one. The image showed a dig site centered in the middle of a desert, but it looked as if someone had tossed the place. He lifted the top picture, then covered his mouth with one hand, stifling a gag. The young woman in the picture was obviously dead.

With an increasing sense of urgency, Fai flipped through the pictures. There were two more bodies: a second woman, and a man Fai didn't know. Cold fear clenched around his heart, and he held his breath, certain that Peter's body would appear in one of the images.

He let out an audible sigh of relief when it did not.

"Where is this?" he asked.

The man licked his lips. "Ur-An."

A thin noise escaped Fai's lips, almost a keening sound. "What did they do to him?" he whispered.

"His body was never found," the man said sympathetically, pausing to take a slurp of his drink. "Nor was the body of his mentor, Samuel Keating."

"Then maybe he's alive?" Fai said hopefully. "Perhaps whoever did this has taken him hostage? Or perhaps he escaped into the desert?"

"I'm sorry, Dr. Chang," said the man. "I can't reveal further details of an ongoing investigation, but I can tell you this with the utmost certainty: your son, Peter Chang, is dead."

5

LOWELL STILL DIDN'T TRUST the aliens, but at a certain point, he was going to have to man up and deal with them anyway.

"Okay, Chang," he said. "I'll talk to your weird grey girlfriend, but I can't promise it's going to go well."

"She's been learning English," Peter gushed. "And she picks up so fast...well, it makes sense after all, she speaks like forty languages...and she's not my girlfriend."

Lowell grunted as he rolled his shoulders. He'd been through the wringer that last day on Enceladus. Back in the day, he was *sure* he'd been tougher, but he was getting older now, and it had taken him longer than he liked to recover from the ordeal.

He'd managed to more or less towel off the remains of the sludge bath before Peter had arrived, but he still felt... sticky. The strangely sweet smell of it clung to him, and it made him feel as though he was still submerged in the stuff, which in turn made his stomach roil. Or maybe that was hunger—the doctor had given him nutritional supplements for the last few days, but he hadn't eaten a real meal since he arrived.

"Can you do me a favor?" Peter asked nervously, smoothing his hair ineffectually. "Can you just, you know, not make fun of me around Muul?"

Lowell rolled his eyes. "What, you want me to *wingman* for you?"

"No! No. It would just be nice if she saw me as, you know." Peter shuffled forward and lowered his voice. "As an *academic equal*."

"You've got a weird kink," Lowell informed him.

Peter opened his mouth to protest, but stopped short when the door opened and the alien stepped in. Lowell was pretty sure that it was Peter's friend, but he still hadn't figured out how to tell them apart. Their smooth, almost featureless faces had all the anonymity of a uniform.

"Muul, right?" he asked, figuring that if he was wrong, Peter would be the only one to tell him off. None of the other aliens knew English, after all.

Her eyes glimmered as she answered, "Lowell."

Lowell hadn't spent much time around animals in the last few years, but he knew a calculated, predatory look when he saw one. Muul's expression barely changed—heck, for all he knew, aliens weren't big on expressions, period—but her movements were deliberate.

There's a reason I've been sleeping with one eye open, Lowell thought. *I don't trust these things as far as I could throw one in zero-G.*

"Shall we walk?" Muul asked, gesturing with one willowy arm toward the door. Her voice was high-pitched and reedy, a combination of an accent Lowell couldn't place and, very possibly, a set of vocal cords built quite differently from his own.

"Yeah," said Peter eagerly. "You've got to see the rest of the ship, Lowell!"

When he and Peter had been pulled onto the ship via tractor beam, or whatever snooty name the aliens called it, Lowell's main thought was that it had looked like a standard UFO: sort of like a frisbee with a hump in the middle, but sleek and chrome-plated. As they left the medical bay, Lowell blinked in the unexpectedly dim light. Muul was dressed in loose, flowing garments that looked more like pajamas than anything else, but the material was oddly shiny. Lowell and Peter's battered Space Corps suits looked like they'd been through hell and back.

"Why is it so dim?" Lowell asked, peering around into the gloom. Walking out into the main part of the ship was like stepping into a muggy August twilight back home.

"I know it's hard to see," said Muul, tilting her oblong head to one side. "We need it so. Our eyes..." She trailed off, then said something to Peter.

"Huh." Peter frowned. "It's... the cones in their eyes, I guess. They refract light differently. It sounds like it has something to do with the atmosphere of their homeworld."

"Uh-huh." Lowell squinted at the walls, which appeared oddly fuzzy. "And where is that homeworld, exactly?"

As they made their way through the corridors, aliens came and went all around them. They all wore the same impassive expressions, and Lowell noticed that they barely glanced his way as they passed. Peter was overawed by them, and Lowell was paranoid, but the aliens didn't seem to care one way or the other about the arrival of their new guests.

And, hey, maybe Lowell was just overthinking it... but wasn't that a little suspicious?

"Home is outside your solar system," Muul said. "We are from —" She emitted a series of strange, sharp noises that made Lowell wish he could take an aspirin.

"As far as I can tell, it's part of Hoag's Object," Peter added helpfully.

Lowell shook his head. "Well, I'm glad one of us understands. So, Muul, what brings you to our neck of the woods?"

The alien tilted her head again. Her expression didn't change, although come to think of it, Lowell wasn't sure that expressions *existed* in her species. Maybe they had some other way of communicating that didn't involve twitching their facial muscles around. They didn't have eyebrows, after all.

"It's an idiom," Peter explained. "He means, *What brought you here?*" Just to be sure, he repeated the question in Akkadian.

Muul didn't answer right away. Maybe she didn't know the words. Or maybe she was thinking of a suitable thing to say that wouldn't arouse suspicion.

"We are here for research purposes," she said at last.

"Research purposes," Lowell repeated. *Pretty impressive vocabulary for someone who's only been speaking the language for two days. Unless she's toeing a party line.* The alien's whole vibe made Lowell's skin crawl.

The way Muul talked reminded Lowell of how he'd been with Lily and Dr. Hansen before their final mission.

Watch your back, he'd told Dr. Hansen.

Her response was going to haunt him to the end of his days: *We always do with you military types.*

He'd given her good advice back then, even if it hadn't been enough to save her life. If he was smart, he'd do the same now.

"Yes," Peter said excitedly, bouncing on the balls of his feet. "It's incredible, Lowell. Muul's people are studying Earth. They want to know all about the life forms that have evolved alongside us, and how many species there are...and they want to know all about us, too. Isn't it incredible? Think of everything we could learn through a cultural exchange like this!"

"You don't know that already?" Lowell asked, lifting an eyebrow at Muul. The significance of the gesture was probably lost on her, but Lowell couldn't help himself.

After all, *somebody* had built those tunnels on Enceladus. *Somebody* had buried the tablet on Earth; *somebody* had created the stellar key and left it on Mars. And given that Muul and Peter happened to speak the same dead language that had made its appearance on the walls of the tunnels, and on the tablet itself, odds seemed high that Muul's people were involved.

But if the Greys had been the one to build the anomaly and construct the stellar key, why pop in to study a planet they'd already been involved with for thousands of years, if not longer?

All this thinking made Lowell's head hurt, and there was no way he was going to convince Peter to be more cautious. Maybe he shouldn't.

Right now, if someone handed him a gun, he wouldn't even know who to shoot.

6

"SORRY," Peter told Muul in Akkadian. *"He's having a hard time. We just survived a war."*

Muul nodded, and Peter could have sworn that she looked sympathetic, even if her facial muscles barely readjusted. *"War is hell."*

Lowell glowered at them. Apparently being left out of the conversation didn't sit well with him, or perhaps he was just generally grumpy. He adjusted his gait slightly, and all of a sudden, his feet shot out from under him. He yelped as the back of his head connected with the slick floor.

Peter winced. "Sorry, I didn't think to warn you. That happens a lot. It's kind of damp in here."

"No kidding." Lowell sat up, rubbing the back of his head and looking more irritable than ever.

"Let me help you," Muul offered, holding out a hand. Lowell ignored her and got carefully to his feet.

"I got along just fine on Enceladus. Now that I know, I'll be more careful."

"*Is he always this stubborn?*" Muul asked.

"Yeah," Peter answered in English. "Grumpy is his baseline emotion."

Lowell narrowed his eyes and flipped Peter the bird. "That means swivel on it," he said helpfully.

Muul tilted her head curiously. "Swivel on what?"

Lowell smirked as Peter stammered. "W-well, it's a, ah, crude term? Involving certain, you know, reproductive... organs..."

"Oh, yes, I forgot." Muul's eyes brightened. "Your species' biology is so interesting. In my species, the females lay a large clutch of eggs and we rely on external fertilization. It's *so* much more efficient." She carried on blithely down the hall, leaving Peter alone with a snickering Lowell.

"I thought you were hurt," Peter snapped.

"I'm suddenly feeling much better."

They left the long, curved corridor and entered a wedge-shaped room. It was much larger than Muul's office, and dwarfed Lowell's small quarters in the sickbay by several orders of magnitude.

Muul deposited them at a table before heading off to retrieve their meals. It was round, held aloft by a single upright leg. The tabletop was comfortingly ordinary, but the same green fuzz that grew from the walls also climbed the leg. The whole ship seemed so much more alive and organic in these inner rooms, despite the fact that the landing bay had been just as sterile and anonymous as the quarters on the Space Corps ship. It had taken Peter several days to realize that this was because the bay was the only part of the ship exposed to the vacuum of space; of *course* the lichen couldn't survive down there.

Peter leaned over the table and lowered his voice. "You're acting all...surly."

"Maybe this is just my face," Lowell murmured back. He, at least, was better suited to the scale of their surroundings.

"You don't like her," Peter said.

Lowell held up a warning finger. "I don't *trust* her. There's a difference."

"She's being nice. She's *helping* us."

"What has she actually told you?" Lowell hissed back. "Has she been forthcoming with *anything*? Or have you just been happy to show off your love of linguistics to an extraterrestrial who's playing you like a fiddle?"

Peter bristled at this accusation, but now that Muul was speaking English, he decided that this conversation was best continued in private. He pulled one of the segmented reclining panels out of a recess in the floor and leaned back on it the way he did in Muul's office.

"Want me to show you how to use these things?" he asked.

Lowell wrinkled his nose. "I'll just stand, thanks."

Muul returned at that moment, carrying a large silver tray with three glasses of water and three sizable covered dishes. At first, Peter had been wary of the food and water, but he'd followed Muul's lead, watching her to make sure that nothing seemed poisoned—although technically, that didn't mean that *his* body would be able to properly digest the food. Fortunately, he'd been able to eat unharmed.

He wasn't an idiot, no matter what Lowell assumed. He was *careful*.

"Here you are," she said, handing them each a pair of two-tined forks the size of spatulas, a glass of water, and a covered dish. "Eat quickly—you don't want to waste it."

Peter watched as Lowell removed the cover and stared down in disgust at the large, brilliant red crustacean lying in front of him. It looked a bit like an oversized lobster or crayfish, split down the back and deveined like a cocktail shrimp. The flesh that was visible through the shell was a pale, minty green.

"Try it," Peter insisted. "It's not bad."

The expression on Lowell's face would only be described as revulsion as he hesitantly reached out to poke it with the tines of one fork. When he did, the creature twitched.

"Christ on a—*is this thing alive?*"

"Barely," said Muul. "That's why we have to cover the dish, of course. Even after deveining, they sometimes try to escape." She dug the tines of one fork between the back of her meal's head and speared the meat with the other, lifting it to her lips. Lowell's eyes widened at the sight of the still-quivering meat as Muul took a bite.

"Mm," she said coaxingly, "delicious."

Peter did the same, wiggling his eyebrows at Lowell as he did so.

"I hate you," Lowell grumbled.

"Don't waste the claws," Muul said. "The front pair is the tastiest, but the back pair has more nutrients."

To his credit, Lowell ate every bite, but he glared at Peter the entire time he did so.

"Lowell," said Muul, after she'd finished her meal, "what can I do to help you trust me?"

Lowell swirled the water around in his glass in one hand and picked a shred of meat out from his teeth with the fingernails of the other. "Nothing comes to mind. You saved our lives, and I appreciate that, but I'm not sold on the idea that you did it for our own good."

Muul was silent for a moment, but Peter had begun to work out her microexpressions. When the muscle at the outside corner of her eye tensed like that, she was trying to understand something. He'd seen it most often over the last couple of days as she'd learned English—and at a truly astonishing rate, too. Her biggest hurdles, if anything, had pertained to parsing idioms.

"Some things will have to wait for another time," she said slowly. "Things that will help you understand. But maybe there are a few tidbits I can tell you? Facts?" The muscle relaxed. "Facts always make me more comfortable."

Lowell sipped his water. His eyes were constantly moving, always evaluating the world around him, always on the lookout for a threat. He didn't seem to understand that they had escaped. Muul and her people had saved them.

"You've been to Earth before," Lowell said.

Muul blinked once. "I have not."

"But your people have?" Lowell waved the glass to encompass the room and all the other aliens sitting around and enjoying a quick lunch. He shuddered at the sight of the table next to them digging eagerly into their still-twitching meals.

"A long time ago."

Lowell's jaw tightened. He hadn't shaved since Muul's crew had scooped them out of the sky, and he looked more like a disgruntled grizzly bear than ever.

Muul steepled her long, slender fingers, leaning forward on her segmented chair until her elbows brushed the table. "There was a war," she said, in clipped tones. Instead of birdsong, her accent grew hard and sharp. She was staring at Lowell with incredible intensity. "I am going to tell your friend a story, and when I am finished, he will translate. Yes?"

Lowell drained his water glass, then set it back on the table. "Yes. Okay."

Muul turned to Peter and spoke in Akkadian. *"I am sorry, but my English is too new."*

"I understand," said Peter sympathetically.

"Our species are not the only two who have ever learned to fly between the stars," she said. *"And we were certainly not the first. Our galaxies are neighbors, but the very first travelers came from a great distance. I do not know if they made Enceladus, or simply altered it, but they were the ones who hid something in its core. A weapon."*

"Wait." Peter held up one hand. "'*Ariru.*' What does that mean, exactly? I saw that word in an inscription recently, and I thought it meant a..." Not sure how to rephrase this in Akkadian, he switched back to English. "A curse? Or a weapon?"

That muscle near her eye twitched again, and then Muul said, "Power."

"Power?" Lowell repeated, leaning in. "You're talking about what happened to Enceladus, right? And it was activated by the stellar key?"

Muul spoke only to Peter. *"Tell him that it is power—in every sense of the word. Yes, it can be used as a tool of destruction, but if we use it correctly, it can also be a source of energy. Surely your species has developed other tools like this as well?"*

"Plenty of them," Peter admitted.

Muul's face became inscrutable. *"Our homeworlds could benefit from this type of power,"* she said.

7

PETER HAD BEEN SPENDING his evenings alone in the small room that had been specifically modified for his comfort. There were two platforms, one projecting from each side of the wall; he had taken up residence on one of them, and now Lowell took the bunk across from him. The lights in the room were brighter, the air a little less thick and humid. Muul had even had the lichen on the walls removed, although Peter suspected that this was because she didn't want it to be damaged, more than out of any concern for his personal comfort.

Muul had given them clothes to wear while they were onboard. Peter changed into them before bed, although the sleeves were so long that they covered his hands, and the hems of the pants dragged on the ground. The fabric was surprisingly breathable; it never quite seemed to touch his skin. Perhaps the aliens' skin was particularly sensitive.

He tucked his Space Corps uniform into a little locker in the wall, and set the stellar key gently inside the helmet. It had been a relief not to have to wear the helmets, and changing back into more everyday clothes made Peter feel that everything was...well, if not 'normal,' at least not as dire as it had been.

"You're not going to sleep in your spacesuit, are you?" he asked Lowell.

The soldier lay back on the bunk, the hard cylindrical pillow that had been provided by the aliens propping up his head. "Never know when you might need it," he said.

"Are you worried that they're going to chuck us out into space?" Peter asked.

Lowell shifted around, obviously uncomfortable. "You told me what Muul said. What did you think of it?"

"That we're better off with her than with anyone else," Peter said.

Lowell grunted.

Peter rolled onto his side. "You don't think so?"

"I think," said Lowell, "that even if she told us the truth—and she didn't tell us much, mind you—that she's still after the exact same thing Munroe wanted. And consider this: if the only thing that key does is 'activate' Enceladus, well then, it's already done."

"Which is good," said Peter. "Right? Because it's already happened, and they're still treating us like guests."

"So then why did they pick us up?" Lowell turned his head to the side, gazing across the room into Peter's eyes.

Peter licked his lips. When they'd first been scooped up out of the void, Muul had indeed told them that they were here because of the stellar key.

"She hasn't asked for it," Peter said. "If they needed it for something, they could just take it, right? But they haven't."

"Not yet," Lowell said, turning back toward the ceiling and closing his eyes. "So maybe I'm just overcautious."

Or maybe I'm naïve, Peter thought, curling into a little ball. *I never questioned Keating's motives, because I wanted so badly for someone to see that I'm smart.* The memory of how excited he'd been by Keating's promise of being named in the research made him squirm. He'd been *thrilled.*

And less than twelve hours later, his friends had been executed.

The lights were on an automatic timer, and they dimmed suddenly, leaving just barely enough illumination for Peter to see by. Lowell's silhouette was just barely visible, solid and familiar.

He's the only one on this ship you can trust, Peter thought, *don't forget that.*

"HAS MUUL TOLD YOU ANYTHING ELSE?" asked Lowell when Peter came back to the room some days later.

Peter shook his head and dropped onto the edge of the cot, rubbing his temples. He was losing track of time. He was fairly sure the days on the alien homeworld were a different length than the days back home, but his circadian rhythm was shot. His best guess was that the timers were on an eighteen-hour cycle rather than a twenty-four hour one, with only four hours a night for sleep, but conversations with Muul about units of time had proven fruitless.

"She just keeps telling me that there's something she needs to show us."

"We don't even know where we are," Lowell said. As far as

Peter could tell, he barely left the room, although there was no real mystery as to why that was: he wanted to protect the stellar key. "We would have been just as well off if the Chinese had taken us prisoner. Any luck learning this alien language of theirs?"

Peter snorted and shook his head. The day before, Lowell had pretended to have an upset stomach so Peter could watch and listen as Muul had translated everything he'd said to the doctor. Lowell had done an admirable job of dragging it out and Peter *had* gotten something out of it. It was a start, but hardly enough to have a breakthrough.

Spoken languages were harder for Peter than written ones, even when they were human in origin. He'd dabbled a little in click languages as part of a project in undergrad, but even if those African tongues were unique and fascinating, they were nowhere near as complex as alien dialects.

No wonder Muul is picking up English so easily, he thought as he eavesdropped his way through the ship. *Compared to her, I'm practically illiterate and mute.*

It didn't help that with every passing day, Peter's anxiety grew. What were the Tiān Zhuānjiā doing right now? What had become of Enceladus?

Who had control of the power source—or, as he was still calling it in his head, the weapon?

Peter had thought that Akkadian in grad school was stressful because of all the other papers he had to write, all of the passages just waiting for him to pick them apart word by word, all of the tests and essays and translations. He'd thought *papers* were the height of stress! He'd been a fool. Now he was trying to crack a code with barely anything resembling a cipher, while for all he knew he'd started World War IV.

"You want a tip?" Lowell offered.

Peter rolled onto his side, examining Lowell's profile in the dim light. "You have some *study* advice? Or is this wisdom gleaned from years of combat?"

Lowell snorted. "Well I was gonna say, *Pretend your life depends on it, and then try harder.*"

Peter groaned and flopped back against the rigid surface of the bunk. "You're the worst."

"Good night, Chang," Lowell told him. The guy sounded almost cheerful.

For the first time since they'd met, Peter resented the fact that he was the whiz at languages and Lowell was the natural fighter. With his particular skillset, there was nothing more he could do to help right now, which meant that all the pressure was on Peter.

He settled back on the cylindrical pillow and closed his eyes, running over his small sliver of known vocabulary in his head.

He had assumed that Lowell was asleep, until the Space Corpsman spoke up again. "You know, back when I was in the Marines, they bounced us all over the place. I tried to learn how to talk to the locals at first, but I didn't have the head for it—I know, what, ten words of Arabic? And I doubt I can even remember that. Then I got bounced around in Africa for a while, so folks were speaking French, Mbaka, Zulu, Swahili... and then I got shipped off to the Philippines, and Malaysia, and Indonesia, and I'd learn two or three words in one town, only to find that they weren't speaking the same dialect two towns over. I kind of gave up."

Peter said nothing. He wasn't usually sympathetic to those who couldn't be bothered to learn other languages, but Lowell's experience was far from ideal, and probably far from unique.

Lowell turned his head so that he faced Peter. "But the thing that I figured out was that even when I couldn't talk to people, I could keep my eyes peeled and start to understand them. People talk with their hands, their eyes, their tone of voice, all of it. And then, sometimes, I could figure out what the *words* meant by keeping my eyes open."

Peter was used to speaking dead languages, using the written word to determine the intention of the writer. In the course of his studies, he'd read scrolls and papyri, tablets and inscriptions, stones and bones and turtle shells.

He'd never tried to read *people*. He'd never had a chance.

Peter sat up. "Lowell. Were you actually... *useful* just now?"

Lowell snorted. "I don't know about that. I just know that it helps if you can tell whether a guy and his goats really just *happened* to wander too close to the base, or if he's secretly planning to lob a grenade over the fence."

"I suppose," Peter said.

Lowell grunted. "If you're going to get real about our situation, I think you'll see that it's not all that different. Where are we, Chang? Where are your good buddies taking us? Name one thing Muul has told you that actually *applies* to anything. One thing that you can take to the bank."

True enough. If Muul wasn't going to tell him the truth, then he was going to have to figure out a way to learn it for himself.

8

RESEARCH OFFICER MUUL was leaning in her office, reviewing the notes she'd taken during all of her meetings with Peter Chang, when Captain Goii stepped through the door.

"Good evening, Officer," he said, lowering himself forward onto the CantiLeaner that Muul had come to think of as Peter's. Watching him sit in it properly struck her as slightly disorienting.

"What progress have you made?" he asked.

"Overall, things are going well." Muul looked up into the captain's eyes. "The larger male makes a terrible subject—he is fit for very little besides observation, but the other one has a surprising intellectual capacity. He's been able to tell me a great deal about his homeworld's current state."

"A fascinating subject, I'm sure," said Captain Goii flatly. "But what about the key? Do you think that he will be able to help, when the time comes?"

Muul drummed her fingers against the base of the textorb. The flat, round, slightly sticky pads of her fingers suctioned to its glassy surface with each pass. "I don't know, sir. Peter—the smaller human—was able to describe several inscriptions from Enceladus, but I don't think he understands the true purpose of the key, much less how to harness it." She had been told, since she was only a nymph, that only traitors misled their superiors. Still, his presence unnerved her. She enjoyed studying the humans, but as far as the captain was concerned, that was an insufficient end goal.

"Then you don't think that the humans on Enceladus have a practical understanding of the weapon yet?" Captain Goii leaned over to examine her notes. "Have you even *questioned* him about their military capacity?"

Muul resisted the urge to darken the dome of her techorb screen. He was her superior, after all, even if he didn't approve of her fascination with an acknowledgedly inferior phylum.

"Officer Muul, if the human fleet has not taken control of the weapon yet, then I would prefer to know *now*. We can coordinate an attack before their reinforcements arrive." He flared his neck pouch at her condescendingly. "You seem like the soft sort who would prefer to avoid bloodshed."

"I'm not sure about the weapon's current status," Muul admitted, feeling like a traitor to a hominid that didn't deserve her loyalty. "And I don't think that our... guests know, sir. Their people are divided into factions, and they do not all communicate with one another as we do. Moreover, I think that P—that the useful human has been holding back."

"Spare me the details," Goii said, rising to his feet and folding away the CantiLeaner. "Backup is on the way, but the longer we wait, the more likely it becomes that *other* forces will get involved as well. Do you take my meaning?"

"What do you intend to do?" Muul asked nervously.

"Your way hasn't worked," said Goii. "I'm afraid that it's time to take action. *Decisive* action."

"Perhaps we have options besides bloodshed," Muul insisted.

Goii's temples rippled with barely suppressed anger. "You seem very concerned for the welfare of your subjects, but make no mistake—I will not tolerate insubordination, either from them or from you. I know what happened to your home colony, Officer. Which means that *you* know that our enemies would be happy to lay waste to everything that you and I have worked so hard to maintain. Think about the possibilities that having a little more... *persuasive motivation* over our enemies could offer."

"We could come to some agreement with them," Muul insisted. "As I told you, one of the humans has evidenced higher levels of brain function than we ever thought possible."

"Are you truly suggesting that we negotiate, Muul? With *mammals*? Their species has only just mastered space travel. I've allowed you to study them while we assess our options, but I have no intention of compromising this mission over a couple of primates." The last word seemed to stick in his throat, and he hacked in disgust. "They deemed the piscine species that inhabited Enceladus exactly as disposable as I deem them. Is that clear?"

After he left, Muul closed her eyes and let her head slump forward onto the chinrest of her CantiLeaner. This was the part that she'd been dreading: the inevitable moment that a commander tired of waiting for her to finish conducting her research. Even worse, she'd come to look fondly upon her subjects. The idea of betraying their trust made her uneasy. A traitorous thought occurred to her: she had more in common with Peter than she had with many of her own people.

But Goii was right. She could hardly go around putting the

well-being of competing species before that of her own. Whoever held the weapon held the power.

And since the weapon on Enceladus was the only one whose location had been confirmed, Muul was obligated to ensure that her people got to it first.

9

HE MING CLIMBED down into the lunar gully. The drones had alerted her to a large object pinned between the canyon narrow walls. The readings they had reported left her confused—surely they couldn't be right.

Then again, if Enceladus had proven anything, it was that the moon was more than capable of defying their expectations.

"What is it?" General Wu asked from behind her. He and Ilin had held back at the peak of the ridge, and their bodyguards had stayed with them. If they could have easily traveled with a larger group, Ming would have sent someone else down in her stead. As it was, every excursion across the face of the moon required perfect balance. Ming wouldn't dare leave the general alone with Ilin and his man, and she was certain that the Russians felt the same about leaving their commander outnumbered. She was certain that the only reason Ilin had agreed to let a third member of the Tiān Zhuānjiā join the landing party was that he didn't believe that a woman could be a threat. The thought reminded her of the American, Peter Chang, and what he had told her during their call. He had seemed like a nice enough young man. Too bad his testimony could have proven so inconvenient for so many people.

Soon the gully would become too steep for her to safely pass. Fortunately, the object in question lay directly before her, surrounded by curious drones.

Ming cocked her head. It was a relatively small vessel, one of the sort that Private Lowell had used to destroy the American warship. In fact, this one could have been its twin. Aside from some damage to the hull caused by its slide into the gulley, the ship seemed largely intact.

How did it get down here without being destroyed when the moon imploded? Ming shuffled forward, looking down into the crack.

"A ship," she said into the mic. "American."

"Good riddance," Ilin grumbled.

"And the drones couldn't identify a ship?" General Wu clicked his tongue in annoyance.

Ming ran one finger over the screen of her control unit, scrolling down through the readout. "They didn't send out an alert because of the ship itself. There are life signs onboard."

Both commanders sucked in a breath, their combined surprise echoing in her ears.

"How is that possible?" Ilin demanded. "Everything else was ejected from the core's atmosphere."

"If the ship was damaged during launch and wasn't able to break escape velocity, they may have crashed after the core restabilized," Ming said. "But here's a thought, gentlemen. Why don't we ask the survivors directly?"

Now that she could see the layout of the crash site properly, she could use the drones more effectively. It would have been far too dangerous to climb out into the ship herself, so she entered a command sequence for three of the closest devices. One located the door and suctioned on to its exterior. When the door refused to come free, she activated its shock feature. She could hear the airlock pop even through the moon's thin atmosphere.

The first drone carried the door off to the side, releasing the suction to drop it down into the chasm below. Meanwhile, the other two sailed through the door, exploring the interior of the ship. If the survivors were lucky, their suits were still intact. Otherwise, they would now be subjected to the moon's inhospitable environment.

Sure enough, the drones soon located the figures slumped inside. They were breathing shallowly, but judging from their readings, they were suffering from the effects of dehydration and malnourishment.

"They're alive," He Ming said. "I'll have the drones extract them."

After she programmed several others to join the effort, she got one to scan the ID plates on the American suits. One of them was named Richard Acosta.

The other was only identified by the codename Hellcat.

10

FAI MISSED the next day of classes.

And the next.

And the next.

At first, he didn't bother to eat or brush his teeth. He didn't even turn the TV on. Simply remembering to drink water was an effort he could barely muster. Instead, he lay on the couch, stared at the textured paint of the living room ceiling, and mourned his son.

The images seemed to linger just behind his eyelids, and Fai sifted through them as if they were old photographs stored in his memory. Peter's first birthday party. Their first visit to Disneyland. The first time they'd looked through a telescope together.

So many of the good memories were old, from before the divorce. Fai had buried himself in his work, and they'd fallen out of sync with one another. In some ways, the Peter of today was a stranger, someone that Fai had always tried to push onward and upward to bigger and better things, although he'd only succeeded at pushing Peter away instead.

I'm sorry, he thought. *I failed you.*

The boy in his memory couldn't hear.

On the third day, Fai got up. He felt empty. He only intended to get a granola bar from the cupboard, but once he started eating, he couldn't stop. He ate dry cereal by the handful; cooked a frozen pizza, and then another. His sister had given him a bottle of *huangjiu* for New Year a few years ago—Fai poured himself one cup, and then a second. Before he knew it, the whole bottle was gone. He collapsed on the couch with an aching stomach, only to realize that eating hadn't filled the emptiness. If anything, he was disgusted with himself for trying.

Four days after the man had found Fai in his class, he sat up on the couch with a hangover. He tottered to the bathroom, splashed cold water on his face, and forced himself to look in the mirror. An old man stared back at him with two bruised-looking eyes.

"Peter is dead," he told the man in the mirror.

Neither of them could believe it.

Fai made himself shower, brush his teeth, and check his phone. He had a dozen missed calls from Susan, and a few from the university. The office was probably wondering where he'd dipped off to.

His ex-wife was probably planning the funeral.

Fai made tea, then drafted an email to the school, explaining that he needed to take time off for bereavement. Then he texted Susan to tell her that he wouldn't be coming, but to bill him for half of the memorial. It would have been kinder to call, but he didn't trust his voice. She would have known immediately that he had other plans.

Over the years, Dr. Fai Chang had become a master of dissociation. He could compartmentalize *everything*. But one thing in particular haunted him:

The man in the suit had claimed that they never found Peter's body, but had assured Fai that he was gone. That meant that he either knew more than he was saying, or that there was a chance—no matter how slim—that Peter was still alive.

Fai cleaned the fridge, packed his bag and his passport, and put a notice out for a rideshare. Then, while he was waiting, he booked a plane ticket to Iran.

FAI PULLED his passport out of the pouch around his neck and smiled at the customs agent. "I'm here on business. My associate, Kavan Behnam, will be meeting me here. We're meeting to discuss our newest book."

The customs agent's blank expression made it very clear that he couldn't care less. He took a quick glance at the passport, confirming that Fai's visa was still current, and ran it through the scanner. "Very good, sir. Enjoy your stay." He handed back the passport and waved Fai through the gates, then gestured to the next person in line.

Fai's academic credentials made entry into Iran relatively straightforward; he'd come to visit Dr. Behnam over spring break—they really had been working on a book together—and his visa was still good for a few weeks. Getting over the border into Iraq, however, wouldn't be quite so simple. Hopefully, Dr. Behnam would be able to help with that.

The temperature in Tehran had climbed to nearly a hundred degrees by the time Fai stepped out of the airport. Even on his second trip to the city, the view left him breathless. The skyline spread out before him, a vast plain packed with glass and concrete and ringed by mountains. In the spring, the slopes had been robed in snow, but now the white caps had retreated to the highest peaks.

It was a beautiful city, and Fai had fond memories of exploring everything it had to offer—but he hadn't come here as a distraction. He came on a mission.

Dr. Behnam was waiting for him outside of the terminal, and he waved as Fai approached. "To what do I owe this pleasure, Dr. Chang?" he asked in heavily accented English. "Your message was... cursory."

Fai hefted his suitcase and slid it into the back of Dr. Behnam's car. "I would like to ask you something, Kavan. Something *private*."

Dr. Behnam's eyebrows rose, and he gestured Fai toward the front passenger seat. "I admit, I am intrigued."

Fai didn't speak until they were both seated in the cab and Dr. Behnam had pulled away from the curb. A few decades ago, the city had stopped issuing licenses to anything but solar-powered vehicles, to combat the high levels of air pollution, and skyhooks had been installed on some of the larger buildings to combat the fact that the city was gradually sinking. The odd structures ballooned out over the tops of major buildings like colorful mushroom caps. Santa Barbara could learn a thing or two from this city. The traffic, however, was terrible.

"I'm sorry to spring all of this on you so unexpectedly, but you're the only person I know in this country," said Fai, folding his hands in his lap. He kept his eyes fixed on the endless line of traffic crawling around them. He and Dr. Behnam were colleagues—friendly colleagues, but what he needed to ask was more than the sort of thing that typically passed between work associates.

"What do you need?" Dr. Behnam asked.

Fai let out a shuddering breath. "A man came to my work the other day. A man I didn't know. He told me that my son had been killed."

"*Allah yrhamoh.* That is terrible news, Dr. Chang. May God grant you peace."

Fai nodded, knitting his fingers together until the knuckles popped. "I believe that the man in question works for the United States government. He made it sound as though Peter's b—" He couldn't say the word *body*. The word formed on his tongue but refused to pass his lips. "His remains were never recovered, although he claimed that the dig where he worked underwent a violent attack. He was working on an archaeological site in Ur-An, just across the border."

"I see," said Dr. Behnam. He was looking directly out of the windshield, his jaw fixed and his eyes cold.

"Do you?"

Dr. Behnam clicked his tongue. The driver in front of them laid on the horn, and an answering volley of beeping echoed back from the surrounding cars. "Of course. You have flown into Iran because you cannot fly into Iraq without certain clearances... and if you applied for those clearances, your own government would deny you. So you have come here in the hopes that I will help you do something illegal and dangerous, is that it? Because you think I want to bring the anger of your government down on my head, is that it?"

Fai leaned back in his seat, wishing that he had stretched more after getting off the plane. He was cramped and sore, and the recrimination in his colleague's voice made him feel about a hundred pounds heavier. "If you will not help me, I will find my own way. If the government comes to you, tell them that you advised me not to go. Or better yet, tell them that I made no mention of my mad plans, and that I fled across the border without your knowledge."

"One thing is true: I do advise against this idea of yours." Dr. Behnam fixed Fai with a look of utter sympathy. "You are grieving the loss of a child, my friend."

"My only child," Fai said bleakly. He had never been a very present father—he'd frequently felt that he wasn't cut out for the job. He and Susan hadn't made a particularly good match, either; they'd gotten married too young and fought too often. Fai frequently felt that he had nothing to offer his energetic, enthusiastic, and outgoing boy. Peter was all the things that Fai was not.

But now?

Finally, there was something that Fai could do that might make a difference.

"What do you hope to achieve?" Dr. Behnam asked with a little less vitriol this time.

"I want to find him. To bring him home. They couldn't show me a picture of his body, and you know how I think, Kavan. He was on a dig with the university with three of his fellow students. The man in the suit showed me the photographs. Three of the murdered students were there, but there was no sign of Peter *or* his professor, and the government isn't looking for them."

Dr. Behnam's dark eyebrows climbed toward the roof of the car. "You do not believe that they were taken?"

"Oh, I believe it." Fai clenched his jaw. "I just don't think it was *locals* that took him."

Dr. Behnam nodded, drumming his fingers on the steering wheel. "I think that you will not be deterred, Dr. Chang. Is that correct?"

"I've come this far," Fai told him, "and I'm not going to accept this quietly. I'll do whatever I have to do to learn the truth."

Dr. Behnam nodded. "In that case, Dr. Chang, I may know someone who can help."

THE LONG FLIGHT had left Fai groggy and exhausted, and as their time in the city's traffic stretched from one hour toward two, he found himself drifting off. Eventually, his head tipped back against the window, and he fell into an uneasy sleep.

He did not so much as stir until someone tapped on the window. The sound roused him from his dreams, which had—as they had for the last few nights—revolved around Peter. Fai groaned, stretched the kink in his neck, and wiped his eyes before turning to look out of the glass.

A short woman in a sleek uniform stood on the far side. Her eyes swept over Fai, then turned to the large tablet held in one hand. She nodded once before saying in English, "It's him."

Fai turned to Dr. Behnam. "What is this? Where have you brought me?"

Dr. Behnam offered him a thin smile, sitting upright in the driver's seat. He did not look at Fai. His attention was focused on the dozen or more uniformed figures circling the car. They were surrounded by scrub and dusty terrain; Dr. Behnam must have driven them out of the city while Fai slept.

"You must know that I have contacts within the Iranian Space Agency. Our space program has been on hold for over forty years—we do not currently have the equipment needed to send a man to the *moon*, much less to Mars or beyond." He closed his eyes and shook his head slightly. "I'm sorry, Dr. Chang. I respect your work, and I sympathize with your loss, but we have so little to bargain with, and forming alliances is more crucial now than ever. I hope that you can understand, even if you cannot forgive me."

Fai gaped at him as the woman outside tapped the glass again before stepping aside. "Get him out of the car," she told one of the uniformed men.

"Who are these people?" Fai demanded. He didn't recognize their uniforms—they didn't look like Marines or Army, but there wasn't a doubt in his mind that they answered to the same people who had allowed Peter to disappear without a trace.

"They're yours," Dr. Behnam said. "And God willing, they will remember that once you are in their care."

A big man stepped forward to open the door. The gun slung across his chest looked unusual, but Fai didn't know enough about firearms to fully recognize *why*.

"We need an alliance for what's coming," Dr. Behnam said. "This is bigger than your freedom, bigger than my reputation. Bigger, I'm afraid, than the life of your son."

"Or me?" asked Fai bitterly.

Before Dr. Behnam could answer, the soldier dragged Fai out of the car, knocking his glasses askew in the process. Another man dragged Fai's luggage out of the back seat. When this was done, the circle of people that surrounded the car parted, and with one last regretful wave, Dr. Behnam pulled away.

Kneeling on the ground and surrounded by people he could never trust, Fai watched as the car kicked up a cloud of ruddy dust all the way along the road back toward the city. He could still make out the profile of Tehran far away.

On his first visit to the city, he'd felt perfectly safe. Why didn't it surprise him that this time around, the greatest danger would come from people who branded themselves as his protectors?

The woman approached again and stood in front of him with her hands folded behind her back. "Search him."

The man who had dragged him from the car lifted Fai back to his feet and roughly patted him down. From the corner of his eye, he watched as the other man rifled through his luggage.

When the soldier found the pouch hanging around Fai's neck, he tensed, but it contained nothing but stacks of rials, his passport, and his driver's license. The man returned all of these items to the pouch, then tossed it to his fellow, who tucked the items into Fai's suitcase.

"No weapons, Dr. Chang?" asked the woman, smiling in bemusement. "Were you going to walk up to the Iraqi border and *knock?*"

Fai didn't answer. He was too busy wallowing in a mélange of fear, disgust, and vindication. He had *known* that something was wrong. The confirmation would have been a sweeter victory, however, if it hadn't landed him in custody.

"Are you arresting me?" he asked, keeping his chin high. "If so, I'd like to know on what grounds. I haven't done anything illegal."

"Yet," added the woman. Now that she knew he wasn't armed, she seemed more amused than anything. "I'm Captain Sanz of the

United States Space Corps. You're lucky we're here, Dr. Chang. Otherwise, you might have gotten hurt on your trip through the Zagros Mountains."

Fai pulled his arm free from the bigger man's grip. "And instead, what? I shall be shot in the back of the head and left for dead in the desert, like my son?"

Captain Sanz's eyes sparkled. "There is a fair bit of evidence to indicate that your son *is* dead, Dr. Chang, but we didn't kill him. In fact, it seems that he did plenty of killing himself."

Fai scoffed. "Peter? Never. Save your lies for someone else, Captain." He didn't have to listen to this—these people might be happy to shoot him, but the certainty of his impending death made him bold.

"It's not a lie," the captain said. She pursed her lips, then turned her head to one side, meeting the eye of the man beside her. "It would be interesting, wouldn't it, Collins, for the three of us to compare notes? You knew Private Lowell, this gentleman knows Peter Chang, and I know the finer details of what happened on Enceladus. Between the three of us, I think we could sort out a few of the things."

Fai blinked. "Enceladus? You mean Saturn's moon?"

Sanz cocked her head to one side. "Listen," she said, "you have two options before you, Dr. Chang. I'm perfectly happy to ship you back to the United States and have you checked into a facility for the next, oh, year or so. By the time you get out, even you will believe that you had a mental break out here in the desert. Loss can do terrible things to a man's psyche."

Fai shrunk back from her, teetering on shaking legs. "And if I refuse you'll make me disappear?"

The captain shook her head. "Nothing that dramatic. My

predecessor was rather more heartless than I am, but I believe that there are other ways to handle problems. In fact, I sincerely believe that if he'd made the offer I'm about to make you, we would've saved ourselves quite a lot of trouble in the long run." She held out her hand between them, and the doctor examined it, not raising his clenched fists from his sides. "How would you like a job?"

11

"I'VE FIGURED IT OUT," Peter hissed, leaning across the mess hall table toward Lowell. "I understood a whole conversation today! Not every word, mind you—I haven't figured out how nouns work, and proper nouns are always hardest because there's no point of reference in translation, so..."

Lowell rolled his eyes and yanked one hand across his throat. "Maybe instead of telling me about sentence structure, you can tell me what you heard." He looked down at the spiny thing on his plate. Just as he'd been coming to terms with the fact that he was stuck eating bogbugs—as Muul had called them—for the foreseeable future, he'd been given some new godawful entree. It looked almost like a starfish, but pointier.

Peter pouted, but within moments he was already leaning toward Lowell and thumping his fingertip on the table again. "They're almost here."

Lowell glared at him, secretly grateful that he didn't have to spear the feebly squirming object in front of him. "Who is?"

"I'm not entirely sure about that yet. From what I can tell, we're waiting for backup. But it sounds like the captain is planning something for today."

Lowell took another sip of water, swishing it between his teeth. All of this sitting around made him irritable—more irritable than usual, even. Especially when his long hours of sulking were interrupted only by eating unsightly decapods. He forced himself to spear the miserable thing, sucking down its greasy flesh. The taste wasn't terrible, honestly, but everything else about the experience was bad enough to make up for that. At least he got to eat them in the more dimly lit rooms. If he could have seen it better, he'd have had an even tougher time horking it down.

"What do you do with the key?" he asked softly. "When we're not in the room?"

"I've got a hiding spot for it," Peter said.

Lowell stood and pushed his tray away. "Then maybe we should—"

He was cut off by the sound of approaching boots ringing across the polished floor. Both men turned to find the door blocked by a cluster of six aliens, all of whom were dressed in the same sort of loose clothing that Peter wore. Lowell still had a terrible time telling the aliens apart, but he recognized Muul at the front of the crowd. He couldn't quite say *how* he knew it was her—her gait, perhaps? Or maybe it was the way that Peter looked at her, with just a *hint* of betrayal in his expression.

One of the aliens at the front of the group spoke. Lowell darted a quick glance at Peter. To his surprise, the kid either had an excellent poker face, or he was genuinely just as lost as Lowell was.

Muul took a step toward the two men. "Please come with us.

Captain Goii would like to request your assistance with an upcoming project."

"And if we don't want to help?" Lowell asked.

Peter frowned at him, but Muul's tone didn't change when she replied, "You will recall that we provided you with shelter and protection when you were floating freely through the vacuum of space. Are we not allies, Mr. Lowell?"

"Until one of us proves otherwise," he replied.

Peter got up, nearly slipping as he did so. The captain's presence seemed to unnerve him. "Sorry, Muul, but you know how my friend is. Of course we're allies. Let's go to the room and retrieve the key."

Lowell glanced sharply at Peter. The aliens hadn't even mentioned the key. But Peter trotted off toward the door before he could catch his eye and Lowell had little choice but to follow. He tried to take stock of every weapon held by the soldiers they passed. He couldn't see any—no guns, no knives, *nothing*, which made Lowell a little nervous. How could he anticipate a firefight if he didn't even know what he'd be fighting?

Keep an eye on it, he thought. *Watch them like a hawk. The moment one of them tries anything...*

But he wasn't sure where to go from there. And what was the point, anyway? Too many people had already died for this key—it was an alien artifact. Maybe the aliens should just have it back.

Behind them, Muul and the captain were engaged in a conversation Lowell couldn't understand.

"I sure wish I knew what they were saying," Lowell muttered.

"Yes," Peter said. "You sure do."

Interesting. So the kid could understand. The whole thing put

Lowell in a precarious situation, one in which he'd never intended to find himself, and yet one that he couldn't deny.

He was going to have to follow Peter's lead. Blindly.

Lowell was still wearing his Space Corps suit, minus the helmet, but Peter had taken to wearing the soft, loose clothing favored by the aliens. If one of them was going to get shot, Lowell was going to have to take the hit, at least until they could get Peter into a uniform.

As they approached their room, Lowell braced for a fight. Even if they did hand the key over, they would become instantly disposable. For all he knew, Muul and the captain would toss them back out into the void.

Judging by his posture, Peter had no such concerns. He was practically skipping as the door slid open. He made a beeline for the locker where he'd stuffed himself while spying on Lowell's bout of 'illness.'

Yeah, Lowell thought, rolling his eyes. *Sure. Real safe hiding spot, Chang.*

Peter pulled out his helmet and reached inside, but his hand came away empty. He frowned at it, then turned the helmet upside-down, as if waiting for something to fall out of it. When nothing did, he tossed it aside, digging through the locker ever more frantically, tossing segments of his suit left and right. When the key didn't appear, he turned to Lowell.

"Did you take it?" he asked.

Lowell shook his head. "What the hell would I do with it? I don't even know what the damn thing *does* anymore."

Peter ran his hands through his hair, then turned to Muul. There was something slightly odd about the way he modulated his voice when he asked her, "Muul? You didn't take it, did you?"

"Of course not," she said. Her tone matched Peter's, and for a moment, Lowell stared at them, wondering what was going on. It was like watching a play, where the actors couldn't quite get the delivery right.

The captain asked a question, and Muul replied in their language. That was the moment when Lowell understood.

Peter was using what he'd learned about their language to put on a show for the captain. He wanted it to look like he was panicking, but in a way that Goii would recognize. *How do you communicate with someone who doesn't speak the same tongue?*

Body language. Intonation.

You clever sonofabitch, Lowell thought admiringly. Peter must have been telling the truth about having a hiding spot for the key, and he was trying to convince them that it was gone.

If the captain's reaction was anything to go by, the aliens were actually buying it.

12

"*WHERE IS IT?*" Goii demanded.

"*He seems to have lost it,*" Muul replied.

"*Lost it?*" the captain repeated incredulously. "*How?*"

Peter made himself breathe harder. He'd barely managed to scrape a B+ out of his improv class in undergrad, but presumably the aliens didn't know too much about human expressions and behaviors. A B+ performance should be good enough to sell it.

"It was right here," Peter said, pointing toward the locker. "It couldn't have just vanished. Someone must have taken it."

"*What is he saying?*" the captain demanded.

Muul translated, while Peter rummaged uselessly around on the floor, as if the stellar key might randomly appear.

"*Who else comes in here?*" the captain demanded.

Peter had to bite back his reply until Muul translated, and when she did, he turned to face her.

"Nobody," he said. "Only me and Lowell and... and you." He

forced himself to go very still, then lifted a shaking finger to point at her. "Muul, are you *sure* that you didn't take it?"

Muul didn't translate that. She only stared at Peter.

This was a risk, and he knew it. If the captain trusted Muul, they might decide to search the ship before leaping to any conclusions. But Peter had spent a lot of time around paranoid, mistrustful commanders in the last few weeks, and he had a feeling that if the stellar key was all that Muul had told them it was, it would inspire greed in the people who hoped to *control* that power.

Sure enough, Goii advanced on her. *"What is he saying?"*

"He... he's confused." Muul's whistling came out higher-pitched. *"He said that nobody else comes in here but me. But the doctor was here. We treated the larger male just the other day."*

"Then who else could have taken it?" Goii asked. *"Who else was in here?"*

"I don't know," Muul whined. *"Sir, I've never even touched the key. We've been waiting for backup."*

Lowell watched this back-and-forth with a mild expression of confusion, his brows pinched together and his arms crossed. He looked utterly nonplussed.

Peter took a step forward, lifting his hands in a placating gesture. *"Please, Muul,"* he whistled. *"I'm scared. Tell him the truth."*

For a moment, nobody moved. Peter was fully aware that his pronunciation was atrocious, and his clauses were all out of order. He could only hope that his meaning came through.

A moment later, Goii's arm whipped out, and he grabbed Muul by the throat. *"What is this?"* he demanded. *"Why does he speak our tongue?"*

"*I don't know!*" Muul cried. "*I didn't teach him. He must have learned on his own.*"

"*No more excuses.*" Goii made a sharp gesture to one of the aliens on his left. "*Is this why you've been telling me to bide my time? Stalling the mission?*"

Out of the corner of his eye, Peter saw Lowell sink into a fighting stance. "He knows!" Peter exclaimed in English. "He knows that we were working with Muul to help buy the Space Corps time to recover the key!" The captain and the other soldiers might not speak English, but if he broke character now, he was afraid that the whole thing would come crashing down around him.

"*Stop this at once!*" Muul told him. "*Why are you doing this? What do you hope to gain by it?*"

"*We can stop lying,*" Peter whistled. "*He knows.*"

Goii growled, and the low, guttural sound echoed through the whole room with a timbre and resonance that made Peter's skin crawl. "*Soldiers, arrest Research Officer Muul, and take these two into custody as well. I want that key in my hands immediately. The Earthlings will send more of their own—we need to secure the weapon now, while their numbers are limited, or we risk them reaching it before we do.*"

If Peter had held the slightest doubt about the captain's intentions, those doubts evaporated instantly. Lowell had been right—the aliens might have been nicer than Munroe, but they wanted the same thing he had. A weapon of war, a power source: it didn't matter. Whatever waited inside the husk of Enceladus would be misused no matter *who* got their hands on it.

"*Sir, I would never...*" Muul pleaded, before Goii tightened his fingers around her throat.

A pang of guilt shot through Peter, but he did his best to ignore it. After all, Muul had misled him, too. Lowell was right. They couldn't trust anyone, not when they possessed something as valuable as the stellar key.

The soldiers were moving in, and one of them reached for Lowell.

"Oh, hell no," Lowell grunted. "I am damn well not going anywhere with you." His fist whipped out and caught the alien square in the face, snapping its head back with such force that Peter could hear the bones in the slender neck pop. It collapsed to the floor, and Lowell frowned at a sticky patch of mucus that lingered on his glove.

"What the —? I swear bastards just got stickier."

"Lowell?" Peter said, gesturing to the other aliens, who had taken a step back.

"Right," Lowell growled—it wasn't as deep as the sound Goii had made, but at least the threat would translate well. "We're fighting frog people. My dad would be so proud."

He flung himself forward, targeting the three soldiers they didn't know. Goii still had his hands full with Muul, and Peter had... well, Peter had the components of a suit and he could whistle comprehensibly.

"You going to help me out, Chang?" Lowell demanded.

"*Help!*" Peter whistled. "*Save us! Muul's crossed us both!*" He wasn't sure that the idiom translated into their language, but it was the best he could do.

"I meant with fighting." Lowell tackled one of the aliens, wrapping his arm around its neck. One of the other guards struck a blow to the back of his head. Lowell seemed uninjured, but the alien's hand left a sticky spot on his hair and neck.

"*Subdue them,*" insisted Goii. He lifted Muul up off of her feet, and she clutched at her arm uselessly. Her face darkened as she struggled against the wall.

Lowell finally dropped the alien he was holding, making a face at the slimy sleeve of his suit. "Their bones are brittle," he said.

Which probably meant that the other two aliens were dead. Peter figured that it shouldn't bother him any more than the death of Munroe and his team had bothered him, but it felt wrong. After a lifetime of wishing that he could meet actual, honest-to-God aliens, the fact that they were just as greedy as regular old human beings was a huge disappointment.

The last two soldiers made a simultaneous grab for Lowell. He managed to grab one by the arm, yanking it closer so that he could get his hands around its throat. While he was preoccupied, the other one leaned in and bit him on the face. Lowell yelped as the bite drew blood, and managed to swing his elbow back into the alien's head. It fell, too, leaving only Muul and Goii standing.

Goii narrowed his eyes at them and lifted his gloved hand to his lips. "*Crew of the Brink, we have a situation. Research Officer Muul has conspired with the humans. All three of them are to be detained immediately if...*" He fell silent when Lowell struck him a blow to the back of the head.

Muul fell to the floor, gasping for breath.

"Well," Lowell said, prodding the captain's limp body with his toe. "That was surprisingly easy."

"What is wrong with both of you?" Muul demanded. She looked up at Peter. The muscles at her temples expanded and contracted at an alarming rate. "Why would you frame me like that?"

"What exactly would your captain have done with us if we just handed over the key?"

Muul looked away.

"Yeah," Peter said coldly. "That's what I thought."

"We should get going," Lowell told him. "I'm guessing that you have the key stashed somewhere?"

Peter smiled sheepishly and climbed up on his bed. He removed the light orb from its socket, revealing the small recess behind it. The stellar key sat safely hidden inside.

"You're a clever little squirrel, aren't you?" Lowell asked approvingly.

"You're both idiots," Muul said, stumbling to her feet. "The captain is going to be *furious*."

Lowell pointed to the limp body on the floor. "The guy whose bones snapped like dry twigs? That captain?"

Before Muul could reply, the first body on the floor twitched. Peter looked down at it curiously.

"You've bought yourself a little time, but they'll regenerate before long. You haven't damaged their central nervous systems," Muul scoffed. "They'll be up and about within the hour."

"Well, I hate that," Lowell grumbled.

A hundred questions sprang to Peter's mind, but now wasn't the time to ask them. He settled on the pertinent one. "But your people *can* be killed, right?"

"As if I would tell you how," Muul snapped.

"I didn't ask how," said Peter reasonably. "But the captain's put out an alert for you—and I bet that whoever's coming after us will know how to hurt you, won't they?"

Muul stared at him, then looked down at her feet; the captain had begun to spasm, and his eyes rolled up to her face.

"So," said Peter with a falsely cheerful tone. "Want to help us figure out how to get off the ship?"

13

AS THEY STEPPED out into the hall, Lowell found himself swaying slightly. The sight of the alien crew lying on the ground left him feeling sickly, which was unusual. He'd seen enough injured men in his day. Hell's bells, he'd *made* enough of them.

The unlikely trio hurried down the hall with Muul in the lead. As they walked, Lowell began to question whether the sight of the aliens was the problem, or if something else was wrong. He felt weak, and the back of his head burned where the alien had slapped him. The bite mark on his face had begun to throb. His feet no longer seemed to obey him, slipping on the slick floor with every uneven step.

"We can't trust your girlfriend," he said aloud. The words came out slurred.

Muul glared over her shoulder at him, her temples fluttering. "No," she said coldly. "You can't."

"Are you okay?" Peter asked.

"Fine," Lowell lied. "Just a little queasy."

They walked through the circle of the outer corridor. Muul kept stretching her hands, and each time she did, the sticky sheen of her skin became more reflective.

Of course they're slimy, he thought. *Munroe was slimy, too.* He giggled.

Peter stopped dead in his tracks. "Lowell? What was that?"

"Funny thought," Lowell said, and to his distant horror, he giggled again. He wasn't a giggler. His niece, Kylie? She was a giggler.

I miss her. Lowell staggered toward the wall, fighting a wave of sadness that threatened to sweep him off of his feet. *I miss Heather. Hell, I even miss Dad...*

"Lowell?" asked Peter urgently. "Look at me."

Lowell did as he was told, and the younger man's eyes widened at whatever he saw in Lowell's face.

"I don't feel good," Lowell admitted.

The sound of marching boots echoed through the hall. There were more of them this time, and they would certainly be armed. They would take the key. And Lowell...

Lowell would die slimy.

He pushed himself off of the wall. "I can fight," he told Peter. "Come on, Chang, let's do this. We can take 'em. We just need to get to a ship."

A whole squadron of alien soldiers came into view. There were more of them this time, and Lowell would need all of his energy to fight them.

Too bad he could barely keep himself upright.

14

PETER HELD Lowell against the wall, looking frantically between his friend, Muul, and the approaching soldiers.

"*Attack them, Muul! Just like you attacked the captain!*" he whistled.

She turned back to face him, and her whole body inflated slightly, as if she was a balloon that had just been attached to a pump.

"What are you doing?" she hissed.

"Giving you some extra motivation to help me," Peter said. "You were supposed to be on our side, Muul."

She started to say something, but one of the soldiers called a warning, and then heaved an object the size of a baseball directly at Peter. He barely had time to hold up one arm and block his eyes before the object hit him square in the chest and exploded.

This is it. I'm dead. It just hasn't sunk in yet. Muul screamed, but Peter just stood there, still propping Lowell up with one arm, breathing hard. When Peter failed to keel over dead, he slowly opened his eyes.

A white powder had exploded over his skin. The empty halves of a silicon shell lay on the floor at his feet; it had burst open on impact, sending a cloud of the pale substance into the air. Peter licked his lips, frowning.

Maybe he was crazy, but it tasted like salt.

Muul's skin had begun to bubble where the substance had touched her hands, and her huge dark eyes already looked swollen and puffy. Lowell and Peter exchanged a glance. Lowell didn't seem to be affected by the powdery substance, either, but his pupils had expanded alarmingly, a rash was breaking out across his neck and scalp, and the bite mark on his face had begun to ooze a dark, tacky substance.

"Dammit," Peter snarled at the assembled soldiers. "*I was your biggest fan. This is why you should never meet your heroes!*"

The soldiers whistled among themselves, and Muul stared at him through watering eyes. "Just hand over the key. They'll let us live."

It sounded reasonable enough, but Peter had been through hell and back trying to stop Munroe from getting his hands on the weapon, and at the moment he was feeling pretty belligerent.

"This thing already wiped out a whole ecosystem, and it hasn't even activated the weapon yet." He waved the stellar key at her. "Sorry, but I don't want to watch another world get destroyed by some jackass with a God complex!"

Muul looked from Peter to the soldiers, who were falling into formation. She sighed wearily. "War is hell, Peter Chang. I know that better than anyone. Let me carry your friend. I can get you to the ships."

Peter blinked at her. "Just like that?"

She reached for Lowell. "You haven't given me much choice, have you? We'll have to work together if we're going to get out of here alive."

She had a point. Peter watched in bemusement as she lifted Lowell onto her back.

"Follow my lead," she said.

In the corridor before them, one of the soldiers moved, and the rest followed suit. Instead of rushing toward them, the group expanded, and Peter watched in astonishment as they climbed the wall on either side of the corridor. Their sticky hands stuck to the lichen lining the wall, carrying them up with as little effort as it would have taken Peter to crawl on all fours.

Muul took a deep breath, then turned and ran the other way.

"Where are you going?" Peter asked in dismay.

"The outer corridor wraps all the way around the ship," she called over her shoulder. "I figured that charging right *at* them would be stupid, so I'm going to circle back around. Come on!"

Peter did as she told him, even as the mass of aliens that circled the hallway from floor to ceiling began their charge.

15

MUUL HAD SERVED in the fleet for most of her life. As a nymph, she'd been raised with her spawnmates who were destined for a life of exploration. By the time that she was old enough to leave the water, her broodmothers had singled her out for her natural aptitude with languages. Studying languages, however, had meant a certain amount of exposure to other ways of thinking. While her spawnmates were raised on a steady diet of homogenous thought, Muul had developed something like empathy.

At the moment, that was presenting something of a problem.

"Faster," she told Peter as she looked over her shoulder. Lowell's head bobbed against her back, and she felt almost sorry for him. A bite like the one he'd sustained could be deadly, and from what she'd read about humans, their bodies didn't regenerate fast enough to outpace the toxin's effects.

At least the paralyzing mucus that had begun to irritate his neck and scalp was probably enough to dull the pain.

"Don't let them touch you," she told Peter.

He flicked his eyes toward her, and didn't ask why. All he said was, "Or bite me either, right?"

She didn't bother responding.

As they ran, the soldiers moving on foot behind them lobbed more saline grenades their way. One hit Peter in his leg, and Muul felt the impact of two more as they struck Lowell's back. That part, she didn't feel so bad about. If the Earthlings were conniving enough to frame her and stupid enough to get bitten, they deserved to take a few hits.

"Is this all that your people use?" Peter asked breathlessly. "Salt pellets?"

Muul flared her neck-flap. "Hardly. Any moment now, someone will…"

She was cut off by a sharp hum, followed by the sizzle of an electrical charge. A bolt of blue light shot past her, scorching the wall on the far side of the corridor.

"Ah, yes," she panted. "There it is."

Electricity was particularly deadly—high enough voltage would make it difficult to properly regenerate, which could result in permanent organ failure. Muul wasn't entirely sure how human biology worked, but she was pretty sure the two men wouldn't react well to taking a direct hit, either.

If she was going to commit to becoming a traitor, now was the time.

"Carry him," Muul said, pulling up short and thrusting Lowell into Peter's arms. The moment that the bigger man's weight had become his friend's problem, Muul peeled away from Peter, heading for the wall. She ignored his cry of protest and ran up the side, no longer away from her old allies, but toward them. It was wildly undignified to go around with bare feet, but fortunately the new regulation boots did a decent job of imitating her feet's natural suction capabilities, and the lichen gave her a little added traction.

What Peter had done to discredit her was bad enough, but she had spent her whole life in service of the fleet. Captain Goii should have known better. They might lock toes, but she had never disobeyed a direct order.

If he was going to call her a traitor, then by the First Spawning, she was going to become one.

Muul didn't allow herself to focus on the size of the group that she was currently charging. Broadening her scope would overwhelm her. It was better to think small. One of the soldiers closer to the ceiling lifted his weapon as he ran, firing a bolt of crackling blue fire her way.

Just like that, he became the target.

Muul timed the jump, measuring the trajectory of the energy blast, her target's speed, and her own arc through the air. If she'd only jumped a little higher, she could have passed over the ring of soldiers entirely. It was tempting to leave the humans to face the mess they had made and escape on her own.

Except for the matter of the key. Peter was right: someone like Goii couldn't be trusted with that much power.

And so, instead of sailing through the center of the ring and out of danger, Muul collided boots-first with her target. The momentum of their collision carried him off the wall, and the two of them tumbled to the floor below. She grabbed his arm, twisting it around behind him until the thin cartilage of his shoulder gave way. He screamed. It was painful, of course, but it wouldn't kill him. Muul had no intention of killing anyone; getting the key away for now might be the best course of action, but she wasn't going to slaughter her crew just to improve her chances of escape. Besides, if she changed her mind, she could always turn Lowell and Peter in along with the key. Goii might not believe her, but another commander might.

The soldier whom she'd just attacked whimpered piteously, but Muul was already moving. She snatched up the bolt gun, yanked a saline grenade out of his utility belt, and bolted back toward Peter. A few of the soldiers had turned to face her, unsure of which target to prioritize. Muul took advantage of their confusion and lobbed the saline grenade right into their midst. When it landed, a few of them cried out in pain.

She certainly wasn't going to make a lot of friends out of this incident, even if she did ultimately return with the stellar key.

Muul jumped again, aiming over the break in the line left by the detonation of her grenade. She spun in the air, firing a few electroshocks wildly. Not close enough to kill, but close enough to make their pursuers think. She landed heavily, and for a moment she was worried about the cartilage in her knees, but all of her bones held. That was good. She didn't have time to sit around waiting to regenerate.

Peter was struggling with Lowell's weight; he appeared to have gone completely limp somewhere along the way. Muul lifted him again, looking back over her shoulder to make sure that the line had scattered. Sure enough, only a few of them had bothered to keep following.

"How's your aim?" she asked.

"Pretty good," Peter gasped. "I think."

"This way," Muul barked. She turned abruptly to the right.

"Are we... close to... the ships?" Peter gasped.

"We don't have time for that," Muul replied. "Besides, they'll never let us take off. We're going to need to find another way off this ship."

To his credit, Peter didn't argue. He followed her to the outer lip of the saucer, the electroshock gun gripped in one hand and the key in the other.

At the end of the corridor was an emergency escape pod. It was outfitted with the necessary survival gear, and a defensive shield that would activate automatically upon launch. On the downside, the pods didn't include steering, but that could be a problem for the future. Right now, they needed to get off this ship.

They stepped through the door into the escape pod just as the first of their pursuers reached the end of the hall.

"Cover us," Muul said, dumping an insensate Lowell in the corner. "But don't hit them."

"Why not?" Peter asked.

She reached for the pod's activation controls. "Because you want me to keep your friend from dying, *I assume*, and I'm not going to do that if you permanently kill members of my crew."

Peter fired off a few shots. Muul didn't bother to check and see if the shots were effective at holding off their pursuers. She set the pod to launch immediately, and to target the nearest heavenly body with an atmosphere capable of sustaining life. The doors hissed closed, and with a jolt that sent Peter toppling to the floor, the pod took off.

As they shot through the void, Muul finally let herself relax for the first time since Goii's fingers had closed over her throat. She expected to feel remorse for leaving the ship behind, but instead she felt almost free. For the first time in her whole life, she had followed her instincts rather than the precepts that the rest of her people subscribed to.

It was unexpectedly liberating.

16

IN THE BEGINNING, Chandran Bhatt had counted the days since his imprisonment by the Chinese space force. He and Tuhin shared a cell in what Chandran had come to think of as the 'upscale' portion of the brig. The rest of the survivors of the Cell were kept in general lockup, but the Tiān Zhuānjiā translator had identified the two-man team of the *Ratri* as the defacto leaders of their fleet, and they had been awarded choice quarters accordingly.

So far, being a POW hadn't been terrible. The rations were good, sometimes better than they had been on the *Kovind*, and with the exception of a few early visits from the Chinese general and his translator, the men had been largely left alone. Drones brought their meals, and their quarters were equipped with a private shower stall and toilet. The space was cramped, certainly, but taken altogether, it wasn't much smaller than the quarters that Chandran and Tuhin had shared.

The difference was that the doors were locked, and every time

Chandran closed his eyes, he remembered the Tiān Zhuānjiā drones swarming over the *Kovind*, systematically dismantling it before his very eyes while the crew inside died horribly.

"Are you awake?" he asked.

Tuhin shifted on the upper level of their stacked bunk. "I am always awake, my friend. How am I supposed to sleep when I am a prisoner in another nation's ship?"

"We haven't moved in days," Chandran said. "Have you heard how quiet the engines are beneath us? We are stuck in place. Waiting. But for what?"

"For our fate to be decided," Tuhin said.

Chandran wanted to press the issue, to speculate about what their captors might be doing now, and whether they had any chance of escape. They'd discussed it many times already. That subject had run dry. They lay in silence, not sleeping despite the darkness. Chandran was trying to think of something to say when the lights abruptly came on.

"Is it morning already?" he asked, sitting up.

Tuhin motioned for him to be quiet, then pointed toward the hallway that passed in between cells. Some faraway mechanism hissed, signaling the opening of a door, and a loud voice could suddenly be heard throughout the hall.

"I don't need some *goddamn robot* like you pushing me around. Acosta? Where are you, Acosta?"

"I'm here," a much calmer voice replied. "And I don't think that the robot cares how much you yell."

Chandran and Tuhin exchanged a curious look.

"Americans?" Chandran whispered.

"Of course," Tuhin said with a wry smile. "Who else would be that loud?"

As the two new prisoners were escorted to their cells, Chandran and Tuhin watched with interest. They were both dressed in their uniforms, minus their helmets, and the United States Space Corps emblems stood out in relief over their hearts.

This could get awkward, Chandran thought. *I wonder if they know that we helped the Tiān Zhuānjiā bring their mothership down?*

Once the prisoners were safely caged, the drones withdrew. Chandran watched with interest as the American woman spat at the retreating machines.

"What are you looking at?" she snarled, making eye contact with Chandran.

"They're looking at you, Moore," said the man in the cell next to her. He was shorter than she was, with curly black hair and skin only a few shades lighter than Chandran's own. "You're making a scene."

"Who are these guys? Are they from the Cell?" The woman scoffed. "I bet they don't even speak English." Her grey-green eyes swept over Tuhin and Chandran, and her lip curled in disgust. Chandran tried to remember what the logo on her suit meant. It marked her as an officer of some kind, he thought, but he'd always had trouble keeping the insignias straight.

"We are indeed from the Cell, Lance Corporal," Tuhin said. Trust *him* to remember that sort of thing. If there was any justice in the universe, he'd have a ranking of his own by now. "And we are, in fact, both fluent." He sat up in his bunk and stretched languidly, barely even bothering to look at their new neighbors.

The woman grunted, and her friend laughed. "Perhaps we should get to know each other," suggested Acosta.

"Why?" demanded Moore.

"We're both prisoners of the Chinese fleet," Acosta said. "Perhaps we should consider an alliance."

"Would you really want to form an alliance with the pilots who brought down your warship?" asked Tuhin, with all the nonchalance of a man discussing options on a dinner menu.

The woman's eyes widened. "You did? I thought that the Tiān Zhuānjiā... Dammit, Acosta, stop talking to them!" She dropped down onto her bunk, glowering at the wall, presumably so that she wouldn't have to look at any of the rest of them.

Acosta sighed. "We'd have done the same to them, if Munroe told us to, Hellcat."

Hellcat. That was an interesting name. It suited her much better than 'Moore.' Chandran swung his legs off of the edge of the bunk and looked at the woman more closely. "Were you the second-in-command?" he asked.

Hellcat turned to him. Sure enough, she had the look of something wild and angry and vengeful. "Of what?" she snarled.

"Of the Space Corps forces."

She snorted. "I guess so."

Chandran dropped to the floor from his bunk and approached the bars. "Which means that you're first in command now." He gestured over his shoulder to Tuhin. "And so, it seems, are we. Perhaps we *should* take advantage of this fact and form an alliance of our own."

Hellcat turned her head sharply away. "Oh, because our alliances have *really* held up so far. No thanks."

"Your commander was the first to fire," Tuhin pointed out. He strolled over to where Chandran stood and leaned against the door. "So, in all fairness, he dissolved the alliance. The Chinese forces have allied themselves with the Russians. It only makes sense that we should do the same."

"Winners versus losers?" Hellcat asked disdainfully.

"Were you planning on forming an alliance with General Wu?" Tuhin asked drily.

Hellcat spat again. "As if."

"Besides, it seems a little early for the Chinese to proclaim themselves the winners," Acosta added. "We're all out here, stranded on this godforsaken rock, waiting to see what happens next."

"And perhaps our alliance could be limited in scope," Chandran added. "Maybe we only agree to work together to find a way out of here."

Hellcat folded her hands and stared up at the ceiling, as if seeking guidance from on high. Acosta approached the corner of his lockup closest to her. "It's not a bad idea," he murmured. "We both have reasons to hate the Tiān Zhuānjiā."

"And the Russians," Tuhin added bitterly.

Hellcat let out a bark of laughter. "Right. I suppose that's true. But I'm not going to risk my ass for a couple of guys who want to ride my coattails out of here."

"We have more to lose than you do," Chandran said. "Some of our crew is still alive, but we're separated. I'm not even sure how we'd get a message to them."

"Funny that they put us all together," Acosta said thoughtfully.

"Probably assumed that we wouldn't play nicely," Tuhin suggested.

"Or they're hedging their bets and putting us in the most

secure part of the ship," Hellcat added. "All right, fine. Let's make a pact. Are we signing in blood?"

"Let's swear on something that actually matters to us," Chandran said. "Not our fleets. Not our governments. To *us*."

Tuhin clapped him on the back and nodded. "I agree, my friend."

Hellcat got to her feet and approached the bars as well, crossing her arms. "Fine. I swear to play nice with you two, so long as we're all on equal footing."

It was a vague promise, but Chandran felt that he could put more faith in an oath like that than he could have in a more diplomatic agreement.

"I swear on the grave of my *abuela*," Acosta said.

"And I, on the grave of my late wife," Tuhin said.

"On the life of my father," Chandran added gravely.

"Well, boys, this has been real cute," Hellcat said. "So what's the plan?"

17

WHEN LOWELL OPENED HIS EYES, he wasn't sure where he was at first. The room was brighter than their quarters on the alien ship had been, but the air was still uncomfortably warm and humid. His vision was blurred, and his face—God, his whole *head* hurt, as though the Devil himself had done a fairly enthusiastic tap dance right on his cheekbones.

Lowell tried to lift his hand to his cheek, but his limbs didn't seem to be in any hurry to obey him. Once, back in Space Corps basic, Vasko had slipped synthetic mushrooms into their rations. Lowell had spent the next twenty-six hours quietly going out of his mind until the effects wore off, and that was pretty much how he felt right now: quietly panicking as his body refused to obey basic commands, while the ceiling spun wildly above him.

"Wha—?" he grunted, but the word came out as a croak. His mouth was so dry that he could barely swallow.

"Lowell?" Peter's face appeared above him. "Are you awake?"

"Depends," Lowell wheezed. "Is this Hell?"

Peter licked his lips and smiled sheepishly. "She said that you were going to feel funny when you woke up. Between the dimethyltryptamine and the tetrodotoxin..."

Lowell groaned and closed his eyes. "Please stop talking. Do we have any water?"

"Oh!" Peter darted away and returned with a pouch; he extended the straw at the top to Lowell's lips. It tasted a little odd—stale, almost, although Lowell had enough experience with field rations to guess that it was mineral-fortified—but he'd have licked the floors of the alien ship at that moment, if it would have given him a little relief.

"Let me try again," Peter said as Lowell slurped. "So when Muul's people are in distress, they can secrete toxins in their mucus that make you hallucinate, and their venom is, like, insanely poisonous. Actually, Muul says that you might have gotten lucky on that front—I guess the trips can be really bad, but since you were poisoned, too, you blacked out before things got... freaky."

Being poisoned is a lucky alternative to a bad trip. Lowell had heard it all now. It wasn't worth arguing over, though, so he just slurped his water.

"Anyway, Muul helped," Peter said. "They had an antivenin onboard, and the worst of the hallucinations should be past, so you're good!"

Lowell slurped the last of the water. His relief was so profound that he swore he could feel the hydration flowing throughout his body, cooling his burning brain and strained muscles as it did so. He let out a contented sigh and spat out the straw. This time, when he struggled to sit up, he was able to do so without tremendous difficulty.

"So where's..." *Muul,* he was going to say, but now that he was able to look around, he had his answer. Their unwilling ally was lying face-down on one of the narrow bunks, her limbs pulled in tight beside her. She was obviously asleep, but her eyes weren't fully closed. Instead, an almost lacy mesh of flesh covered her partially narrowed eyes.

"Er, yeah, she's taking a quick nap." Even Peter, usually so quick to accept the alien's quirks, seemed a little shaken by the sight. "I guess that's an evolutionary thing for when they need to stay alert while resting, but..." He leaned toward Lowell. "*It's freaking me out.*"

"Good to know you draw the line somewhere," Lowell said. He still felt weak, but his head wasn't spinning anymore. In another few minutes, he was going to be able to relax enough to be royally pissed. It was just typical, wasn't it, that nobody had warned them about the specifics of alien biology. There had to be a way to kill them for real—even if breaking bones didn't work, exposing them to the vacuum of space would probably do the trick. Holding a guy prisoner while pretending to be allies? Rude, but expected. Biting a man and bringing him to the brink of death? Tactically specific, but still within the moral bounds of engagement. Making a man trip like crazy after rubbing your gross skin-spit in his hair?

Unacceptable.

"Where are we headed now?" Lowell asked.

Peter winced. "Um, so, funny story—the escape pod picks a target before launch and then just *goes*, and we don't get to change our minds mid-flight—"

"Skip to the punchline."

"We'll reach Enceladus in about two hours," Peter blurted.

"Enceladus?" Lowell repeated. "No, hold on, the moon blew up."

"The ship IDed it as the nearest habitable object," Peter said. He got to his feet and began pacing back and forth through the small cabin. There was only enough room for him to take about four steps, but he managed to do it in a state of grave agitation. "And by now, whatever's left of it is probably crawling with soldiers. It's a war zone."

"And all of those soldiers are going to be after the weapon."

Peter held up the stellar key. "A weapon that they can only get with this."

Lowell stared at it, torn between resignation and annoyance. It was such a small thing, barely bigger than a man's closed fist. What was its body count up to now? How many people had died to get this stupid chunk of bright metal from Mars to Earth to Enceladus? And those were only the people that Lowell *knew* about.

"So are we viewing this as an asset, or a liability?"

Peter stared at him. "A liability, obviously. Everyone who's known that we have it has tried to kill us! And every time we've tried to bargain, or make allies"—he frowned at Muul's sleeping form—"they've stabbed us in the back the minute they get the chance."

"A valid point," Lowell said. "But may I remind you that we're about to be back where we started, except that instead of having every government on Earth targeting us, we've now got *toxic frog-monsters* on our tails?"

"They're not frogs," said Peter absently, rolling the stellar key between his palms. "They have newtlike characteristics as well... I know that's not the point," he hurried on, before Lowell could interrupt. "But even if we could make a solid alliance, I hate the idea of just handing over the key to whoever's willing to take us in. If we give it to Muul's people, Earth could be in trouble, but I'm not sure that most people would be better off if we handed it over to an Earth faction. My parents live in the US, but my paternal grandparents still live in China. Who am I going to throw under the bus, just to save my own skin?"

Lowell's familial loyalties might not be as divided, but the idea of protecting his own family, at the cost of handing the key over to the Space Corps after everything they'd done to him over the years, rankled.

"So maybe we don't bargain with the key," he said.

"And do what instead? Squat on Enceladus until someone comes along to pick us up?"

"Or," said Lowell, "we could get the weapon ourselves."

Peter's eyes widened. "What would we do with it?"

"Depends. We don't even know what it *is* yet." Using the wall to help himself balance, Lowell slowly scooted himself up into a standing position. "But Muul said it's 'power,' right? And whoever holds the power is going to have the most options."

Peter stared at him, not nodding, but not refuting him, either. Lowell could understand his hesitance. It was one thing to control access to whatever the inscriptions on those underwater tunnels had referred to, and another entirely to hold what was very probably the fate of their species in their hands.

"If you've got a better idea, let's hear it," Lowell urged.

But Peter, as he'd expected, remained utterly silent.

18

ALL HIS LIFE, Fai had dreamed of visiting deep space. He'd studied it from afar, first at the Yunnan Astronomical Observatory, then at the Las Cumbres observatory in Santa Barbara. He'd consulted, albeit in an ancillary capacity, on the first manned mission to Mars. When Peter was a baby, he'd even visited the lunar colony; the number of NDAs he'd needed to sign had seemed outrageous at the time. He'd applied for a mission to Mars and made it to the second round of interviews, but then Susan had filed for divorce, and their lawyer had told him that he would likely lose all future visitation rights with Peter if he went ahead, and Fai had made his choice.

Which made it all the more ironic that now, more than two decades later, he had been drafted as a civilian consultant for the Space Corps, all with the intention of *getting* to Peter.

Captain Sanz had pleaded his case without asking for his input—Fai got the distinct impression that her superiors weren't thrilled about his presence, but the whole mission had a tense, frenetic quality that made it seem as though things were *perhaps* not going the way the Space Corps wanted. And still, nobody had been able to tell him what happened to Peter.

Fai was trying on a spare spacesuit, with the help of Will Collins, when he finally got up the nerve to ask for more details.

"Who is this Lowell fellow that people keep mentioning, and what does he have to do with my son?"

The broad-shouldered, square-jawed man looked down at him with something like sympathy. "He's an old buddy of mine. Sounds like he and your kid got into some trouble out there."

"On Enceladus?" asked Fai, who still couldn't quite believe this. It seemed too wildly improbable.

"Yeah."

"But I still don't understand how he got there," Fai said. There was a pleading note in his voice.

Collins sucked his bottom teeth. "Do you know your prescription?"

Fai blinked at him.

"For your glasses. Can't wear glasses with your helmet. Are you near- or farsighted?"

"Nearsighted." It didn't take a genius to realize that he was going to be stonewalled on this front. Captain Sanz hadn't been forthcoming, either, but at least she'd been civil. Not that Fai presented much of a threat.

Collins trotted over to the other side of the armory, then returned with a small box. "Tilt your head back and open your eyes," he said.

Fai obeyed, but when he saw the contacts held in Collins' hands, he waved the soldier away. "No, I can't use those. Normal contact lenses are fine, but I have trouble with the digital ones."

"These aren't the civilian version," Collins assured him. "And like I said, if you opt out, you're going to be flying blind any time we need full gear."

Reluctantly, Fai agreed, frowning as Collins picked them up on the sterile dropper and lowered the first one onto Fai's eye.

The moment the contacts fell into place, Fai's vision sharpened. The world came into startling focus, and after he blinked a few times, he realized that he could read the smallest tags on the farthest side of the room.

"Oh!" he exclaimed. He lifted his hand toward his face, and his vision instantly refocused, bringing even the smallest wrinkles on his palm into sharp relief, as if he'd somehow zoomed in on it.

"They take some getting used to, but you'll get the hang of it." Collins tapped one finger below his eye and smiled. "A bunch of us wear them now."

"It must make it easier for you to shoot your enemies in the back from a distance," Fai said. "And your allies, too."

Collins' mouth snapped shut.

"I saw the photographs of what your people did to those children," Fai told him. "So as much as I appreciate the use of your new tech, Mr. Collins, I think you can appreciate my concerns. I want to know what you can tell me about my boy."

Collins reached out and closed one hand around Fai's shoulder, pulling him closer. Fai's heart pounded in his chest—but it was true, wasn't it? The Space Corps couldn't be trusted. No one could. Dr. Behnam had made that crystal-clear.

"Listen," Collins muttered, "if anyone gives you shit, you let me know, okay? That goes for Sanz, too. I don't have a read on her yet. But Vasko and me? You can trust us. Even if our orders change, we're not going to let anything happen to you."

Fai's mouth fell open in surprise.

"And for what it's worth?" Collins added, in a voice so low Fai could barely make out the words. "If your son really was hanging around with Lowell? I bet he's still alive. Lowell's not the kind of guy who'd go quietly. If your kid's dead, it means that Lowell died first."

"Oh," Fai breathed. This was the first hint that anyone had given him that Peter might have survived, and although Fai hadn't let go of this hope entirely, the confirmation that he wasn't completely delusional felt like a blessing.

They heard footsteps behind them, and Collins quickly stepped away as Captain Sanz stepped into the armory.

"You've been cleared, Dr. Chang. We're heading out now, before one of the bigwigs changes their minds." She looked over Fai, nodding solemnly. "Make sure you've got your helmet, Doctor. Collins, show him how to secure it and make sure he's on our channel. We're counting on him to be useful, and that means keeping him in the loop. We'll brief you on the way." She lifted her own helmet into place and strode past them toward the waiting ship. Collins grabbed a spare helmet and thrust it into Fai's hands, then led the way.

There was nothing to celebrate, really. The circumstances could hardly have been grimmer. For finally, Fai stood on the brink of launching outside of Earth's orbit, not just to the little tourist trap that was the lunar colony, but out into the sky beyond.

For just a moment, he let himself savor a thrill of excitement.

19

HE MING WAS BECOMING INCREASINGLY irritated. General Wu wanted results, and she had nothing new to give him. What was she supposed to tell him? That the drones had mapped ninety-nine percent of the moon's surface, and they still had nothing to show for it? That they might have to start from scratch?

That would be bad enough, but Ming's real fear was that they had come all this way and gone to all this trouble for nothing. Perhaps the Americans had sabotaged them in some way—perhaps letting Mr. Lowell and Mr. Chang die had been a hideous mistake.

"It's been more than a week," Ilin complained. "A whole week for the *mudaki* back home to argue and fuss and generally make trouble. I don't like it. Before too long, we'll have other visitors to contend with."

Although Ilin hadn't said so outright, Ming had no doubt that the Russian fleet would be sending backup. It also stood to reason that the Americans would be hastily scraping together a new crew. She could only guess how many of the other fleets would be tripping over themselves to send reinforcements, and when they did, General Wu would have to dedicate more of his attention to diplomacy—or warfare, depending on how the former went. Their time for unhindered searching grew short.

And she had nothing to show for it.

"We hold a tactical advantage," Wu reminded them. He was standing on the lunar surface, his hands folded behind his back, looking up at the sky. Saturn was visible from here, one sliver of its profile turned gold in the light of the sun. Ming did not often look skyward. Doing so left her unsettled, and reminded her just how far they stood from the habitable zone. When she kept busy, she could almost imagine that she was back on Earth, moving around in an admittedly bulky suit. When she looked up, she was confronted with the gas giant and its distinctive rings, which dominated the sky. It was always visible from this face.

Even now, Ming had to bite the insides of her cheeks to control her breathing. *We do not belong out here. This environment is hostile. If my suit failed now, I could die in a hundred different ways, and all of them would be a result of my own hubris in stepping out onto a world where my species does not belong.*

"Ming?" asked the general.

"Hm?" she asked, unable to form words.

"Are there any other anomalies that we should investigate? Anything that the drones have pinged?"

The question gave her mind something to do, and she turned gratefully to the control device on her hand. "If we withdraw to the ship for a while, I can review the readouts. We may have missed something, or...or dismissed it as extraneous data."

"I wouldn't mind a break," Ilin admitted. "Would you like to join me for supper? I'm happy to host."

Her language services weren't needed here, but Ming found herself translating all the same. *I don't want to let you out of my sight for a moment, in case you're saying all this to hide the truth from me.*

"We might decide to rest, as well," the general replied. "And I wish to speak to a few members of my crew."

Translation: *If we come with you, I'm concerned that you will try to kill us, imprison us, or hold us hostage.*

"But we must be close, General, surely. It seems a shame to part ways at this crucial juncture."

Translation: *If we part ways, I cannot guarantee that you won't fire on my ship, and I might be forced to fire on you first in order to mitigate the risk.*

General Wu considered this, then nodded. "I see your point, Ilin. Very well, perhaps…"

"Oh!" Ming cried, pointing skyward. She had just let her eyes wander back to the heavens, in the direction of that implacable view, when something burst through the atmosphere. It burned like a shooting star, diving toward them at a sharp angle. It passed over their heads and out of sight around the tight horizon of the much-diminished moon.

"What was that?" asked Ilin suspiciously.

"I don't know," Ming said, but her fingers were already on the controls, ordering her drones to do a sweep of the dark side of the moon. "Something entered the atmosphere, but I'm not sure where it went down."

"It was big, though, wasn't it?" General Wu asked. "Not just a little meteor burning through the atmosphere—it seemed more substantial than that."

Big enough to be a ship. "Yes," Ming said.

They tumbled back into the transport, all thought of rest and sustenance forgotten. That was for the best, Ming thought. When they were working toward a common goal, Ilin's anxieties faded, and Ming didn't trust him when he was anxious.

The drones had just spotted something, and Ming was about to relay the coordinates when her mic kicked on.

"General?" said a nervous voice. Ming recognized it as belonging to Wan Xu, the junior officer that General Wu had left in charge of their ship. "I'm sorry to interrupt, sir, but we have a situation. We have eyes on another ship."

"Did it just land on the surface?" the general asked.

"No, sir." The young man sounded nervous. "It's...well, sir, I think you're going to need to see this for yourself."

20

CAPTAIN GOII'S head was still ringing from the blow that the human had dealt him. When he probed the back of his skull with his fingers, he could feel the fracture. He was angry at the man, but the humans, after all, were not the real problem.

The real problem was Muul.

"Stop touching it," the medic scolded. "And lie back—the sooner you heal, the sooner we can act."

Goii inflated his neck pouch in irritation, but he did as the medic said, lying back in the regenerative gel tank. As the medicated gel came in contact with his skin, his mucus glands absorbed it, making him heal at an even faster rate than usual.

Not fast enough. Muul was already gone, and she'd taken the key with her.

"Have we found them yet?" he asked.

The soldier standing at his tankside nodded. "Yes, sir. We have a tracker on the escape pod. They were headed straight for Enceladus."

"*Enceladus?*" Goii repeated, sitting upright so fast that a bit of gel splashed out onto the floor below. "The audacity!"

"Sir, please," the medic protested.

"We don't have time for this." Goii stood up and stepped out of the tank, reaching for a change of clothes. He didn't bother wiping off the gel; it would gradually permeate his sebaceous glands, just as the medic intended. In the meantime, he had droughts to end.

He strode toward the door, and his junior officer followed.

"She knew that we were supposed to wait until backup came," he muttered. "We have no way to transport it, and if we interfere with the human fleets..." He puffed up without meaning to. Muul knew the consequences. She had seen with her own eyes what could happen when the hierarchy collapsed.

"Shall I send a message to the high commanders, sir?" asked the young assistant.

Goii stopped so abruptly that his assistant nearly collided with him. He turned slowly, flaring his neck pouch as he did so. "Juaa, isn't it?"

The young male recoiled. "Yes, sir."

"Do you have any idea what the high commanders will do to me if they find out that I've let the stellar key fall into the hands of a spawntraitor?"

"N-no, sir," the young male whistled.

Goii opened his mouth so that Juaa could see past his maxillary teeth, right into his throat. As he did so, he rolled his eyes inward, so that his pupils could focus on Juaa through the thin membrane beneath. The membrane blocked his view slightly, but Juaa's expression of undisguised horror was easy enough to make out. Goii could understand; the parasite that had latched onto the stump of his tongue was enough to make his own stomach turn anytime he looked inward and saw it.

"S-sir? What is that?" asked Juaa.

Goii closed his mouth and spun his eyes back outward, refocusing on Juaa. "It's a louse—it has eaten my tongue beyond the point of regeneration, and if it were to be removed, I would neither be able to speak nor eat. Accepting its placement was one part of the conditions of being given a ranking post."

"But, sir..." Juaa couldn't seem to take his eyes off of Goii's lips.

"So long as I serve high command, my *tongue is theirs*. Everything I am, I owe to my spawnbrothers. Everything I have was given to me by the graces of my spawnmothers. If I betray our people, the parasite will be removed, and I will gradually waste away. But do you want to know something?" He stepped even closer, and the youth leaned back on his heels. In a state of agitation like this, Goii might poison anyone he touched. Usually he would be more sensitive to the threat of danger his state of mind presented, but if this young male wanted to lock toes over a matter of protocol, Goii would happily oblige him.

"No, sir," Juaa breathed.

"I accepted it *gladly*. Unlike some, I am loyal to our people's best interests. My tongue? My life? I'd give it all in service to the greater good. The sooner we subdue Spawntraitor Muul, the better off we will be. So now, we won't be sending a message to high command admitting defeat. Instead, we will be charting a course for Enceladus, and we will be getting back what is rightfully ours."

Somewhere along the way, Juaa had regained his composure. "Yes, sir."

"Good," said Goii, finally backing away. "See to it. I need some time to prepare myself, but when I am prepared, I will make for the landing bay. Have a crew ready to accompany me."

"You intend to lead the party yourself, sir?" asked Juaa.

"Of course," said Goii. "I've let the key get away from me once already. I will not make the same mistake again. And I'll be leaving you in charge of the ship."

Juaa shuddered, but he didn't argue. At least he'd be good at following orders, even if he didn't have two cranial nerves to rub together.

If Muul was killed in the mission, so much the better. But if he brought her back alive, Goii reflected as he began the walk to his quarters, he could think of all sorts of interesting ways to pay her back for her betrayal. Their people could regenerate extremities for a very long time, but there had been no practical studies done about the limits of their regrowth, only anecdotal evidence and scientific theory.

Perhaps, Goii reflected, they'd have a chance to develop a more complete data set in the very near future.

21

PETER HADN'T SPENT much time on Enceladus, all told, but his prior excursion on the moon had been memorable for a number of reasons. He'd seen the icy surface fracture and give way, and the liquid plume slowly turn down, like a spigot as its water pressure drained away. Still, when he thought of Enceladus, he recalled it as an icy sea. As they careened toward it, he was shocked to see that it was now nothing but smooth, almost white stone.

"Hold onto something," said Muul casually. She braced her boots against the floor and clung to the wall with her sticky fingers. Peter looked around for something stationary to grab, but without the evolutionary benefit of adhesive skin, it was too late.

The turbulence of the escape pod entering Enceladus' atmosphere sent both Peter and Lowell toppling to the floor, and then rolling sideways toward one wall. Peter landed in the corner with a grunt, and then squealed in dismay when Lowell's weight all but flattened him. The artificial gravity of the escape pod gave way to the very real, but very low, gravity of the little moon, disorienting Peter even further.

Fortunately, this also meant that Lowell's weight suddenly became much less crushing, and Peter was able to shove him aside and suck in a deep breath of air.

"Hold onto something?" asked Lowell incredulously. "Was that supposed to be helpful?"

"Sorry," said Muul, without sounding sorry at all. Sometimes, her unusual inflection was the result of a subtle difference in linguistic convention, but apparently sarcasm sounded the same among her folk as it did in English.

Lowell started to say something else, but he was interrupted by a deep, shuddering thud that echoed throughout the ship. Metal grated against stone. Peter slapped his hands ineffectually over his ears, but the noise persisted until they finally ground to a halt.

"That went well," said Muul as she let go of the wall.

Lowell rolled to his knees, then struggled to his feet, while Peter slowly righted himself. He expected Lowell to say something rude, but the Space Corpsman must have still been feeling under the weather since his twofold poisoning, and all he did was glare at her.

They'd already changed into the suits included in the escape pod's supply locker. Peter somewhat liked the powder-blue suit that Muul had handed him. Given the size differential between her species and his own five-foot-seven frame, he'd expected the suit to be uncomfortably large. Unlike the Space Corps uniforms, however, they actually adjusted. The suit was comfortably conforming without being too tight. It made sense that Muul's people wouldn't want their outerwear to sit too close to the skin, given what he'd learned about their mucus glands over the last few days.

Now that they had landed, Muul crossed over to the utility locker again and removed three small, insulated packs. She tossed one toward each of the men.

"What's in here?" Lowell asked, reaching for his.

"Supplies. I'm not sure that we'll be able to use them here, but it's better to be prepared than not."

Lowell opened the bag and dug into it, removing a flat rectangular object wrapped in what looked like a vacuum-sealed banana leaf. "What's this?"

Muul glanced over her shoulder. "Food."

Lowell waved the object at her. "Hold on. Are you telling me that you've had me eating live bugs when I could have had MREs this whole time?"

"They're much more nutritionally dense when they're fresh," Muul said dismissively. She pulled an armload of objects out of the locker and approached the two men. As she untangled the objects, she slung one around Lowell's waist and buckled it into place, then did the same to Peter. "Emergency kits. I'll tell you what they are if we need anything."

"You could tell us now," Lowell protested.

Muul strapped on a belt of her own. "I think not. For one, we *know* that Goii will be coming after us at the earliest opportunity, and two, I don't want you deciding that I'm disposable the second we step off this ship."

Peter looked down at the belt. One thing was immediately recognizable: the squat, round-barreled gun held in place over his left hip.

Muul pulled on the gloves of her suit, slung her pack over her front as if carrying a baby, and reached for her helmet.

"What channel are we on?" Peter asked.

Muul tilted her head. "Channel?"

"How do we talk to each other?"

"We'll connect automatically within a certain range," Muul assured him. She pulled her helmet on, then came over to check that they had attached theirs correctly. The helmet was the only overly spacious element of the suit, but wearing it still made Peter claustrophobic—the second he put it on, the smell of damp, slightly swampy air engulfed him.

"Ready?" asked Muul. When they both nodded, she opened the airlock.

The vast, icy tundra that had once been the surface of Enceladus was now gone. A thin layer of ice had formed over the surface of the otherwise bare stone mantle, but it was otherwise unrecognizable.

Peter took an unintentionally large step and nearly overbalanced; the gravity was so low, he wasn't sure how to compensate. His arms pinwheeled, but he stopped moving abruptly as the stellar key glittered between his fingers. Peter experienced a vivid mental image of what would happen if he accidentally dropped it, how it would skip away out of sight, barely encumbered by the low gravity.

He was going to have to learn to be more careful, especially if they really did end up retrieving the weapon. Once he righted himself, he swung his pack around to his front and slipped the key inside, clipping it firmly shut.

"Walk on your heels," Muul suggested. "If you put your weight to the back of your foot, the boots will suction to the surface. If you lean toward your toes more, it will be easier to run, but you won't get a good grip."

Peter tried her suggestion. Finding the right balance was hard, but once he got the hang of it, he discovered that she was right. Lowell grunted in what Peter assumed was admiration of the boots' capabilities.

"Any idea where we're headed?" Lowell asked.

"Not really," Peter admitted. "I was kind of hoping that Muul might know."

"I've never been here," Muul said. "You said that there were inscriptions somewhere? What did they say?"

"We found them under the sea bed," Peter said. "In a cavern alongside the deepest trench. But I would think that they would have been destroyed by the disturbances on the surface."

"Not necessarily," Lowell said. "They were pretty deep underground, remember? And that seems like a good starting point. If there's anything left here, it's going to be under the old sea bed, after all. Besides, now we've got someone who can actually *read* them."

"How are we supposed to find them?" Peter asked.

"Remember what you kept going on about?" Lowell said. "The giantess's face, or whatever?" He pointed to the sky, where Saturn hung above them, low on the horizon. "I told you, one face of Enceladus always faces the planet, so we can use the location of Saturn in the sky as our north star." Without waiting for Peter's response, Lowell set out across the barren plain in the direction of the planet.

"I may have underestimated your species' intelligence," Muul said.

"Yeah," Peter mumbled. "Me, too."

Lowell led them onwards and, as Saturn rose higher in the sky, Peter saw the great chasm come slowly into view. Enceladus may have shrunk, like a massive jawbreaker after its outer layers were dissolved, but the chasm was as deep as ever. The memory of Sharkie and their adventure into its digestive tract made him shudder. Was that what it was like for the bogbugs as he swallowed them down alive?

Seriously, knock it off, brain. If you keep thinking like that, you're going to be sick in your helmet.

Even with the suction on their boots, they made good time. Peter couldn't have said with any certainty how long it had been since they landed, but as they sprang across the wasteland, he felt a profound sense of relief. There was no sign of the Tiān Zhuānjiǎ, and no indication that Goii had managed to track them just yet. Maybe, for once, luck was on their side.

As if to confirm this, Lowell pointed ahead, down the slope of the crevasse wall. "Should be around there," he said.

"Move faster," Muul said. When they turned to look at her, she pointed to the sky, where four objects glinted like airplanes flying overhead.

"What are they?" Peter asked.

Lowell cursed. "Ships. The atmosphere's so thin here that you can see them even before they hit orbit. One of those is a USSC vessel."

"And one of them," said Muul, "is mine."

22

OFFICER CADET ARTYOM ZIMA had been in charge of the Russian spacecraft *Knyaz Bayan* in his commander's absence, and he was getting comfortable in his new role. When the radar first alerted him to the blip, he didn't concern himself too much. The Tiān Zhuānjiā ship had been hovering nearby for days, and it was inevitable that the other fleets would send new vessels in eventually. Zima settled himself down at the comm, sat up straight, and smiled serenely. He was a better diplomat than Ilin. He could handle this.

Then the new ship flew closer, and Zima's jaw dropped.

"What is that, sir?" the navigator asked.

Zima blinked at the screen, wondering if he'd started to go a bit mad. It looked a great deal like...

"A UFO?"

Zima and the navigator exchanged a puzzled glance, and she shrugged. The squat, squashed-looking vessel was the same shape he'd seen in a hundred films and online articles: a disc with a lump in the middle, the outer edges of its perimeter illuminated in sickly green lights.

"It looks like one to me, sir," she said. "Is this the Americans' idea of a joke?"

"No," he breathed. "I doubt it." The hair on the back of Zima's neck stood up. He hadn't spent too much time thinking about the damage that the ship had taken during their altercation with the Cell, but until now, there'd been no one to fight. All of their munitions towers had been knocked out, and while the compromises in the hull had been patched, they were still operating without firepower. What was the likelihood that an alien ship would fly up and want to make polite chitchat?

Somewhere close to zero, presumably.

Zima suddenly and desperately wished that Ilin was here to make decisions.

"Hail the major general," he said. "And activate our defenses—anything we have."

The communications specialist's hands were already flying over the keys, and the navigator cleared her throat several times. "Sir, there's something else." She pulled an image up onto the main screen, and Zima bit his tongue in silent frustration.

The Americans had arrived. And if someone decided to start a fight, they were going to be completely dependent on the Chinese warship to defend them in combat.

23

"DR. CHANG!" barked the captain. "Get over here and tell me what the hell I'm looking at."

Fai hurried to her side. Out of habit, he reached up to push his glasses up his nose, only for the contacts to readjust wildly. He hadn't quite gotten the hang of them yet.

"It appears to be a UFO," he said matter-of-factly. The flattened profile was so familiar, Fai was tempted to laugh. He'd given a lecture at Stanford a few years ago about how the image that sprang to mind when people talked about UFOs was an altogether unlikely design. It was neither aerodynamic nor fuel-efficient.

And yet, here one was.

I suppose the egg is on my face, then, he thought.

Captain Sanz narrowed her eyes at him and pointed to the screen. "I can see that. I was hoping that you might have something more useful to add, Professor."

"You're the one who has access to state secrets," Fai said mildly.

"Can we hail it?" Collins asked.

Sanz got up from her chair on the ship's bridge and crossed toward the screen. Fai discreetly looked around the room, measuring up the expressions of the other soldiers at their various posts. Their usually impassive features had grown tense; this, then, was unexpected.

Is it possible that this is our species' first contact with other intelligent life? Or at least, the first official, documented contact in the present day? Unlike the rest of the crew, Fai was practically bursting with excitement. The idea that all this should happen while he was *here* was almost more than he could stand. For just a moment, all thought of his son was pushed completely aside, replaced by awe.

"No answer," said the young man seated to the left of the captain's chair. "I'm trying them on all frequencies, but they're jamming us."

Captain Sanz stopped at the base of the steps that connected the lowermost section of the bridge to the upper deck. "And what about the moon?"

"I'm getting two distinct sets of heat signatures from the surface of Enceladus," said an older woman seated along the back wall. "They've moving toward one another."

"I don't like this," muttered the captain. She bit down on her thumbnail, then seemed to realize her tic and quickly folded her hands behind her back. "I don't like not having a damn clue."

She turned to Collins. "Take Vasko and get to the surface."

"Ma'am?"

"You two have the most experience out here. And if Private Lowell is somehow still involved in this, you know how the man thinks. Get down to the surface and get me some intel."

Collins nodded. "We should take Chang with us."

Fai startled, and Sanz's eyebrows rose. "To what end?"

"Based on the mission parameters, he's more useful down there than up here," said Collins, with a little shrug.

Mission parameters? What mission parameters?

Sanz took in Fai's surprised face and nodded. "Fine, take him. PFC Tallin, get a picture of this thing to Washington and see what they want from us. Sergeant Petersen, trying hailing the other fleets. I want a clear picture of what's going on, and I want it *yesterday*." She walked back up the steps, barking orders to the men and women she passed, all of whom lurched onto motion.

"Come on, Doc." Collins ushered Fai to the door. "You heard her—we're grabbing Vasko and going to the surface. You ever fired a gun?"

"I'm capable," Fai assured him.

Collins grinned. "Well, look at you, Doc. You're just full of surprises."

———

FAI HAD SPENT a great deal of time with Collins over the last few days, but he was wary of Vasko. He struck Fai as erratic, the sort of man who made snap decisions without considering the consequences.

So of course, he was the one put in charge of flying the ship.

"A hundred bucks says that the Tiān Zhuānjiā have people down here," he said as they skimmed over the moons' surface toward the smaller of the heat signatures. "And if they do, I'm gonna pop 'em one."

"We're allies again," Collins reminded him.

"They killed Munroe," Vasko pointed out. "Don't get me wrong, the guy deserved what he got, but does that sound like an alliance to you? You're not seriously going to report me if I open fire, are you?"

Collins considered this for a minute. "Just don't do anything stupid."

Vasko cackled, which didn't strike Fai as a good sign.

Fai didn't quite understand the readings, but they seemed to be closing in on their first target. "If we do encounter enemy soldiers, what do we do?"

Collins drummed his gloved hands on the steering panel. "Guess we see how they respond."

Vasko's arm jerked suddenly, and the ship shuddered.

"For God's sake, Vas, what was that for?" Collins demanded.

"Drones," said Vasko sweetly. "I know that I'm not supposed to be shooting anyone, but I didn't think drones counted."

"Quit being an idiot. What's that?" Collins pointed out the window.

Fai's eyes widened at the sight of the silvery, bullet-shaped object lying on the surface of the moon below. It was smoother than any of the other vessels that Fai had seen over the last few days, and the iridescent casing glimmered against the dull stone on which it rested.

"It's empty," Vasko said. "But there are life signs up ahead."

He brought them in to land on the far side of a deep chasm, evidently with a lot more grace than the other ship had come down. They secured their helmets, and Collins tossed Fai one of the large but lightweight rifles that both soldiers carried.

"We don't know what we're going to run into out there," he warned. "So follow our lead, okay?"

"What about the ship?" Fai asked. "If there are other people out here, aren't you worried about somebody stealing it?"

Vasko chuckled, then yanked the panel around the steering controls free. "Let me show you a little trick, Doc." He leaned the panel against a wall, then disconnected two of the cables within. "Ship won't go without that connection, but it's an easy enough fix. We can't stop them from blowing it up, but we can make it look like she's dead." He snapped the plastic panel back into place and pretended to dust off his hands. "All better. You see what to do if you're the only one who makes it back out, right?"

Fai nodded, trying to get used to the airflow in his helmet. The oxygen blend must have been higher than usual, and it left him feeling giddy and punchy. The casual way in which Vasko brought up the possibility of his own death would have unnerved him under other circumstances, but things were different out here—it only made sense that the humor would be darker as well. When the other two men disembarked, he stepped out on the moon's surface, following close on Collins' heels.

Collins had brought a tracker with him, and three heat signatures stood out against the frozen stone. Fai let himself hope against all logic that Peter might somehow be one of them.

24

GETTING DOWN to the entrance of the tunnels had been easy enough when they were piloting a pod as though it were a sub. Now that they were forced to get there on their own two legs and could only move along two axes, the tunnels seemed a hell of a lot less accessible.

It didn't help, Lowell reflected, that they were standing on the wrong damn edge of the chasm.

The gap between them and the other side of the cliff was easily fifty feet wide, but that was nothing compared to its depth. Despite the fact that they were standing on the bright face of Enceladus, and that there was now no primordial ocean filling the void with its impenetrable blue, the chasm narrowed into utter darkness below. If they slipped into it, there was no saying how far they might fall.

"You think it goes all the way to the core?" he asked.

"No idea," said Muul. She squatted down on the edge, peering deeper. "The good news is that if we fall in, gravity will likely be kind to us; we probably wouldn't be flattened against the rocks."

"Mm-hmm," said Lowell thinly. "And the bad news?"

"The surface was recently destabilized, and for all we know, we're one rockslide away from this fault line turning into an active volcano," Peter told him. "Or something else entirely might happen, something so bizarre that none of us can even grasp the possibility. That seems to be the way things have been going lately, doesn't it?"

"Well, you're just a regular goddamn ray of sunshine, aren't you?" Lowell asked. "All right, Mr. Positive, who's jumping first?"

"*Jumping?*" Peter squeaked. "Can't we just walk around?"

Muul stood up again, pointing to the far edge of the trench. "It's not a bad idea, actually. I might be able to make that jump even under normal circumstances, but in the lower gravity present here? It shouldn't be a problem."

"With a running start, we should be capable," Lowell added.

"I don't know." Peter looked in either direction. "That seems like an unnecessary risk."

A flash of light on Lowell's peripheral vision made him turn. A ship was skimming over the surface of the moon, and its proportions were unmistakable: it was the same model of Space Corps ship that Helena Moore had used to hunt them, and the same kind that he and Peter had used to bring down Munroe.

They'd spent too long on that alien ship. The Space Corps already had people out here, and if they weren't specifically after the two of them yet, it was only because they were most likely presumed dead.

"I don't think we have the time to spare," he told Peter. "Come on, you can do this. You weigh, at a guess, half of what I do."

Peter shuffled toward the lip of the chasm and let out a shuddering breath. "It's so *deep*."

"I'll go first," Muul offered. She took a few shuffling steps back, lowered herself into a crouch, and then charged forward. With all the grace of an Olympic diver, she raised her arms above her head, pushed off with her toes, and sailed through the air.

Lowell had no reason to want to hurt her especially, not now that she was ostensibly on their side. That said, if she'd tumbled to her death at the bottom of the chasm, he wouldn't have complained *that* much.

But she didn't. Instead, she sailed clear over the divide, landing in a smooth crouch on the far lip.

"There," she said proudly into her mic. "Let's see if you can make it."

Lowell bit back a growl, but he allowed himself an eyeroll. Of course it was a contest. If one of them slipped, she damn well wasn't going to help them out.

"You want me to go next?" Lowell asked.

"Mm." Peter shuffled closer to the edge, staring down into the darkness. "Mm-hmm."

"If I can do it, you can do it," Lowell said, clapping Peter on the back with one large hand. "And if I *can't* do it, you'll know to take your time walking around, right?"

Peter let out a strangled squeal, and Lowell thumped his shoulder again. Then he backed up, crouched down, and took a running start. At the outermost edge of the cliff, Lowell pushed off with his toes, spread his arms, and held his breath. Looking down into the gap below made his heart hammer in his throat. It was a little bit like flying, in a way that even space travel wasn't. When he came to rest, he dug in his heels, activating the suction feature of the boots Muul had given him.

"Impressive," she said, almost grudgingly.

"Told you." Lowell shuffled a safe distance from the edge, then turned to face Peter. "Okay, kid, come on. You've got this."

"Yup." Peter's voice came out in a rush. "Definitely. I'm just gonna... just gonna..."

"You've got this," Lowell assured him.

"Right." Peter exhaled loudly and did a sort of wiggling dance, as though amping himself up for a sports match. "Ready. Steady. Go!"

He broke into a run; even factoring in the low gravity, he was pretty fast. Lowell watched as he pelted toward the edge with unexpected grace.

And then he pushed off with his heel.

"No!" cried Lowell. "You've got to use your toes!"

It was too late. Instead of flinging himself high into the air, Peter's heel stuck to the icy stones for just a second too long. His arms windmilled, his weight continued moving forward; then his heel released, and he tumbled headfirst into the rift.

Lowell didn't stop to think.

"Hold on, kid," he grunted, and he threw himself headlong after him.

25

TRANSLATOR HE MING kept glancing over at Ilin. The man's face had gone shockingly pale inside his helmet.

"Perhaps we should return you to your ship?" she offered.

Ilin rounded on her. "What a novel idea, Miss He. Perhaps while I'm facing off against an unidentified force in an unarmed ship, you can go track down the object that fell from the sky. If you're lucky, you'll be able to get a leg up on the Russian forces. If you are luckier still, I might be killed outright without you having to intervene!"

"Now, Major General, there's no need to speak to her in that way," General Wu said calmly. "Her suggestion is a valid one. We are, of course, not making you do anything. Your nerves are overtaxed."

Ilin sat back, knocking his gloved fists together in an obvious display of irritation. She could practically see the thoughts whirling through his head. If he left them now, he might fail in his mission. If his ship was destroyed, he would be stranded on a hostile world in the company of forces he couldn't entirely trust.

"We shall carry on," he said at last. "Zima is fully prepared to handle the situation."

Ming wasn't sure if the man was lying to her, or trying to fool himself. Their own ship, of course, was in a rather precarious position, but Ilin's was unarmed.

But going back to an unarmed ship wouldn't make it any stronger, would it? Ming folded her hands on her lap and didn't say a word, but she could feel the slight shift in the balance of power between them, with Ilin falling into a more and more precarious situation.

They would have to be careful with him. The more he doubted the security of his position, the more likely he was to take dramatic, uncalculated action.

Which wasn't necessarily a bad thing, so long as it wasn't being used against them. Perhaps it could be redirected against a mutual adversary.

"Do you see that, sir?" Ming pointed at the screen of her scanner. "A small American ship has just arrived on the surface. They've just taken out one of our drones."

Ilin groaned and pressed his hands to either side of his helmet. "Of course, they're after us, too."

The man's defeatist attitude was, frankly, tiresome. Ming zoomed out on her scanner to give Ilin a moment to gather himself. When she did, she spotted an unusual reading. "There appears to be an opening in the side of the trench, General. I'm seeing three heat signatures at its mouth."

General Wu nodded. "Chart a course for it, then."

"And what about the new batch of Americans?" Ilin asked. "They're sure to come after us."

The general's voice was as cold as the tundra outside when he responded. "We will handle the Americans, Ilin. Make no mistake about that."

26

PETER WAS TOO surprised to cry out when he fell, and by the time he realized what was happening, what was the point? Instead of crying out, he kept his mouth shut and tried to think. A fall from this height would almost certainly kill him on Earth, suit or no, but the gravity here was so much less powerful that he figured he had a good chance of surviving this intact. All he had to do was relax; people survived falls from tremendous heights when they didn't tense their muscles.

The impact that he hoped to prepare for never came. Instead of landing on a flat surface at the bottom of the crevasse, he hit the wall and skidded for a while. It hurt, but the suit absorbed most of the damage, and after a solid minute of grating against the canyon wall, Peter became wedged between two outcroppings of stone. He was trapped upside-down, and his leg was stuck fast, but at least he hadn't broken a seal.

Yet.

Better not think about that at the moment.

"Lowell?" he asked in a thin voice. "Muul? Can you hear me?"

"Coming," Lowell's familiar gruff voice replied. Peter twisted around and was greeted by the sight of Lowell practically skiing down the rock face. He'd figured out how to use the suction of their boots to his best advantage, because of course he had. Only Peter could have made such a simple, stupid mistake.

Lowell came to rest just above him, not quite as gracefully as Muul would have, but with effortless confidence nonetheless. He hadn't done well as a guest on an alien ship, but now that they were back in action, Lowell seemed more at ease. Smug, cocky bastard. If he wasn't his only friend out here—and saving his life—Peter would really hate him.

"Are you hurt?" Lowell asked. He leaned forward, bracing one arm against the far wall as he moved close to get a better look.

"Not badly."

"Can you unstick yourself?"

Peter made a valiant attempt to lift himself up by his trapped leg and brace his arms against the wall, but even in the low gravity, he wasn't fit enough. After a brief and fruitless struggle, he groaned. "No."

"Hang on, then, and stop me if this hurts." Lowell reached his free hand down and wrapped his gloved fingers around Peter's ankle. He tugged once, sharply, and Peter whimpered. He lifted his arms again, hoping to wedge himself between the two rock faces. Only when he saw his empty hands did Peter let out a gasp of horror. He patted his shoulders, hoping that his fears would be put to rest when he found the straps of his bag. There was nothing there.

"Lowell!" he moaned. "I dropped my pack!"

Lowell tugged on him again, but instead of helping, Peter

twisted around to get a better view beneath him. The bag was small enough that it would have had no trouble slipping between the crack that had trapped Peter fast.

"Quit squirming," Lowell grunted. "I can't quite..."

"Lowell, wait!"

"It's just a bag, kid. Who cares about Muul's supplies, anyway? It's not like we can eat MREs in a vacuum, not unless we want to choke on the atmosphere or lack thereof..."

"The key was in my bag."

Lowell let out a frustrated grumble. "Oh, come *on*, Chang. The one thing we're risking our necks to save just got thrown down a moonhole? Are you *kidding?*" His helmeted head moved, though his grip on Peter never slackened. "Muul? Can you hear us?"

The line went dead for a moment, other than the sounds of their breathing.

"We must be out of range," Peter sighed.

"Yeah," Lowell said darkly. "That's one option."

Even in the canyon, it was bright. The pale surface of the moon reflected light from Saturn's face all the way down to the bottom of the trench. Peter could see it now, only a hundred feet or so below them, although only a sliver of it was visible from here. When Peter twisted around, he saw his small blue-grey pack dangling by one strap from another protrusion in the wall below. He let out a little yelp of excitement and reached down, but it was still a good two feet out of reach.

"I've got eyes on it," he said excitedly. "Can you lower me down a little?"

"You're not as light as you look, Chang." Lowell sighed. "Are you sure you can reach?"

"Yeah," Peter lied. "Just another couple of inches." Lowell was a strong guy. He could handle it, especially with the aid of the suction boots.

"One second, then." Lowell bent his knees and shuffled his hand slightly down the wall. "How about now?"

"Almost, almost..." Peter wiggled his fingers ineffectually. Below the place where he was stuck, the trench widened again. If Lowell could just lower him enough, he'd have plenty of room to grab the bag and possibly even right himself. First things first. He had another six inches to go.

"Dammit, Chang, can you reach it or not?" Lowell's voice was strained, and Peter would have felt bad if the future of the universe hadn't been on the line.

"Almost... just another inch..."

"I'm not sure I can do this, Chang. Let me just—"

It happened in the span of a few seconds. First, Peter's fingertips brushed against the strap of the bag. Then it slipped, and he had to scramble to keep the damn thing from freefalling the rest of the way to the bottom.

"Gotcha!" Peter crowed.

Then Lowell's knees gave out, and the two of them plummeted through the air once more.

At least Lowell didn't land on top of him when they hit the ground.

Peter lay against the stone, breathless and dazed. He was half-prepared for the rock below him to give way and for a bubble of molten lava to spill forth from the moon's core. When it didn't, he opened one eye.

People who didn't know better, even in the world of academia, tended to conflate archeology and geology. Other than knives, axe heads, fishing weights, and other manmade stone tools or carvings,

Peter didn't know much about mineral deposits. He didn't *have* to. He might not know exactly what he was looking at, but it was certainly beautiful. The floor of the once-underwater cavern where they now found themselves was mercifully flat, but the roof above them dripped with stalactite-like formations freckled with blue, green, and purple gemstones. It reminded Peter of Ali Baba's Cave crossed with the Northern Lights, the sight made all the more wondrous by the sliver of Saturn's face still visible through the fissure above.

"Wow," he breathed as he sat up, clutching the pack to his chest.

"Wow is right," Lowell growled. He sat up, dusting off his chest. If the wonders of their surroundings had any effect on him, he did nothing to indicate as much. Instead, he rolled his head to one side and tapped his palm against his neck. His spine popped so loudly that Peter could hear it through his mic. "What the heck were you thinking?"

"I couldn't lose it," Peter told him stubbornly.

"Then you shouldn't have dropped it in the first place. What's the plan now? You think we're going to climb all the way back up there?" He pointed to the wall above them. Even if Peter had any hope of being a decent rock climber, the cavern roof was at least twenty feet from the ground.

The place where they stood was dimly lit, but ten feet on either side of them, the light failed. Struck by a sudden spark of inspiration, Peter knelt down and rifled through his pack. He wasn't sure what *everything* was, but to his relief the stellar key was sitting right on top, and a bit of digging produced a familiar orb. It looked just like the ones that had been installed in the ceiling of the alien ship.

"I think this is a light," he said, although closer inspection didn't reveal how it worked. He tried poking it, shaking it, even tapping it against the floor to no avail.

"Wish we knew what these things did," Lowell said. "Too bad your girlfriend couldn't be bothered to—"

A lean figure blotted out one segment of the visible sky, and a moment later Muul dropped to the ground in a crouch as Peter's side. Without a word, she took the orb from him and twisted each hemisphere in opposite directions. It instantly lit up, although like the lights on her old craft, it was a bit dim for Peter's liking.

Peter grinned up at her. "You came."

"It seems I did," Muul replied.

Lowell didn't sound half as pleased as Peter felt. "Let me guess: you could hear us the whole time, and you waited until you knew it was safe to join us?"

Muul opened her pack. When she spoke, her tone was cool. "I am not the only one who weighs the pros and cons of our relationship before involving myself unnecessarily." She produced her own light orb, powered it on, and closed her bag again. "Besides, there was another vessel headed for the mouth of the tunnel, and since I haven't got a clue who are allies and who are enemies, I thought it best to stick with you."

"I'm afraid everyone's an enemy now," Peter sighed.

Lowell was still bristling, but now that the light worked, Peter's gaze wandered over the walls of the cavern. He'd underestimated how many of the formations were coated in a geode-like mineral that sparkled in the light.

"Lowell," he said slowly, "remember when we were in that cavern where all the tunnels met? Do you think this might connect somewhere up above?"

Lowell turned toward him, and Peter gestured with the light to indicate a passageway through the stone. The walls dripped with mineral deposits, but beneath them, the tunnel seemed perfectly smooth, almost as if it had been made rather than simply formed.

The three of them peered off into the darkness, and Lowell sighed. "Only one way to find out."

27

FAI NO LONGER TRUSTED ANYONE. The trouble was, he'd been put in a position where his life depended on the two men he was traveling with.

"Do you see what happened to the folks who were out here?" Vasko asked.

Collins looked down at the readings on his palm-sized scanner. "Nope. But I've got a reading on that Tiān Zhuānjiā ship we spotted earlier. It looks like they just landed." He glanced over his shoulder at Fai. "Keep up, Doc. I wouldn't want to lose you."

Fai obeyed. He had some vague notion that he might be able to slip away, but to what end, he still didn't know. They'd seen fit to arm him with a small gun, but Fai had never handled one before, and he wasn't entirely clear on the mechanics of it. Not enough to be effective, anyway.

He didn't trust the two men he was traveling with, but he still didn't want to be left behind. Fai quickened his pace.

Collins led them to the edge of a deep ravine, then frowned

down at his scanner. Without explaining himself, he shuffled forward until the toes of his boots extended over the ledge.

"There's a tunnel down there," he said. "I can see the mouth from here."

Vasko stepped up beside him, while Fai hung back. "Yup, I see it. Are we doing this?"

"It's our best bet."

Fai sucked in a breath as Vasko stepped over the ledge without another word. A moment later, a grunt echoed through the mic. "Easy peasy, gentlemen. And look, that Chinese ship is down here. We're right on the money, Collins. It's empty. I'm guessing they took the tunnel. I can't see the end of it."

"We're coming down." Collins gestured for Fai to join him. Despite his little squeak of discomfort, Fai went. What were his options, really? Hang around on his own until someone hopefully came back for him?

Besides, Peter might be there. He'd steeled himself to walk into a war zone to get answers, and even if this was a bit more extreme than what he'd had in mind, it was too late to turn back now.

"You first," Collins said. Perhaps he could sense the older man's hesitation.

Fai leaned out over the edge. He could see Vasko below. *It's not that far,* he told himself. *You can break your own fall.* Before his rational mind could kick in, Fai leapt. He landed in a graceless heap on the ground at Vasko's feet, and the soldier applauded. It was disorienting, to see his hands meet but not hear the sound of applause.

"Nice work, Doc." He reached out a hand and helped pull Fai to his feet. "You're full of surprises, old man."

"I'm not that old," Fai grumbled.

Vasko slapped his back. "That's the spirit." They stepped inside, making room at the mouth of the tunnel for Collins, who joined them a moment later.

The abandoned ship was only a few yards away. Fai didn't know enough about spaceships to know one from the next, but Vasko kicked this one with his boot. "We should sabotage this thing," he said. "Strand those Tiān Zhuānjiā bastards on this godforsaken rock, I say." He said the name of the Chinese Space Corps with a flat American accent that made Fai cringe.

It had been many years since Fai had thought of himself as a Chinese citizen. He'd left Yunnan as a young man, and most of the good parts of his life had taken place on American soil. Most of the bad parts, too, come to think of it. Even so, the idea of stranding anyone on a hostile world was wretched, much less people who might have grown up on the same land where Fai was born.

That sort of logic might not sway the Space Corpsmen traveling with him, so he employed another line of thinking instead. "I'm not sure that's a good idea. May I remind you that we have no easy means of reaching our own ship?" He pointed up at the tunnel's ceiling toward the moon's surface. "Maybe we're better off leaving this vessel intact so that we have a handy means of escape later."

Vasko was obviously put out, but Collins nodded. "Fair point. In the meantime, we should—"

Fai couldn't hear the weapon firing, but the bolt of light that fired over their heads was startling, as was the shower of sparks and sand that resulted when it connected with the wall. Collins had somehow sensed it at the last possible moment, and dropped on the floor to his belly just in time to avoid being hit. Without really thinking, Fai dropped, too, and Vasko rolled off his feet, landing in a crouch behind the abandoned ship.

"Bastards," Vasko grumbled. "Got a read on 'em, Collins?"

"Follow the source of the laser fire, dipstick," Collins snapped. He whipped out one hand to catch Fai by the back of his suit, and dragged them both toward Vasko. A few more blasts threw sparks up from the ground as they went. Vasko cursed—at least, Fai *thought* it was a curse. The string of sounds that passed through his lips was essentially meaningless. He leaned around the side of the little ship and fired back, apparently at random.

"Can we talk to them?" Fai asked.

"Sure," Vasko said. "Take off your helmet and give them a shout, why don't you?"

"I don't know the handshake for their main channel," Collins said. "Not like it matters. So much for a truce, huh?"

"Should we radio the captain? Tell her what's happening here? Can't she beam us up or something?"

Vasko stopped shooting long enough to turn to Fai. "Just shut up and don't get killed, okay?" Then he launched himself out from behind the ship.

On Earth, Fai had never been one for physical combat. He'd run track in college, but he'd never been competitive enough to make a good athlete, and the one time he'd been mugged, he'd quietly handed over his wallet and waited for the armed man to leave. Running into a battle had quite literally never occurred to him; the only victims of gunshot wounds he'd seen were on the news or social media or—he shuddered to think of it now—the pictures of the murdered students at Ur-An that the man in the suit had shown him.

Vasko, it seemed, didn't have that problem. He darted toward one side of the tunnel, where a curve in the wall afforded him a little protection, and fired at the source of the laser beams. Collins did the same from his vantage point.

Fai, however, huddled there shivering like a useless coward. How much use had he really thought he'd be to anybody if he panicked the moment things got real?

Don't think of this as a gunfight, he told himself now. *Think of it as a logistics problem.*

The near-silence of the helmet made that possible, and Fai forced himself to relax as he took in the variables. If he'd been confronted with the sound of gunfire, it would have been impossible. Instead, he could only rely on sight.

Easy enough. Collins was firing from one angle, Vasko from another, but neither of them had a clear line of sight on their opponents. Besides, it was dark in the tunnel.

The contacts that Collins had given him were going haywire, but Fai took a deep breath and concentrated on the deeper parts of the tunnel. Zooming in and out was all well and good, but soldiers had to fight in darkness, too. Surely there had to be a way to make them switch to night-vision...

Maybe there was still too much light in the tunnel for the contacts to switch over. Wondering if he was a fool for even thinking of it, Fai cupped his hands around the visor of his helmet and squinted.

There. He could see the Chinese soldiers further down the tunnel, five bright beacons of heat in a dark world. Judging by their position, Vasko and Collins would never be able to hit them at this rate.

"You need to get up on top of the ship," he told Collins.

The soldier held his fire for a second and glanced at Fai. "What?"

"On top! You'll have a clear shot. I can direct you, but I don't know how to use a gun. Some of them have already retreated, so if you just get higher..."

He expected the soldier to argue, but to his surprise, Collins simply did as he said, letting his gun dangle over his shoulder long enough to scramble to the top of the ship.

"One o'clock and down, about thirty degrees," Fai instructed.

Collins fired off a shot, and one of the figures dropped. For a fraction of a second, Fai's heart leapt with excitement. He'd managed to be useful after all.

Except that now, a man was dead. Because of him.

"Did I get him?" Collins asked.

Fai gagged. He had to close his eyes and take two long breaths with his mouth open before he could answer. "One of them, but the others..." He opened his eyes again, then stared in confusion at the place where Collins had fired. One figure still lay splayed on the ground where he'd fallen.

The others had disappeared entirely.

"Where are they?" Fai murmured.

Collins slid off the side of the ship to land next to him. "Where are who?"

"The other soldiers. I could see them one moment, and the next it was like they just... vanished."

Fai had no idea what to do with this information, but Collins just sighed, as if he'd been expecting this. "Are you thinking what I'm thinking?" he asked.

Vasko held his position along the wall. "That those bastards figured out a way to apply a cloaking device to something smaller than their ships? Like their suits, for example?"

"Yup." Collins sighed. "Perfect. Nothing I love more than fighting blind. Think they're still out there, or did they take off?"

"One way to find out." Vasko stepped abruptly away from the wall, right into the open ground where the stone was still smoking from the previous blasts. He stood there for a moment before slinging his gun back over his shoulder. "Looks like they moved on. Think we should follow them?"

Collins shook his head disapprovingly in Vasko's direction, then checked his scanner. He let out an exasperated sigh. "Other than our dead friend, I'm not seeing a single thing on here now. How did we lose *everyone*?"

"Perhaps we should steal their ship," Fai suggested. Getting out of danger certainly seemed like an attractive alternative to their current situation.

Vasko snorted. "Nah, screw it. Let's go hunting. Captain's got her hands full, and our targets are still down here. I like a challenge."

Fai might not have trusted anyone, but that didn't leave him with a lot of choices. As the two soldiers set out down the hall, he followed nervously, keeping his head down. When they passed the dead soldier, Vasko made a rude gesture at him. Collins knelt down to pick up the fallen soldier's weapon, and thrust it into Fai's hands.

"I told you," Fai protested, "I don't know how to *use* this."

"The enemy won't know that," Collins pointed out. "And besides, if you have it with you, there's always a chance you'll figure it out."

Yes, Fai thought grimly. *On the other hand, there's a chance that*

I'll accidentally shoot someone on our side. But they seemed to have few enough allies out here, which made the likelihood that much lower.

They passed into the darkness, where Fai's night vision fully kicked in, but there was no sign of their quarry.

Assuming, of course, that they were the ones doing the hunting, and not the other way around.

28

CHANDRAN BHATT WAS SLEEPING when the door at the end of the hall opened and a pair of drones entered. The lights came on abruptly, and Chandran sat up in his bunk, rubbing his eyes. He'd lost all sense of time since he'd been captured by the Tiān Zhuānjiā, but he was still fairly certain that this was a deviation from the usual routine.

On the bunk below, Tuhin grunted. "What do you think they want now?"

Chandran peered down at him with bleary eyes before glancing across the hallway at the Space Corps prisoners. Acosta had sat up, too, but Hellcat was lying perfectly still, her hands folded over her belly, her dark eyes fixed on Chandran's face.

The smooth, featureless planes of the drones gave Chandran no indication of what they were in for next, but as they approached the bars of his cell, a screen flared up on one of those blank surfaces. That was new. The general and his translator had only visited on a few occasions, but when they had wanted to speak, they'd come in person. Why send a drone to delive message this time?

Because they can't come. Chandran's heart skipped a beat. *Because something's gone wrong.* He might not know the details, but it didn't take an extraordinary amount of imagination to figure out where the problem stemmed from. The Tiān Zhuānjiǎ were currently at a disadvantage.

The avatar that appeared on the screen was unmistakably CGI. Technically speaking, it was almost perfect, except for being uncomfortably symmetrical and slightly too androgynous to be real.

"Greetings," the drone said with a slight smile. "Due to our current situation, General Wu has requested the Cell's assistance once again. As you may recall, you are currently prisoners of war, bound by a standing agreement to assist the Tiān Zhuānjiǎ in battle as necessary. This ship is currently under attack by enemy forces, and your ongoing compliance is requested. Those who are unwilling to take up arms against our current foes will face immediate repercussions." There was something slightly stilted about the voice's intonation.

This only confirmed Chandran's theory: if General Wu had been available, he'd have come to discuss the matter himself. This wasn't a planned attack on the part of the Chinese fleet. This was a defensive maneuver.

It wouldn't be so bad, would it, to climb aboard the Ratri *and take action?* The general wouldn't have been stupid enough to deploy them against other Indian forces; they would have defected immediately. Most likely, they were going up against some new threat from the United States Space Corps, or offing the Russian ship once and for all. In his heart of hearts, Chandran had no objection to fighting the Americans, and once he was on his ship again, he and Tuhin might be able to work out an escape plan.

Hellcat was still staring at him, watching for his response.

"Of course." Tuhin got to his feet, and Chandran slid off the bunk to stand beside him. "Will we be able to speak to the other members of our fleet before we launch?"

"All communications will go through our channels," the drone informed them. "And all of your ships have been updated with tracking devices. We will be watching you closely. Deviation from the approved plan will not be tolerated."

Tuhin nodded. "Of course."

Chandran watched the pilot's back, trying to judge his intent from the set of his shoulders and the tension in his spine. When it came to people, Tuhin usually took the lead. He was better at understanding people, and Chandran trusted him completely.

At the moment, Chandran's head was spinning with the possibilities that lay before them. If they went along with the wishes of the Tiān Zhuānjiā, they would probably be kept alive for the time being. More importantly, the other members of the Cell would also be afforded whatever level of protection that the Chinese space forces were willing to extend. On the other hand, this might be their only chance to escape. Hellcat and Acosta had made a deal. The question was, who could they place more of their trust in: their Tiān Zhuānjiā captors, or the USSC aggressors?

Tuhin would decide, and whatever choice he made, Chandran would follow his lead.

The drone slid the bars of their cell aside, and Tuhin dutifully extended his arms. As he did, two small, jointed arms extended from the front face of the obelisk and secured a pair of magnetic cuffs to his wrists.

All right, then. They'd play along for now.

Tuhin shuffled to one side, and Chandran caught one last glimpse of Hellcat's eyes, of the slight curl of her upper lip, of her exposed canine. She'd clearly just as soon spit on him as look at him.

Just as he was reaching out his arms to accept the cuffs, he caught Tuhin's eye, and he saw the question etched on the man's face.

He'd miscalculated. Tuhin might be the leader when it came to negotiation, but a navigator's job was to line up the shot. Tuhin was waiting for his signal before he pulled the trigger.

The decision to fight or comply rested on Chandran's shoulders.

He didn't stop to give himself time to think. That wasn't how he'd learned to fight, after all. Instinct was king, and Chandran's instinct was to disarm the enemy first and ask questions later. He caught the drone by its spindly arms and yanked as hard as he could, driving the reinforced toe of his boot into the side base of the device.

The force of his attack wasn't enough to knock the drone over, but it teetered precariously on its electromagnetic base, careening sideways into its neighbor. The arms were stronger than they looked, and the drone's three metallic fingers wrapped around Chandran's wrists with a force that would have doubtless crushed the bone if he hadn't been for the protection of his suit.

If he'd been forced to fight both drones on his own, he would have been overpowered within seconds, but fortunately Tuhin was already in motion. He threw himself at the drone whose screen still showed that placid, androgynous, inhuman face. The force of his attack carried them both to the ground. From the corner of his eye, Chandran saw his friend drive his cuffs toward the screen, and heard the electric crackle and the shattering of tempered glass as the reinforced metal struck home.

"Get down!" Chandran called in English as he tried to topple the drone once more. Hellcat dove off of her bunk, taking refuge beneath it. He couldn't see Acosta from here, but he had to trust that the other man had done the same.

As he lashed out at the drone's base again, it fired a bolt of light that passed close enough to his cheek to sear the skin. Chandran risked a glance over his shoulder; the smoking hole in the wall of his old cell was proof that his suit wouldn't do much to protect him from the blast.

It also gave him an idea.

Still holding the metal arms, Chandran swung the drone around to face Hellcat's cell. He could see where the bolt would fire from, and he moved his head to one side, lining up the shot. The instant the laser powered up, Chandran whipped his head to the side so hard that something in his spine popped. He hissed and gritted his teeth as the bolt seared his earlobe, then yanked again. If he was lucky, his aim had been good. If not, he was in no rush to try again.

The next time the drone tottered, it was of its own accord, yanking Chandran sideways so that he lost his balance. Between the pain in his head and the jerky, fumbling movements of the machine, Chandran fell. When he tried to catch himself, the drone released him, and he landed on his back, cracking his head against the floor of the ship.

Keep moving. If it fires again, you're done. On your feet, Bhatt. Chandran blinked as the drone towered over him. *Roll, damn you. Out of the way.*

He couldn't make himself move. Fortunately, he didn't have to.

His aim had been good; Hellcat threw the door of her cell open and lunged at the drone, leaping at the last moment so that she hit the top half of the machine. She let out a howl worthy of her namesake as the drone fell. Unlike Tuhin, she didn't restrict herself to lashing out. The fingers of her gloves drove into metal paneling and tightened, tearing a hole through the sheet metal. Before the drone even hit the ground, she was tearing into it like a wild animal, clawing at the mechanical guts.

At first, Chandran lay there panting, eyes fixed on what looked like a mindless attack. Soon enough, however, he realized that it wasn't random.

She's removing the weaponry. He hoisted himself up on one elbow despite his injury. Sure enough, Hellcat had already disabled the machine, and was now yanking the laser blaster out of the drone's shell. The moment it was free, she whirled toward Tuhin.

"It's done," Tuhin said. The Cell pilot was breathing hard, but he seemed to be uninjured. Sure enough, his drone was reduced to smoking wreckage just as surely as Hellcat's.

Without a word, Hellcat stalked over to Acosta's door and fired a single blast at the mechanism. The drone's weapon fizzled alarmingly, but for all Chandran's concerns, Hellcat was either oblivious or simply indifferent. She kicked open the door and stepped away.

"Not bad, gentlemen," she said. "For a moment, I thought you were going to bail on us."

Chandran and Tuhin exchanged a look, and the pilot's eyes widened. "What happened to your ear, Bhatt?"

Chandran lifted a shaking hand to the side of his head. The

drone hadn't just hit his left ear. By the feel of it, it had been practically sheared off the side of his head.

"Nothing to worry about," Hellcat said. "What's done is done, and anyway, the laser will have cauterized it, right?" She smirked down at him as she approached, but she held out her hand. After a reluctant moment, Chandran took it.

"What now?" asked Acosta.

Hellcat helped Chandran steady himself, then went to Tuhin. She held his hands steady as she fiddled with his cuffs; a moment later, they clattered to the ground.

"Now we yank the guts out of that other drone, see what we can salvage, and get to work on the rest of our jailbreak." She nodded approvingly at Tuhin and Chandran, offering them a toothy approximation of a smile. "The other Cell crewmembers are still on lockdown, and anyone else they've taken prisoner. We're going to bust as many of them free as we can."

"They said that the Cell vessels have been equipped with tracking devices," Tuhin pointed out. "And we're still in deep space, unless you think we stand any chance of being picked up by friendly forces." The fact that friends of the Cell didn't always overlap with friends of the Space Corps went unspoken. "How are we supposed to leave?"

"Who said anything about leaving?" Hellcat stalked toward the other drone. "I'm not hoping to get off this ship, boys. I'm planning to take it over."

29

JUAA PACED the captain's private quarters, sticking and unsticking his increasingly mucous-y palms. It was lucky, he mused, that he was immune to his own venom. Then again, it would be nice to have an excuse to pass out right now. He wasn't looking forward to speaking to high command.

The junior officer hadn't spent a great deal of time in these quarters. Most of his duties could be completed down below, among the males and females of the general crew. Until only a few hours ago, he'd been eager to receive a better posting, or a promotion that would lift him out of obscurity. Now that he'd seen the parasite occupying the captain's mouth, however, his feelings had shifted.

It was one thing to swear to live and die for his spawnbrothers. Juaa would make that oath in an instant. To give up his *tongue*, though?

Calm down. If high command calls in and sees that you've got the anxiety slimes, they're going to have you replaced. Juaa might well decide that he was done pursuing a higher rank, but he wanted that to be *his* choice, not the result of bungling a battle that had been a few centuries in the making.

He forced himself to lean belly-first against one of the plush captain's chairs and focus on his breathing. This room was one of the nicest on the whole ship, with some of the dimmest lighting and the lushest walls. There were even a few ancestor plants clinging to the ceiling, two of which were in bloom. Their granulated, yellow blossoms smelled reassuringly of decay. Juaa closed his third eyelids and allowed his systems to temporarily suspend.

He was still sitting like that when the screen on the far wall came to life. *"Captain Goii, please respond immediately. Captain Goii, incoming call."*

Juaa lifted his head to examine his hand one last time. His venom secretion had slowed to a trickle. It would be barely noticeable on a call.

Perfect.

"This is Junior Officer Juaa, answering on Goii's behalf."

The screen came to life, and Juaa had to press his maxillary teeth together in an attempt to hide his surprise. Most of their people looked relatively similar: the same mottled grey skin, the same wide black eyes, even a similar posture and height, minus a slight disparity among males and females. High command, however, might as well have been another species entirely.

The closest figure was a male with brilliant yellow skin and protruding eyes that sat near the top of his head; next to him sat a hunched-backed older male whose inky black skin was dappled with bright blue splotches; and behind them both sat a tall female with a pointed face and scarlet pigmentation.

"Junior Officer Juaa," chittered the blue male. "Where is your captain?"

"He's leading a landing party on the surface of Enceladus," Juaa replied.

The yellow male's voice was much deeper, a booming bass that made the mics thrum. "Does he have the key?"

Juaa hesitated. Goii hadn't been explicit about what to say on this front, but he was fairly confident that his superior wouldn't appreciate being undermined in front of high command, especially given what Juaa knew about his circumstances.

"He didn't give me all of the details," Juaa said after only the slightest pause. "Captain Goii made it quite clear that my job was to await your orders and then proceed accordingly. We have three human vessels in range, and they have been continuously hailing us, but for the moment we have held our fire."

The female at the back of the group spoke for the first time. Her voice reminded Juaa of an engine firing, the steady *pit-pit-pit* of a machine coming to life. It made his pores prickle and tighten with alarm.

"These humans are only valuable if they hold the key," she chittered. "I appreciate that Muul has logged several reports about their baseline intelligence, but frankly, any large-scale study of their species is a waste of time. You are familiar, Officer Juaa, with what became of her world?"

Juaa tipped his chin down to stop his throat pouch from inflating involuntarily. "Yes, Broodmother."

"Then you know why she might be tempted to sympathize with a disposable species."

Her physiognomy was sufficiently different from Juaa's that he found her expression difficult to read, but his pores tightened even further at her words. There were rumors about high command being another species entirely: not as different as the humans, certainly, but more advanced than his own.

They say the powerful are just as amphibious as the rest of us, he thought bleakly, but now he could see that for the lie it was. They were something else entirely, something dangerous and lovely and unsafe.

"Eliminate the enemy vessels," the elder said. "Whatever stands between us and the power source is a mere inconvenience. You know what to do, I take it?"

"Yes, Broodmother."

The yellow male—an equal? or a temporary mate whose power would only last until the Broodmother tired of him? Juaa was no longer sure—pressed the sticky pads of his fingers together. "Excellent. We are headed your way, Officer Juaa. We will arrive at your location in approximately one solar cycle, and I expect you to have dealt with the problem by the time we arrive."

They didn't give him time to answer. The video cut out, and Juaa was left in the silence of a room whose lavish mosses no longer felt quite as soothing as before. He had passed beyond the nervous slimes now, and instead his skin felt cold and clammy and much too dry.

There was no time to worry about that now. With a reluctant sigh, Juaa crossed to the ancestor plants and plucked one powdery flower from its drooping spike. With his other hand, he scooped up the Control Orb from its cranny in the wall. Then he settled into the cleared space in the middle of the floor and set the Control Orb in the dip at the center of the circle.

Balance was the tricky part. At first, he arranged all of the toes on his free hand and his feet so that his palm-pads rested against the control orb and his digits kept him upright. Then he placed the ancestor plant in his mouth and brought that hand into position as well.

How would this work for Goii? He couldn't hold the blossom on his tongue. Perhaps the parasite...?

As the powdery coating of the ancestor blossom dissolved on his tongue, Juaa's thoughts receded. The experience wasn't quite as disorienting as being poisoned, although the effects were similar: his consciousness faded, dulled by the mildly hallucinogenic effects of the ancestor plant. It was easier to see in this state, and to keep tabs on every section of the ship at once.

His worries evaporated, and his fears vanished. The only thing that mattered was the orders of the elders in high command.

The humans were disposable, and it was time for them to go.

30

ZIMA STARED down at the instructions that had come in from Major General Ilin.

Handle it.

That was all.

Zima couldn't have said what he expected. After all, Ilin had a mission of his own, and the Tiān Zhuānjiā were temporary allies, at best. But surely the arrival of an American vessel and an alien ship warranted a bit more advice than *Handle it.*

Unless Ilin was just as out of his depth as Zima. It was comforting, he'd found, to assume that his superiors had all sorts of secret information to which he was not privy. He was quite content with the notion that his commanders made their decisions based on an elaborate system that Zima himself was patently incapable of comprehending.

It was, frankly, terrifying to think that they were flying by the seat of their pants, just as he was.

"Hail the Space Corps vessel," he demanded. If the

newcomers refused to answer, he was going to find someone who would.

A moment later, the main screen lit up to reveal a sharp-faced young woman. "Commander Ilin...?"

"You are speaking to the acting captain of the *Knyaz Bayan*," Zima barked. "What is the meaning of this?"

"I was hoping you could tell me," the American commander replied grimly. "Our... specialist seemed to think we were in the midst of an alien encounter."

Zima pursed his lips and glanced around the bridge. The navigation officer's face had gone very pale, and everyone else was staring not at the screen, but through the glass at the rotating disc outside.

Perhaps this is a dream. It certainly doesn't feel real. And if it's not, there's no precedent, no protocol going forward.

"I propose a truce," said Zima. "I understand that the situation is complicated, but if this is a first encounter, don't we owe more to our fellow man than to whoever these interlopers are?"

The American bit her lip, her eyes flicking back and forth between Zima and something just off-screen. "I suppose..."

"Officer Zima." Engineer Rada Morozova lifted a trembling finger to point out at the unfamiliar ship. "What is happening?"

"What was that?" asked the American sharply.

Zima tilted his head to the side, puzzling over this new development. The silver disc had begun to spin, its green lights blinking in an unfamiliar pattern. It swung to one side so that the bottom of the ship was visible, a perfect gleaming circle set against the stark blackness of space beyond.

"I don't know," he began.

Suddenly, the whole room was bathed in a soft green light.

Zima wasn't sure if the power on his own ship cut out, but he found himself floating out of his chair, drifting toward the ceiling. He could still breathe. Whatever was happening wasn't painful, exactly, just puzzling. It was a bit like flying.

It isn't bad, he thought woozily, smiling, although there was really nothing to smile about. He simply felt good. *Perhaps they come in peace.*

A moment later, the bond between his atoms gave way, and he expanded impossibly, with vast gaps in his mass that rendered his organs nonviable. Before his consciousness had even truly dissipated, the gaps in his biomass closed, condensing him and the ship around him, along with the rest of the crew, to a single pinpoint of matter.

It didn't hurt. It didn't feel like anything at all.

"WHAT WAS THAT?" Captain Sanz demanded, slamming her palm down onto the emergency alert. In the microsecond before the video chat cut out, she had seen Zima's blissed-out expression; the next moment, the Russian ship was *gone.*

"Captain?" asked a voice at Sanz's shoulder. "What are our orders?"

Sanz took a shuddering breath before powering on the ship-wide audio, so that her answer would reach everyone onboard at once. "I need everyone at their battle stations. We've encountered a new threat; priority goes to evasive maneuvers, with offense as a secondary concern."

"Do we retreat, Captain?"

For a moment, Sanz pictured Collins and Vasko on the surface of the little moon, ignorant of the bloodless carnage she'd just witnessed. The civilian, too. She didn't know what she was up against, and leaving them behind might be the most prudent course of action.

Sanz had been trained to deal with all manner of problems, and to make snap decisions at a moment's notice. It took a bit of humility to admit that she had no idea how to deal with this particular problem.

"My orders stand," she said at last. "I'm going to contact Washington. Hold the line."

A call out and back could take upwards of six minutes, even if Washington was able to make an immediate decision. If they said to abandon this post, she would, and Collins and Vasko would be left on their own. They knew the risks.

But she wasn't going to bow out yet, and not just out of a sense of loyalty that had been hammered into her since the first day she enlisted in the Corps. There was no chance in hell that the silver ship was the only one of its kind.

If one of them could implode a Russian transport ship, what could more of them do to Earth?

31

PETER WAS GETTING CHATTY AGAIN, a sure sign that he was beginning to relax, but Lowell didn't feel the same at all. For one thing, he had no idea where they were. For another thing, the person—creature—he trusted the least was walking along beside him.

About half an hour into their ascent through the tunnels, something wet touched Lowell's leg. *That shouldn't be possible,* he thought in alarm, before realizing that the dampness was climbing his body, engulfing everything but his head in a sticky, damp substance.

"What the *hell?*" he yelped, looking down at his suit. There was nothing visibly wrong with it, but the damp sensation persisted.

"Lowell?" Peter asked. "What's...*aah!*" He did a writhing dance of discomfort, and nearly dropped the ball of light clutched in one of his hands.

"It's just the suit's automatic misting feature," Muul said casually. "You wouldn't want to dry out, would you?"

"So it's just water?" Peter asked nervously.

"Of course not. It's an electrolyte and enzyme compound designed to keep your skin at peak moistness."

Lowell groaned. "How many words are in the English language, Chang?"

Peter frowned at him. "Roughly a million? More, depending on how you count..."

"More than a million words, and you've already taught her *moist*? You're a monster." He turned an accusing gaze on Muul. "How do we turn off the houseplant feature?"

"I told you," Muul said coolly. "It's automatic. Besides, you spent plenty of time submerged in the substance back on my ship, and you showed no adverse effects. If anything, it significantly improved your health."

Lowell's gorge rose at the memory of that slimy grey substance he'd been submerged in while in the care of their 'hosts,' but Muul had a point. He'd recovered from his injuries quite well with the help of said goo. Maybe it wasn't a bad thing, even if it currently rendered parts of him uncomfortably sticky and damp.

"Ooh!" Peter pointed ahead and scrambled over toward one of the walls. "Do you see that? There's a carving there. Too bad it's covered by the mineral deposits..."

Lowell followed him over to the wall and held up his own light orb. Muul joined them, examining the visible portion of the inscription with interest.

"This seems to be a set of instructions," she said. The hostility had faded from her voice. She was so like Chang: they were two nerds in a pod.

"You can read it?" Peter asked excitedly. "What does it say?"

"I can only make out a few words..."

With a weary sigh, Lowell made a fist and then drove it into the layer of stone that obscured the rest of the writing.

"Lowell!" Peter gasped. "What are you doing?"

"Call it excavating," Lowell retorted drily—or as drily as he could, given that he was now unpleasantly moist from the neck down. "This is kind of like what you did back on Earth, right?"

"You could damage the inscription," Muul chided him.

"And the mineral deposits are a natural wonder," Peter added. "For all we know, they formed over millennia..."

Lowell groaned and drove his fist into the wall again, shattering the fine layer of limestone-like material that obscured the rest of the inscription. "Spare me, Chang. I know you want to preserve everything, but I think we both know that this moon's about to go the way of the armor-plated space fish that used to live here. We've got at least three enemies on our tails, if not more, and if you haven't somehow managed to lose it again, we're carting around what I'm guessing is one of the most valuable objects around. We don't have six weeks to piss around taking samples and preserving alien relics. We need to *move*."

He peeled away another brittle chunk of stone to reveal the rest of the writing. Even he could see that the segments above and below it were in another language, and as satisfying as it would have been to turn the whole wall into dust, there was no sense in getting the linguists all worked up just to burn off a little steam. His task accomplished, Lowell stepped away and gestured to the wall.

"Go nuts."

It was a clear sign of their obsession with dead languages that neither Peter nor Muul objected any further. Instead, they stepped forward, crowding Lowell out of the way.

"It's a bit like your language," Peter said. "I recognize the accents and vowel qualities..."

"The vocabulary is archaic, though," Muul replied, letting one finger hover over the stone. Even after Lowell had pummeled his fists against it, she was still solemnly respectful of the ancient inscription. He would have said it was an alien thing, except Peter was doing it, too.

"It says to go up to the Grand Chamber," Muul said.

"Grand Chamber?" Peter asked. "Where are you seeing that?"

"It's a rough translation," Muul admitted. "The word actually means something closer to"—she let out a high-pitched whistle—"but I'm not sure how to capture the gravitas of the meaning in English..."

"We know what it means, anyway," Lowell said. "We were there, remember? We just keep heading upward until we reach that weird room from before. You know the one, Chang."

"Right." Peter laughed awkwardly. "I guess that the specific translation doesn't matter all that much."

"Damn right it doesn't." Lowell was reaching the end of his rope. "So up we go."

He set out at once, and only looked over his shoulder when he was half a dozen strides through the hall. Peter was reluctantly following him, but Muul was still standing in front of the inscription, giving it one final contemplative look.

I don't like that Peter can't read that language, Lowell thought darkly. *Muul could tell us anything, and she already heard Peter talking about the cavern up top. What if she's got us chasing our tails? What if she's using us?*

At least once they reached the chamber above, Peter would have a point of comparison. Everything they were doing now kept them one uneasy step ahead of trouble, and at some point trouble was going to catch them.

Lowell adjusted the straps of his pack as he looked at Muul. *Unless trouble's been along with us for the whole ride.*

32

PETER HAD NEVER HAD anyone in his life who could skim ancient languages with the same natural ease he did. In high school, his interests had gotten him stuffed in more than one locker; in college, surrounded by like-minded geeks, they had become a sort of party trick. Amira had thought that his ability to sight-read was cute, or even hot, depending on her mood. But nobody had ever met him on his level, much less pushed him to try harder.

Until Muul.

He was well aware that Lowell would give him flak for trusting her even one iota, but surely someone as dedicated to the linguistic arts as she was couldn't be *all* bad. In a war, it was usually the academics who stuck to their moral guns and rebelled against fascism and mindless murder.

Well, most of the time. Sure, Peter could think of a *few* counter-examples, some of them quite upsetting—proponents of the Manhattan Project, the Tuskegee Experiment, and the 2043

Eradication Initiative all sprang to mind—but that was rather besides the point. Statistically, Muul was probably on their side.

So what if statistics had never been Peter's strong suit?

As they stepped into the Grand Chamber, however, Muul's gasp of delight was a balm to Peter's spirit. It almost made up for the fact that he was now thoroughly moistened.

"Look at this," she marveled, hurrying over to the wall. "I've read about rooms like this, but to be here! It's truly remarkable."

"What have you heard?" Peter asked curiously. "About the weapon—or rather, the power source?"

Muul examined one portion of the inscription carefully. She'd chosen a section that was written in a language Peter didn't recognize, but she didn't translate aloud. Instead, she spoke absently, as if the majority of her brain was more occupied with the written words than spoken ones. "These tunnels were built to house the source."

"*Built?*" Peter looked around. "Carved, right?"

Muul pulled away from the wall again. "What are you talking about?"

"Oh!" Peter held up a finger, pleased to be able to teach Muul something else she didn't know. "To say that they were built would imply that the tunnels were created from the ground up, rather than cut through the moon's existing core."

Muul was apparently nonplussed by this information. "You heard what I said the first time. Enceladus is a structure built to house the power source."

Peter shook his head. "Hang on... the moon was *built?*"

"Think about it," Lowell said softly. "It makes perfect sense. Enceladus isn't natural. It's practically a machine."

Peter spun toward his friend, mildly annoyed that Lowell

thought he understood the situation better than Peter did. "What do you mean?"

"That thing on the ocean floor," Lowell said. "That silver thing, remember, with all the markings? Everyone was calling it the Anomaly, like it was something unusual that got stuck in the ground. But I don't think it was. I think it protruded from the moon's core."

Peter scoffed. "How did you come to that conclusion?"

"Yes," Muul said softly. "I'm also curious. When did you guess?" Unlike Peter, there was more curiosity than skepticism in her tone.

Lowell sighed, as if he could read Peter's rather uncomplimentary thoughts. "Look, I know that I'm not the smartest guy in this room, but I do know weapons. If you wanted to destabilize something the size of Enceladus, I can think of a few things that might work. Hell, I bet you could even do it with a sound cannon, if you had one that was big enough. But if we'd set off a sound cannon powerful enough to destabilize the whole moon, we'd have been turned just about inside out, and we'd have been swimming in the alien equivalent of a seafood boil. Everything in that ocean would have been chum. The same goes for any other weapon I can think of. Something that can radically alter the surface of a world without destroying it entirely? I've never experienced anything like that."

Muul was usually open about her derision whenever one of them said something utterly stupid. Peter couldn't help the feeling that Lowell's assertions fell into the latter category, but when Muul kept silent, he considered Lowell's ideas more thoroughly. When he did, a rather nasty thought occurred to him.

"But you have, right, Chang?" Lowell said softly. "You grew up on the West Coast."

Peter had spent most of his life in California, where earthquakes had occurred with increasing regularity ever since his childhood. None of them had been on the same scale as what activating the Anomaly had done to Enceladus, of course, but the parallel was unnerving.

"Are you suggesting," Peter asked slowly, "that someone *built* Enceladus to house...whatever it is Muul's people are after?"

"I told you," Muul said calmly, "it's a power source."

Lowell said what Peter was thinking: "Bullshit."

"Are you calling me a liar?" she asked.

Lowell took a few steps forward. "Cut the crap, Muul. When you fed us that line about how your people wanted this thing for nothing but good, you were still using us. You really expect us to keep buying that? No way. Goii isn't looking for a battery, for God's sake—he doesn't really strike me as the *love and peace* sort."

By the light of their spheres, Peter could only dimly make out the profile of Muul's face through her helmet, and it was impossible to read her microexpressions from here. He had a feeling, however, that she was considering her next words very carefully.

Peter spoke first. "How are you still loyal to them?" he asked.

Muul exhaled heavily; from a human, it would have sounded like a sigh, but Peter suspected that she'd just inflated her neckpouch as a defensive gesture. "Why would I be loyal to you, either?"

"Because we're both trying to stop our asshole bosses from getting their hands on something that could wreck the universe," Lowell pointed out.

Muul snorted. "That's your best argument? You aren't going to try to sell me on the concepts of, as you put it, love and peace?"

"Hell, no," Lowell shot back. "I'm not a liar. When has a weapon ever brought *anybody* love and peace?"

Muul glanced back up at the inscriptions. "I suppose that admission makes your argument more compelling, at least. All right, then." Her huge, dark eyes traveled over the stone in search of something. When she spotted it, she waved them over to a series of images cut into the smooth wall of the cavern. To Peter, the pictures would have looked like nonsense, but as Muul began to speak, their meaning came into focus.

"Listen," Muul told them. "And I'll explain what I know."

IN THE BEGINNING, *even before the Spawnmother laid her first great clutch of eggs, there was another species who made their original home on a faraway planet, in a galaxy much closer to the center of the universe than either yours or mine. They began quite simply as single-celled organisms, floating in the primordial soup of amino acid chains without a care. Then these tiny cells became eukaryotic...they learned how to feed, and to grow, and to multiply. As time went on, individual cells banded together, at first in a loose cluster, and then gradually, into larger and larger aggregates, which eventually came to be possessed of a single mind.*

For a long time, they made their home in the soil of their homeworld, seeking nothing but nourishment and moisture and light. Over millennia, these people—the Photosynthians—grew in complexity, and developed specialized behaviors that allowed them to become more and more independent. At length, they became as intelligent as your species, and then later as intelligent as mine.

And then, as all self-aware species gradually do, they began to turn to the stars, and to wonder if there were other species like them, or if they were alone in the universe. They found ways to travel and explore, but over the course of unnumbered eons, they discovered the truth:

That first world was the only one of its kind.

At first, this was disheartening. But these people had never lost their connection to the lifecycles of their homeworld, so they put down vestigial roots—no longer life-giving since the olden days when they had first become epiphytes—and set their collective mind to pondering what made them special.

They found it eventually, deep within the core of their world: the spark. The thing that made their planet unique. They could not remove it without killing themselves off, of course, but they were advanced enough to understand how they could synthesize it. So they developed a reliable method of synthesis, built a fleet of experimental ships, and set out. They took an abundance of their single-celled progenitors with them, as they were still plentiful in that time, and set out on a voyage of discovery.

The Photosynthians were long-lived, but even so, their voyage lasted generations. They visited star after star, galaxy after galaxy, in search of habitable zones. When they found them, they constructed untold numbers of moons and planets, each with a bit of this synthesized, life-supporting energy at its core. They seeded each world with the earliest versions of themselves—and at the heart of each world, they built a kill switch, in case the experiment failed.

Time passed before their species returned to examine the fruits of their labor. Millions of years, to be exact. They discovered that the life they had seeded had developed in myriad ways, according to the bioavailability of that particular world, its relative placement in the habitable zone where it had been established, and other factors too numerous to name. On some worlds, reptiles flourished; on others, amphibians triumphed; there were worlds like Enceladus where the piscine species dominated, and those where invertebrates ruled. Some worlds had died out altogether, but more than half of these seeded colonies were thriving...

"TIME OUT." Lowell held up a quelling hand. "So you're telling me that aliens are responsible for seeding all other life throughout the entire universe?"

"It's not as crazy as it sounds," Peter offered. "In fact, space seeding is a widely accepted theory for how single-celled organisms first arrived on Earth—"

"Theories are all well and good, but how could anyone know for sure?"

"We know," Muul said, "because they told us."

Both men stared at her.

"On their second pass through the universe, they encountered our species and explained our origins. I must say, it was very helpful in codifying our religious texts."

Peter felt as if he was standing on the brink of madness and staring down into the void below. The worst part was that it all made a convoluted sort of sense. Hadn't he and Lowell remarked that the creatures in the moon's oceans bore a striking resemblance to creatures that had evolved on Earth? And Muul's people did seem to bear some resemblance to the amphibians of Earth, albeit overgrown.

"Hold on," he rasped. "So the thing at the heart of Enceladus, the thing everyone's been after, really *is* a power source?"

"A power source with a kill switch?" Lowell amended.

That was a disturbing notion, especially if it applied to Earth as well. If the wrong person got their hands on the stellar key, things could go very badly indeed.

Muul's next words brought with them a new concern. "Exactly, but that's not the worst of it. Life on Earth evolved in parallel with life on Enceladus because of a number of shared factors related to your sun, but Earth's position was better suited to hosting life, so things moved along much more quickly. There is a similar situation in my galaxy, but *my* species is from the inferior worlds."

"You don't say," Lowell muttered smugly.

Muul ignored him. "Several small sister-worlds evolved near-identical species; Goii's people and my own are almost genetically indistinguishable. But the dominant species—including the members of our High Council—decided to exert control by using their own stellar key to activate the kill switch. In the end, they not only destroyed my homeworld... they were able to reverse-engineer the power source to wipe out a neighboring galaxy."

"How?" Lowell croaked.

Muul shook her head. "I'm not sure. But the stellar key does more than simply activate the kill switch. Whoever has it will also need it to retrieve the synthesized spark from the moon's core. And if the High Council gets there first..." She trailed off into silence, although her meaning was perfectly clear.

Peter froze, and even Lowell seemed lost for words. It was easy to imagine a hundred ways that this might end badly. If Goii got his hands on the stellar key, he could either use it to destroy Earth directly, or to extract the power source at the center of Enceladus and use *that* to destroy Earth, and pretty much everything else while he was at it.

"Do you think Munroe knew that story?" he murmured.

"No." Lowell shook his head. "Not the whole thing—not at his rank. If you want my guess, he was the gopher. I bet he knew that it was a weapon. Something powerful. Maybe he even knew what it could do. That would explain why he was willing to do whatever it took to get his hands on it."

"We need to find a way to warn someone," Peter said.

Lowell grunted. "Who?"

It was a straightforward enough question, but Peter didn't have an answer. He'd spent too much of his life thinking that, by and large, people were comparatively good, and that he was relatively safe from any real danger. In the movies and the old cartoon reruns he'd grown up on, people who figured out the big bad conspiracy simply had to alert the proper authorities, and then something would be done off-screen to rectify the problem.

But in this case, who *were* the proper authorities? Not the Space Corps, certainly. Not Muul's leaders, either. Peter had been harboring the vague hope that once their little quest was complete, he'd be able to go over Goii's head and talk to the higher-ups.

From what Muul had told them, though, that wasn't going to be an option.

Maybe we can get in touch with the people who started this all. The ones who seeded Earth and Enceladus to begin with. Although who was to say that they weren't just as awful as everyone else?

"I think you're right," Lowell murmured. "I think we need to find a way to warn someone, just in case the folks in Washington don't realize they're playing with fire."

Muul's amusement was obvious. "Oh, come now, Lowell. They already know. The Photosynthians told my ancestors what was really happening—and I'm certain that they told yours as well."

Lowell and Peter exchanged another distressed glance. That did absolutely nothing to make Peter feel better. Of all the people in the universe, there were only a few people to whom Peter would willingly hand over the stellar key, and Lowell was one of them. He trusted that Lowell would do the right thing, even if he was a military man.

Anyone else? Not so much.

Peter would find a way to destroy the key before he let it fall into the wrong person's hands, even if it killed him.

33

AT FIRST, He Ming hadn't understood what was happening when their party stumbled across the trio of strangers. Their pale, powder-blue uniforms were unfamiliar, and she couldn't make out a crest.

What she *did* know was that her speakers crackled to life, and two familiar voices—along with an utterly strange and unfamiliar one—became suddenly audible through the static. She must have stumbled across an open channel.

She held up a warning hand and shooed the men back, gesturing for them to wait until she could return. Ilin had been quiet for some time, ever since his subordinate had been shot down by the Americans. Whether it was sorrow for the loss of the soldier himself, or more likely distress about being left alone in the company of Tiān Zhuānjiā soldiers and outnumbered three-to-one, Ming didn't know and didn't care. Perhaps he was simply uncomfortable with being rendered invisible by the personal cloaking device General Wu had slapped onto his suit as they retreated.

Officers in particular seemed distressed about disappearing from sight. Ming found that it suited her.

Once she was confident that the men would hold their positions, she crept back toward the three figures in the open part of the cavern. The tallest of them had a very unusual accent, and even with her years of linguistic experience, Ming found herself struggling to understand.

The other voices, however, she knew all too well.

Carpenter Lowell and Peter Chang. What are the odds? On further consideration, Ming discovered that she wasn't all *that* surprised. Some people, like some viruses, were frustratingly difficult to eradicate.

Despite the difficulties, Ming eventually began to piece together the thrust of the conversation. The third member of their party seemed to know a great deal more than the rest of them; more, certainly, than Ming herself.

They were quite a long way through the conversation when Ming finally put together something that hadn't made sense. Judging by what Ming could hear, the third member of their party wasn't human.

So those simpletons made friends with extraterrestrials? That was both vexing and very slightly impressive.

When she'd heard enough, Ming withdrew to where the men were waiting, and briefly summarized what the Americans and their companion had said. From this distance, she could no longer hear them over her mic, and it seemed safe to assume that if she couldn't hear them, they couldn't hear her.

When she was finished, the men were silent. The private

seemed justifiably stunned and Ilin still hadn't spoken since they'd left the ship. General Wu, however, was thinking. The general could maintain his composure at the best of times, but when he was thinking, his silence took on a new quality.

"And you are quite certain that you heard all this correctly?" he asked at length. "There is no room for misinterpretation and error?"

Ming nodded, but of course the general couldn't see her, so she added, "None."

"Can you imagine what might be done with a weapon of this magnitude?" Ilin asked. "Why, the man who held such a weapon might do anything he liked. Enough to annihilate a *galaxy...?* He would be treated like a god."

Only an idiot would choose to wield such a weapon, thought Ming. *If he could annihilate a galaxy, then he would run the risk of destroying everything in a temper tantrum.*

Ming had served in the Tiān Zhuānjiā for most of her life, but that didn't make her a soldier. No matter what they said to the contrary, most of the soldiers she knew had been trained to think in terms of black and white, us and them, in broad but rigid categories and unshakeable absolutes. Translation was different. Ming's primary duty was to understand, on a fundamental level, not only the literal meaning but also the underlying intent of whoever she spoke to.

Men like Ilin had one intent, and one only: to gain power, and then wield it in a way that benefitted them.

She was still wondering what to do about him when the man spoke again. "They have this stellar key, you say? Then I suppose we'd better take it."

"Yes," General Wu agreed. "The Americans cannot be trusted with anything so sensitive."

But who can *be trusted?* Ming wondered.

And for the first time since she had gone to work for General Wu, she did not know the answer.

34

LOWELL WAS FED up with aliens. Until quite recently, he'd been conveniently convinced that they didn't exist, and even at his most miserable, he had been a hell of a lot happier in his ignorance. Peter, of course, was over the moon, but the kid had proven himself certifiably nuts in other regards...like when he'd thought that being surrounded by hungry prehistoric fish was *cool*.

Point in case: the kid was a weirdo. He didn't have the brains God had given an eggplant. Lowell, on the other hand, was a heck of a lot more sensible.

If he'd had a nervous temperament, the revelation that aliens had designed the planet he called home might have frightened and disturbed him. The creek behind the house where he'd played as a boy before the water shortage? That was part of an experiment. The woods behind the house where he, and later Heather, had thrown secret parties with their high school friends: an experiment. The scorpions that had hidden in his boots on his first tour in the Middle East: experiment. The island where he'd taken his only serious girlfriend when he was on a two-week leave from the Marines; the sheer stone faces of Yosemite, where he and his dad had once hiked before their estrangement; dammit, his whole freaking *species*: experiment.

This realization didn't frighten him. On the contrary. It made him angry as hell.

"Anything else you'd like to tell us?" he demanded.

"I think that covers it," said Muul in that oddly lilting, deeply condescending way she had.

Lowell glared up at the etchings on the rock face. It would have been one thing if the images were pretty. He felt, irrationally, that fine art might have softened the blow. Instead, the story was laid out before him in blunt, utilitarian ideograms.

What a way to break it to a guy, he thought dismally.

"I guess we'd better go retrieve this thing, then," he said. "Can't just leave a universe-destroying bit of tech lying about, can we? Damned irresponsible."

"*Galaxy*-destroying," Peter corrected. "It wouldn't be powerful enough to level the whole universe, or we'd know. Or rather, we *wouldn't* know, because Muul's people would have blown us up and we'd all be dead now."

"Don't get angry at *me*," Muul said. "My planet *was* destroyed! Besides, I'm helping you now."

"I'm carrying around one of the most powerful objects in *existence!*" Peter wailed. "I hid it in a *lightbulb socket!* You couldn't have thought to mention at any point that I might perhaps want to be more careful with it?"

"Look, if you're too idiotic to keep track of priceless artifacts, that's no concern of mine—"

Lowell wasn't sure what tipped him off. Call it intuition, call it experience, call it plain dumb luck, but whatever it was that set off the alarm bells in the back of his brain, they did so just in time. Just as the flash of light became visible, Lowell threw himself at Muul, knocking her off of her feet.

"Get off me, you Spawn-cursed *monkey!*" Muul snarled.

Lowell's gaze flicked upward to the smoking crater that now marred one of the images above.

"Oh," Muul said softly. "*Waste-pellets.*"

They rolled apart in opposite directions. Muul was already reaching into the bag slung across her chest, but Lowell's hand flew to his belt first. The small gun still rested at his hip, and he yanked it loose, aiming into the darkness.

The light of their little spheres did a decent job of illuminating the inscriptions, but whoever had fired on them had done so from a distance.

"Get down," he snarled.

Peter immediately fell to the floor, covering his head with his arms, as if that was going to do anything to keep him safe. Honestly, how had he survived to adulthood with so little sense?

I suppose most people don't have to survive gunfire on a regular basis from a young age, Lowell mused. He truly couldn't relate.

The next bolt that fired out of the darkness wasn't a laser weapon of the type favored by the Tiān Zhuānjiā; this one was a chemical weapon. The shot splattered against the stone beside Lowell's shoulder, and the mineral face immediately began to corrode. That didn't bode well. The Russians and the Chinese must be working together against them.

Typical. They'd been stabbed in the back by the Tiān Zhuānjiā once already. Now the Russians wanted a turn.

Get in line.

The first attack had taken him by surprise, and his first thought had been the safety of his team, but on the second shot, Lowell was able to track the source of the round. He tossed the light orb toward the source of the shot, then lifted his weapon and took aim.

But there was nothing to shoot. The hallway was empty.

Lowell frowned. Had his aim been that far off? He was certain that he was in the right vicinity, but—

Hang on. Something moved on the periphery of his vision, not a person but the *silhouette* of a person. A shadow. *What in the hell...*

The shadow was blurry and dim, almost as if someone had passed midway between the light of the sphere and the wall itself, but there was no one there.

It came to him all at once: *the cloaking device.* Lowell had gotten good at spotting hidden ships back in the day, but he'd never seen one scaled down to hide an individual soldier. That was clever. But how was he supposed to fight an opponent he couldn't see?

Muul answered for him, firing at random into the center of the cave. The room exploded in electrical static, and although she didn't seem to hit anything directly, the voltage fanned out like a Tesla coil. For a moment, Lowell saw four figures lit up in relief; it reminded him of lightning striking at night, revealing the land as bright as daylight for less than a second. Someone swore.

"Are you bastards on our channel?" Lowell snarled.

A stream of furious Russian echoed back to him. Lowell fired near where one of the figures had been, and someone else swore in Mandarin.

"You *are.* Stand down, you ugly sons of bitches, or have the decency to *shoot me to my face!*" Lowell knew that he wasn't making sense, but he'd had enough for one day—enough for one lifetime, probably—and if he couldn't exchange a few choice words with the plant people who'd seen fit to go gallivanting around the universe sowing their wild oats, so to speak, he could at least shoot the enemies that were here.

"Lowell, I can't *see* them," Peter said.

"Because they're invisible cowards." Lowell fired again, just for the hell of it. "Don't even know who they *are*."

"You know at least one of us, Mr. Lowell," said a crisp, feminine voice.

"Oh, great." Lowell grumbled. "Miss He. What an unexpected pain in the ass."

He saw the beam headed his way and rolled to the side, firing right back toward its point of origin, but she must have been on the move, because he didn't hit anything. Presumably, if he did, they'd at least hear the injured person crying out.

From the corner of his eye, he saw Peter squirm against the floor. "Ah! Lowell! What the... *getitoffgetitoffgetitofff!*"

"What now?" Lowell demanded. His brain hadn't quite caught up with him. There *was* a way to negate the cloaking devices, but he couldn't quite remember.

Peter rolled onto his back. "Lowell, help! Someone's going after my pack!"

For a split-second, Lowell was on the brink of telling him, *I don't give a rat's ass about your pack,* until he remembered what was inside. If the stellar key fell into enemy hands, they'd be in trouble on a galactic scale. Nothing that could cause species-level extinction should be left in the hands of an enemy force.

And given that everyone was the enemy these days, their odds weren't looking good.

Peter lashed out with his fists and feet like some sort of overturned beetle. He'd dropped his light, and Lowell could see the silhouette of a person in uniform clawing at the bag's straps. Lowell lifted his gun to fire on the person, but before he could, someone struck him in the back of the head. His helmet cushioned the blow, but it sent his aim wide.

Lowell spun toward his own attacker, but his light was too far away to provide him with even the slightest advantage. Something struck his hands, and the gun went flying.

Fighting in a spacesuit was always a disadvantage. Lowell couldn't hear the telltale sounds of an attack before it arrived, or feel a change in pressure. In fact, with the exception of anything that he could hear over the feed, fighting in space meant being robbed of all senses but sight.

And now the Tiān Zhuānjiǎ had figured out a way to rob him of that, too.

His attacker brought his full weight down on Lowell. He said something in Mandarin, and then Lowell felt a pressure on the back of his neck.

Someone was trying to unclasp his helmet.

"Get off." Lowell struggled, but figuring how to grapple with one invisible person, much less two, was nearly impossible.

"Stop wasting time," said General Wu's ever-placid voice. "Shoot it off." He could have said it in Mandarin, of course, which by Lowell's accounting meant that the man wanted him to understand what was coming.

A second later, Lowell was blinded by an explosion of light, and Muul clicked something in her language that might well have been a curse of her own. A strange sensation passed through

Lowell, like a static prickle but all over his body. He twitched involuntarily, but the sensation wasn't unpleasant.

Presumably, the guy screaming above him as the current passed through him didn't feel the same way. Then the full weight of a man's body in uniform collapsed onto him.

General Wu had put up a good fight, but dead weight was less of a problem. Lowell got his arms under him and shoved himself away from the floor, then rolled over, locking his arms and legs around whatever he could reach. Too bad that Muul hadn't hit the general while she was at it. On the other hand, it gave Lowell an excuse to pound his face in.

There was another blast of light as Muul fired toward Peter, and then another round of Russian curses, which presumably meant that her aim on that shot hadn't been as accurate as the first one.

"Give it *back!*" Peter snarled.

Lowell would have helped him if he hadn't been so busy trying to deal with his own scuffle. He reached for the alien weapon he'd dropped, but the general hauled him back.

"You invisible, cowardly *fu—*" he began.

He didn't understand what happened next. It was as if someone had turned the lights off, but only on one side of his head. Someone was laughing, and a dark red liquid was splattered across Lowell's field of vision.

Aw, hell. He must have shot me in the head. On the bright side, when the pain sets in, it'll only last a moment. The vacuum and the cold will take care of the rest, even if the laser didn't do it.

But instead of a light at the end of a long dark road and a chorus of heavenly voices—or demonic chanting, which honestly seemed like the more plausible option—Lowell was next beset by a maniacal laugh.

"How much did that damn cloaking tech cost to develop? A couple billion? And it *still* gets knocked out with a simple paintball. What a bunch of dimwits in the lab, am I right?" The unhinged laughter continued, followed by another burst of light from Muul's weapon.

"Oh, good," she said drily. "More humans to kill."

Lowell flipped over on his back to look up at his assailant. General Wu wasn't entirely visible, but parts of his uniform were now picked out in scarlet.

Paint. That was it. Between that and the laughter, a whole set of complicated memories came rushing back to Lowell. Mostly about getting stabbed in the back by the men who were supposed to be on *his* team.

"That's right, Muul," he growled. "Shoot the bastards."

Without further explanation, he flipped the general off him and reached for the gun.

35

THEY WERE in a meeting when the call came. It might have seemed like a stunning coincidence to anyone who wasn't involved in their private enclave, but the meeting was running into its twenty-eighth hour, and Vice President Perez was riding the latest caffeine high to the bitter end.

It had been hours since anyone had said or done anything productive. They'd gathered at a perfectly sensible eight o'clock meeting on the morning that Captain Sanz's ship was scheduled to approach Enceladus, and Perez had calmly informed them that nobody would be allowed to leave until they could be properly updated regarding the situation with that damned frozen moon.

Looks like one of those spherical ice cubes reserved for good whiskey, Perez thought woozily. *Wish I could have a whiskey. Could do with a bit of a pick-me-up.*

Defense Secretary Owens was leaning back in his chair, his head rolled back and his mouth open; a less professional man would have been tempted to toss little wads of paper into it.

General Reeves sat beside him, curled up slightly in her chair. Only Press Secretary Kelley was still awake, looking bushy-tailed as ever, except for his bloodshot eyes.

War is exhausting. Perez took another slurp of coffee. The rim of the mug was still pressed to his lips when the alarm went off. Reeves shot upright in her chair, and Owens jumped so abruptly that Perez heard his teeth snap together, even from across the table.

"It's Sanz," Kelley observed, casually lifting his hand to flick the button and accept the message, broadcasting it onto the main screen.

Little bastard doesn't know when to quit, does he? Overstepping bounds left and right... bet he thinks he's in line to become VP next, well, we'll see how that goes...

Then the video message from Enceladus appeared on the screen. Instead of Sanz's face, which Perez had expected, the image was that of what looked like an old-fashioned science fiction film: a silver disc with a lump in the center, casually spinning against a starry backdrop in immediate proximity to a modern Russian warship.

"Is this some kind of joke?" asked the defense secretary. "Someone's idea of a prank? These military boys have a terrible sense of humor. If they want to play games, now is certainly not the time—"

Sanz's voice piped through the speakers. "Operation Cascade has encountered an unprecedented issue..."

Perez stopped listening, because a light spilled out of the UFO —*might as well call a spade a spade*—and then, quite abruptly, the Russian ship was gone.

He reached out to shove Kelley's hand away from the controls, and played the video back.

"...unprecedented issue..."

The ship was there, and then it was gone.

Perez played it once more, rotating through the images frame by frame. In real time, the Russian ship seemed to simply blink out of existence, but when he slowed it down and played it frame by frame, he could see that it seemed to collapse inward in one frame and expand in the next. In the third frame, the ship was nothing more than glimmering green flecks against the background of the night.

The four of them stared at the screen, stunned.

"It's not *real*," Owens repeated.

Reeves frowned at him with undisguised contempt. "Of course it is."

Owens flapped his hands at the image before them. "But... how?"

Kelley's eyes met Perez's, and the two of them stared at each other for a long moment.

"You know, don't you?" Kelley asked softly.

Perez didn't consider himself a violent man, but at that exact moment, he would have happily hurled Kelley out of the fifth-floor window with no questions asked. The man knew too much. *Far too much.*

"We should tell the president," Perez said aloud. He could feel a trickle of sweat spilling down the back of his neck, just below his hairline. He had hoped that it wouldn't come to this, that they would be able to handle things quietly.

If they played their cards right, they still might, although it would be a very tight window of opportunity indeed.

"I'll go get her," he said. Not that she'd know what to do either. Standing on the brink of war over a scuffle with the Space Corps was one thing, but if extraterrestrials got involved...

Perez knew what could happen as a result. Technically, he and the president were the only two people in the White House who knew the full scope of the danger, but judging by the way Kelley was staring at him, word had gotten out.

The president would want to skin Perez alive for keeping her in the dark this long. *Smart, in a way,* he thought grimly, *to put off telling her until that became the least of my problems.*

"Tell Sanz to stand by and wait for our orders," he said.

"Yes, sir," Kelley said smugly. He was already recording a response before Perez reached the door.

36

SOMEONE WAS SHOOTING AT LOWELL, but Peter didn't have time to worry about that. At the moment, he had bigger problems: namely, the ghostly figure that was currently trying to kill him.

Peter had never been a big scrapper as a kid, but as he wrestled an invisible man for control of the key that could destroy the Earth in its entirety—or the Milky Way or whatever—he discovered an underlying store of energy that he hadn't known he possessed.

Lowell, of course, had reached for his gun first, because he was a soldier and he had what a civilian like Peter might call *honed reflexes*. Peter's reflex, by contrast, was to bite.

It was stupid, in hindsight. He'd spent enough time in spacesuits recently that it should have occurred to him that his head was wrapped in an airtight bubble and that, barring that, his opponent was wearing a suit made of equally impervious metal. If he'd been thinking, he wouldn't have thrust his head toward the point where unseen fingers grasped at the bag's strap.

But he wasn't, so he did, and the results were quite different than anything he intended.

Muul had made it clear that biting was a natural defense mechanism among her people, although a helmet should have rendered that somewhat difficult. Apparently, rather than learning to do without that skill, Muul's people had simply adapted their defensive armor to allow them to carry the tactic into the stars with them. As Peter's chin bumped against his attacker's invisible fingers, a lower segment of the helmet swung upward to meet a portion that swung down from over Peter's head. For a moment, his entire field of vision was obscured, and when the two segments of the helmet retracted, someone was screaming.

It must be me, Peter realized. *Lowell would never scream like that, and Muul would drop dead before making such a spectacle of herself.* It took him a full second to realize that, although he had let out a little cry of alarm when the world went dark, the screaming was coming from someone else's throat. It was so painfully loud that it rattled Peter's bones.

Then he looked down and saw the glove lying on his chest, completely limp, as if it had been dropped by some careless person as they passed. Except they were in space, and dropping a glove would mean that its owner had one unprotected hand.

That was about the point when Peter worked out why someone was screaming loud enough to wake the dead.

The weight on his chest shifted away suddenly, as if the screaming person had been hauled off of him. Peter sat up, and the glove flopped to the ground, revealing the interior of the wrist. Sure enough, there was still a hand inside it.

Peter reached for his gun, trying to aim in the direction of wherever his attacker was now, only to be confronted by a sight even more disturbing than the hand: three American soldiers, in those all-too-familiar Space Corps uniforms, each of them carrying a laser gun. There was also a silhouette splattered in red, standing between the two groups.

Paintball. Someone had said something about paintball. That was a clever solution to the invisibility problem, Peter had to admit, but that solution had come from someone sporting the same uniform that Munroe had worn. Peter had a definite feeling about people who wore that uniform, and apparently Muul did, too, because she fired on the trio.

One of the figures crouched down, pulling away from the action. *Odd move for a soldier,* Peter thought, *that's more my style.*

"Don't shoot *us!*" yelped one of the Americans. "Shoot the paint guy—"

The paint-splattered man gestured sharply, and the whole world stopped.

The screaming that echoed in the speakers was bad enough, but the sound that suddenly tore through the mic was enough to make Peter pant and whimper and crumple to the ground. It was worse than speaker feedback, an impossibly high-pitched tone that seemed to constantly be rising just to the edge of Peter's range of hearing. The Space Corps sound cannons were deep, too low to hear but powerful enough to turn a man's organs into *paté.* This was a different kind of suffering, one that made Peter want to claw at his ears until the sound stopped. Bile rose in his throat, and he had to bite his tongue to keep from losing his last bogbug into his own helmet.

Someone had to make it stop. If they didn't, Peter's eyes were going to liquefy and his bones would leap out of his body. It *hurt.*

Then Lowell's voice, swearing imperceptibly, cut through the noise, and there was a crunch, and the sound stopped.

When Peter returned to his senses, he was lying on his side on the cavern floor, one arm clutching his pack to his chest, the other pressing one hand to the exterior of his helmet in a vain attempt to block out the sound. Lowell was standing in the middle of the floor, his boot planted on the wreckage of some small machine. Muul lay in a small heap on the floor, curled in on herself. At first, Peter thought she was dead, but then a soft keening noise echoed through his helmet, and her voice repeated a mantra in her tongue, over and over: "*It hurts it hurts it hurts...*"

"Damn," muttered one of the Americans. "Freakin' sonic grenade, I hate that crap..."

"Drop your weapon," Lowell snarled.

"Hey, I just saved your bacon, Lowell. You could try unpuckering and *thanking* me."

"I helped ice Munroe." Lowell walked over to the soldier and kicked the gun out of his hands, aiming point-blank at his head. "I'd have shot him myself if the Tiān Zhuānjiā hadn't beaten me to it. Give me one good reason that I shouldn't shoot you, Vasko."

Peter scrambled to his feet and drew his gun, aiming it at the other competent-seeming soldier. "You were with Munroe?"

"Back in the day," the second man said casually. "At the same time Lowell was. Believe me, I know how much of a jackass the lieutenant could be. That's why I testified against him, if you recall."

Lowell didn't speak, but Peter knew well enough how much of a sore spot his history with Munroe was, and truth be told, Peter was harboring some bitterness of his own. Given what Muul had just told them about the stellar key, the idea of letting it fall into Space Corps hands again seemed downright backward.

They were traitors by now, after all. They could become traitors again.

Vasko, the chatty one, made a rude gesture at Lowell. "Oh, screw you. I've stuck my neck out for you twice, man, and if this is the thanks I get—"

"Don't bait him," the calmer man said. "Here, Lowell, will this help?" He laid his gun on the ground and backed away, hands held above his head. "We're all just tetchy from the sonic scrambler, so let's take a minute and breathe."

"Tetchy?" Peter snapped. "Listen, mister, I don't know you, but you have no idea what we've been through, or how many times people wearing that same uniform have tried to kill us with lasers and harpoons and *giant freaking fish*. Getting our ears blasted off with that thing isn't the problem, it's the last freaking straw."

Vasko snorted and gestured toward Muul. "Tell that to your friend."

The soft clicks and whistles of Muul's mutterings had persisted throughout the conversation, and Peter turned to look at her now. She hadn't moved a muscle since the sound stopped. Either her hearing was more sensitive, or she was more responsive to whatever other sonic vibrations had been emitted by the scrambler.

Peter only looked away for a minute, but before he was able to turn his attention back to the standoff, the calm speaker had burst into action. He leapt forward, grabbing Peter's wrist and deftly twisting the gun out of his hand. Before Peter knew what was happening, he was on his knees, yelping as the man pinned his arm behind his back.

"Let's try this again, Lowell," said the man in the same, easy tones as before. "Who's the kid?"

Lowell's feet shifted nervously, but he didn't take his sights off of Vasko.

Stoic silence had its place, but this wasn't it. "I'm Peter! Peter Chang. A graduate student. Munroe killed off the rest of my dig team, so you'll have to forgive me if I tell you to go to hell. Shoot him, Lowell. I don't care what happens to me, just make sure that they don't get it."

To Peter's immense relief, nobody shot anyone. Instead, the third figure rose to his feet and took a trembling step forward.

"Peter?" asked a soft, shy voice.

"See?" the calm man said. "I told you we'd find him."

"Even if he turned out to be a bit of a prick," Vasko muttered.

Peter ignored them. His head was still spinning from the sound, and from the surprise attack, and from the fact that he'd somehow managed to bite a man's hand off with mechanical mandibles. He pushed all that aside and looked up toward the man standing less than fifteen feet away from him, on a dead moon that had been built by aliens.

"Dad?" he croaked.

37

SANZ WAS WATCHING her messages intently when a new alert came in from Washington. She breathed a premature sigh of relief, until she watched the brief video attachment. It was that little worm, Kelley. He was well-informed, savvy, and condescending as hell. Sanz hated him.

"Please stand by for further instructions," he said cheerfully. That was it.

"Dammit!" Sanz slammed her palm down on the console. "Are you kidding me?"

"Captain?" asked Boswell. "What are our orders?"

"Sit around and twiddle our thumbs while we wait to get vaporized," Sanz spat.

Every eye turned toward her, and Sanz privately wished that she'd restrained herself from reaching out to Washington. They were never helpful, and they never seemed to understand the concept of speed. *We might as well leave the military in the hands of little boys whose only experience with conflict comes in the form of turn-based games and pausable VR.*

She tapped her fingertips on the console. If she was going to earn the right to complain about the stiffs in Washington dragging their heels, she'd have to do better.

"We don't know if our shields work against these things," she said aloud to no one. "And we don't know if our weapons work on them—or if Washington is ready to engage." If they told her to withdraw, that would be ideal; she'd happily pull all of her troops out of harm's way. She'd do it now, in fact, if it didn't involve leaving Vasko and Collins behind.

And Fai Chang, too. They should never have dragged a civilian into this. Her soldiers knew the risk, but abandoning a civilian behind enemy lines?

What they needed was time, and some reasonable assurance that they wouldn't be vaporized in the process.

"Boswell," she said slowly, "are you familiar with the Coburn Tactic?"

"Oh." Boswell's eyes lit up. "The Polyhedron Maneuver? Of course I am."

"Chart a course." She held up a warning finger. "And keep it..."

"Erratic," Boswell finished. "Yes, ma'am. I know the theory."

"Perfect." Sanz scrubbed her hands across her face. "Make it happen."

She kept one eye on her input and the other on the screen, dividing her attention equally between the two. The UFO was turning toward them now with the languid confidence of a cat hunting a mouse.

They think they've got us.

It was a disconcerting thought, in part because if their enemy had a way to counter their maneuver, the next message from Washington might arrive to find nothing left of Sanz and her crew but empty air.

But Boswell, at least, was more competent than her superiors. Within moments, the ship lurched sideways, and they appeared at a different vantage point on the far side of the UFO, safely out of range but still in view. The UFO rotated again, trying to bring the Space Corps vessel in range of the vaporizing weapon it had fired on the Russians. Just before it did, they jumped again, appearing at another point that was now—in the grand scheme of things—rather higher than before. Every time they jumped, they appeared at another random point, and the UFO had to course-correct to bring them into its sights.

The Coburn Tactic always made Sanz slightly sick to her stomach, and it was hell on the engines, but the random nature of their course across multiple axes in space made it difficult to predict where they would end up next. It also made them almost impossible to hit.

There, she thought smugly as the UFO spun uselessly in an attempt to target them. *That ought to keep them occupied for a little while.*

38

FRANK GRADY, Jr. had never been the sort of man who held high aspirations. He'd enrolled in the military at eighteen, mostly because it seemed like something to do. In the part of rural Ohio where he'd grown up, most people were still wasting their time with phones and computers rather than upgrading to the *good* stuff: the contacts that let you stream VR directly into your field of vision, the earrings that allowed you to play music right into your ear canal with nobody being any the wiser, or—Grady's personal favorite—Catapult Cars. Grady's father had always told him that if screens had been good enough for him, they should be good enough for Frank Jr. as well. *There's no need for all those knobs and bobs, sticking out of your head and making you look like some kind of freak.*

Well, Grady had shown his father, because he'd gone to space.

Basic Space Corps training had been fine at first. For the most part, people just yelled at you and told you what to do, which was all right so long as you did it. Some of the other cadets had fought back, angry at having to take orders. Grady had simply knuckled down and done as he was told. His squad leader had taken a liking to him, mostly on account of his malleability.

Working for Munroe had been the worst part of Grady's career so far, but then the Chinese general had killed Munroe in front of him, and Grady had become a POW, and everything had gone back to normal. His days had a routine again, and as long as he puttered along and did everything he was told to do, life was good.

When the Tiān Zhuānjiā had imprisoned Grady, they'd thrown him in with a group of Cell members, but Grady didn't speak Indian. Early on, one of them had tried to explain to him that there was no such language as 'Indian,' and that there was instead a wide array of languages spoken by the Cell members, including Hindi, Tamil, Bangla, and Punjabi... Grady had held up his hand to stop the flow of unnecessary information and told them that if they wanted to speak to him, they could speak English just fine.

After that, they left him alone, which was fine by him.

GRADY HAD LOST track of the days, but he knew the order of events. Being imprisoned on the Tiān Zhuānjiā ship was a lot like getting sent back to Basic. It was bedtime, and Grady had fallen asleep the moment the lights turned off. So when the lights came on again, well before Grady's internal clock nudged him awake, he felt baffled. Unmoored. Worst of all, he wasn't sure what to do next, and so far nobody had told him.

He sat up in his bunk as a row of drones trundled in from the main room, scrubbing at his eyes with the back of his knuckles. One of the screens kicked on, and a monotone voice began reciting a message in one of the many languages that Grady didn't speak. The Cell members exchanged meaningful glances laced with confusion and fear, all of which was lost on Grady. His only question came as the drones split off and approached the Cell cages one by one.

"Hello?" he called. "What about me? Excuse me? I'm Frank Grady, with the Space Corps? Do you have any instructions for me?"

If one of the drones had turned to him and flatly demanded that he go back to bed, Grady would have done so in a heartbeat. But they didn't, so he simply stood there, staring and waiting for someone to tell him what happened next.

More than half of the doors were open, and the Cell pilots and their navigators were being cuffed one by one, when the door at the end of the hall opened again.

Oh, thank God. Grady nearly went limp with relief. At last, someone had come along with instructions. He was expecting General Wu and that pretty assistant of his—it was a shame, in his opinion, how many attractive women went to waste in military careers where their senses of style and humor were inevitably drained away.

What greeted him was something else entirely.

A few blasts of laser fire rang out, and Grady ducked involuntarily. If someone was going to be shot, it stood to reason that it would be him. He was the only American in the room, after all, and the only person who hadn't received an assignment.

Instead, one of the drones wobbled and fell, and the figure at the head of the little party let out a triumphant whoop. "That's right, you sad sacks! This is my house now!"

Grady looked up in surprise. "Hellcat?" he asked.

"Hey, Grady," she said, smiling ferally. "I hear you lost Munroe, huh?"

He tried to answer, preferably with some excuse that would get him off the hook, but she wasn't listening. Instead, she lifted her arm. It was wrapped in what looked like the guts of a drone, and each time her hand clenched over the firing mechanism, the blaster went off. A ripple of sparks passed down her arm, and she flinched, but Hellcat was one of the strongest people Grady knew, and she didn't let her distress show on her face.

The Cell members were shouting, and a second figure followed after Hellcat, wearing a homebrew weapon just like hers. This man was shorter and darker than Hellcat, and he was calling out to the Cell members in what seemed to be a rallying cry. One of his ears was missing, and the wound looked raw and fresh.

One other detail stood out to Grady: the man was wearing a sage-green jumpsuit just like the one Hellcat wore, and the one worn by Grady himself. Everyone in that hall wore one just like it, and while the Tiān Zhuānjiā had probably chosen them because they made everyone look shapeless and impersonal, Grady saw the jumpsuits for what they were.

Uniforms.

He was wearing the same uniform as everyone else in the room, which meant that they were all on the same side.

The gears in his head were slowly creaking toward the logical conclusion when Hellcat called, "Come on, Grady, don't sit there staring like an ass. Help us!"

That was all Grady had been waiting for: a command. Now he had a job, and he knew exactly what he had to do.

When he'd served under Munroe, he'd been given a capsule for use in dire circumstances. He'd managed to smuggle it into captivity through means that he wasn't entirely proud of, and he'd managed to keep it hidden in a pocket of his jumpsuit for just such an occasion. Now, Grady thrust his hand into his pocket, popped the capsule in two, and let the neon blue powder inside pour onto his tongue and dissolve.

The results were instantaneous. He'd tried the powder once before in training, under the supervision of his team leader. It had been fun.

There was no time for fun now. Grady had orders.

He reached up to place his hands on the top bar of his cell door and yanked for all he was worth. Ordinarily, this would have been enough to rattle the door in its automated track and nothing more, but this time the muscles in Grady's arms bulged, straining against the sleeves of his jumpsuit, and a vein pulsed painfully in his forehead. Riding the Neon didn't feel good, but it felt *right,* and not having to yield to the natural constraints of his body and his muscles was a real power trip.

With a metallic groan, the door tore free from its track. Grady grabbed it in both hands and swung it toward the nearest drone. When the machine toppled, he lifted the door above his head and brought it down hard, shearing the machine clean in two.

Hellcat, in the midst of her own rampage, paused to stare at him in surprise. "Nice work, Grady."

Praise. The only thing better than knowing what was wanted of him was knowing when he'd done it right.

The drones were firing on them, and Hellcat was forced to

duck and weave between the press of bodies and machines. Grady wasn't afraid of being shot, however. Riding the Neon made him strong, but it also limited the output of his pain receptors, meaning that a little thing like taking a laser bolt to the chest wasn't anything much to get worked up over. Instead, Grady picked his next target, hauled back, and struck it with the door so hard that the nearest drone went down, taking two more with it. When it tried to right itself, Grady brought his foot down on it with enough force that the metal buckled and he nearly dislocated his knee.

That was all right. All pain was gain when he was riding the Neon.

39

IT HAD BEEN a long while since Helena 'Hellcat' Moore had gotten to participate in a decent brawl. Her recent attempt to take down Lowell had been an embarrassment, and for years before that her team had operated in silence, in the dark, unheard and unseen but desperately feared.

Being an assassin had its charms, certainly, but firing a faulty laser cannon into a mass of confused drones and enraged soldiers? That sort of thing satisfied like nothing else, and Helena had missed the chaos like crazy.

The one downside was her weapon itself. Every time she fired, the guts of the drone hit her with a wave of electrical blowback that made her teeth ache and her hair curl. If she wasn't careful, she was going to electrocute herself.

She'd always thought that Grady fellow was a bit of a wet blanket, but apparently he was full of surprises. Watching him topple drones was, quite frankly, a delight. Chandran Bhatt wasn't what she'd expected, either. Judging by his frazzled hair and his bloodshot eyes, his weaponry was as faulty as hers.

The other Cell members weren't standing by idly, either. Helena watched in surprise as two of them approached one of the drones Grady had severed in half and began to dismantle it, then used the shorn panels as shields while they attacked one of its fellows.

Technically, the Cell and the Space Corps weren't allies. Nobody back in Washington would hold Helena accountable for the health and safety of a militia that had turned against them. If Munroe had been in her shoes, he'd have been delighted to use the Cell members as human shields.

But Tuhin and Chandran had helped her out, and there was no way that she and Acosta would be able to take on the Tiān Zhuānjiā alone. If Chandran had her back, that made him an ally, and the Cell members were his people.

Which meant that, at least for the time being, they were her people, too.

With a feral scream, Helena charged deeper into the fray, dodging Grady's makeshift battering ram and the drones' erratic laser fire.

A few of the Cell members went down, but as the drones were taken out one by one, their remaining reinforcements soon found themselves outnumbered. In the end, Helena was surrounded by the ruins of some two dozen drones; two of the Cell soldiers were dead, and more were injured, but they'd gotten off more lightly than she'd dared hope, mostly thanks to that lunatic Grady.

"Now what?" he asked, tossing his weapon aside and storming up to Helena. His eyes looked bloodshot, but on closer inspection, the blood vessels glowed deep blue; the color pulsed in time with his racing heartbeat. Riding the Neon took an incredible toll on the body, and Helena had seen more than one dosed-up soldier succumb to a heart attack or an aneurysm or just sheer, mindless stupidity. Still, for the next four hours or so, Grady would be more or less unstoppable.

She could use that.

"You need protection," she told him. The twisted hulk of a downed drone lay at her feet, and Helena prodded it with her foot. "Looks like our Cell friends have the right idea."

"Friends?" Grady looked around at their East Indian counterparts. "Are we working with them now, boss?"

Helena nodded firmly. "Yes. They're on our side, Grady."

Even through the stiff canvas of his jumpsuit, it was easy to make out the muscle spasms that passed through Grady's limbs. "Understood, ma'am." Grady knelt down and peeled back the sheet-metal casing of the downed drone as if it was nothing more than wrapping paper, then bent the sheets around his arms and his chest. It was crude armor, but it would get the job done.

Chandran was showing a few of the Cell members how to repurpose the drones' guts when the doors opened. Acosta and Tuhin had taken up watch in the hall, but now they came barreling through the doors.

"We've got company," Acosta panted.

Helena spread her feet into a fighting stance and braced for combat. "More drones?"

Acosta shook his head. "Soldiers."

"You heard that, folks?" she asked loudly. "We've got Tiān Zhuānjiā incoming."

She was used to taking charge, but they'd never really

discussed who'd be taking the lead. It came as a surprise to her when Chandran waved to the soldiers.

"I want pairs together, funnel formation! Navigators in front—you know the drill. If your partner went down, I want you up front with a shield. Nobody gets behind us. If someone falls, leave them. We'll come back for the wounded when we can, but we're taking this ship. *Chak de phatte!*"

With one voice, the other soldiers pumped their fists in the air and replied, "*Chak de phatte!*"

Helena had never seen a unit follow orders as quickly and accurately as the Cell members did...not even *her* team. Despite their makeshift weaponry, they seemed to know exactly what to do.

"What about us, boss?" Grady asked loudly.

Helena looked up at him. "Looks like we're in front, Private, unless you're afraid of taking a little friendly fire?"

Grady grinned a little too widely and cracked his knuckles. "I'm not afraid of anything."

They wouldn't have long before the Tiān Zhuānjiā came in, so she used her time wisely. She gutted another drone and wrapped its firing mechanism around her free arm—no reason to waste time with a shield when she could double her firepower instead—before taking her place at the head of the ragtag army. Acosta stepped up beside her, bearing a weapon of his own.

"It's been nice serving with you," he said, smiling wryly across at her.

"Don't get all maudlin on me now," she told him. "We're taking these bastards down."

Acosta grinned. "Love the confidence."

There was no time to say anything more. A platoon of soldiers, dressed in the Chinese fleet's uniforms, came barging in through the open doors. Grady bent over, rolled his shoulders forward, and charged. *"For the Space Corps!"* he bellowed.

"Chak de phatte!" the Cell soldiers called again, and began to fire.

Helena didn't waste her breath on a battle cry. She was too busy laughing as she fired into the mass of faceless black-clad bodies. The Tiān Zhuānjiā clearly hadn't expected to find their opponents armed and ready. They broke formation within seconds, and their troubles were compounded by the squat, muscular figure wrapped in what looked like old tinfoil who plunged into the midst of their ranks, fists flying. Grady's impromptu armor looked utterly useless, but it did a decent job of repelling laser fire. He grabbed one soldier's blaster, shoved its barrel back toward the soldier's throat so hard that the man went down, and wrenched it out of his hands. He repeated the maneuver with his other hand, and within seconds of reaching the front line of Chinese soldiers, he was holding one rifle in each arm, stocks propped against his elbows, firing laser rounds into the crowd like some sort of deranged cowboy, laughing like a madman all the while.

Maybe it wasn't elegant, but it was effective as hell.

Helena, meanwhile, was putting her sharpshooter training to good use. She knew all the weakest points of the Tiān Zhuānjiā uniforms, and while their enemies focused on the unstoppable chaos of a Neon-dosed Space Corpsman, they left their pulse points unprotected. Helena aimed for throats, kneecaps, the weak seam between chest- and backplates, and the soft joint at the armpit. Acosta wasn't as quick a shot, but he was even more accurate.

And all the while, the Cell was pushing forward, forcing the Tiān Zhuānjiā soldiers back out into the hall with all the patient brutality of a hoplite formation.

Maybe we should talk strategy when this is over, Helena mused. If she could get her recruits to work as well together as the Cell crews did, nobody would be able to stop her.

The Tiān Zhuānjiā numbers were dwindling, but the little allied army no longer had the element of surprise. As their enemy troops rallied, they managed to pick off a few of the Cell pilots. Helena heard the anguished cries of their fellows, but their formation held until they reached a place where their corridor ended in an intersection.

Helena and Acosta fell back behind the shield line, while Grady continued his reign of terror and mayhem out front. An almost continuous stream of laser fire issued from his twin rifles. He was no sniper, but the chaos he brought with him was enough to draw the majority of enemy fire while Helena consulted Chandran and Tuhin.

"You want to keep them from getting behind your lines, right?" Helena said, crouching down beside Chandran.

"We could divide our force," Chandran said warily.

"Your team works well together," Helena said. "Here's my thought: we can sweep the main force down one corridor; Acosta, Grady, and I will take the other and stop anyone who tries to flank you. We'll meet at the bridge and take out whoever's left at the controls."

Chandran and Tuhin exchanged a silent glance.

"You're asking us to put a lot of faith in you," Tuhin said. "How do we know that you won't turn on us to buy favor with the crew?"

Acosta butted in. "And how do we know that you won't head for your ships and leave us to die?"

Chandran shook his head firmly. "We won't. You can trust us."

"And you can trust *us*," Helena replied. "We're short on time here. If we keep second-guessing each other, they'll kill us where we stand."

Another scream from the front line of Cell soldiers drove her point home.

Tuhin shrugged slightly, and Chandran took a deep breath. Then he nodded to Helena. "I hope this is the right call."

Helena grinned back at him. "*Chak de phatte,*" she told him.

Chandran stood up abruptly and shouted instructions in Punjabi, and the Cell forces swept to one side of the corridor, driving the Tiān Zhuānjiā forces ahead of them.

"Grady!" Helena bellowed. "You're with me!"

With a whoop of delight, Grady came charging back, literally bouncing off the wall in order to get past the Cell. "Where are we headed, ma'am?"

Helena gestured sharply down the hall. "We're sweeping to this side. Meeting in the middle. Think you can handle it?"

With a maniacal cackle, Grady bounded down the hall, laser rifles blazing even though there was no enemy in sight.

Acosta sprinted after him, keeping pace with Helena. "I *hate* it when they ride the Neon. Makes 'em stupid."

Helena shrugged. "How bright was he before?"

They met a handful of soldiers at the far end of the hall, and this time, they weren't taken aback by Grady's unpredictable behavior. *Must have been watching us on the cameras,* Helena reasoned. They were still grunts—not a sharpshooter in the bunch—but until now the Space Corpsmen had been fighting as part of a small army. Now there were only three of them, and only one with armor. Grady's high was going strong, but while a few of the Tiān Zhuānjiā were still standing, Helena risked firing both of her weapons at once. The individual jolts were bad enough, but the combined blowback of two faulty currents left her gasping for breath, and while she was still reeling, Acosta screamed and went down in a flash of light and a splash of scarlet blood.

Not Acosta, dammit. In the field, Helena thought of the other soldiers as pieces in a game, and losing subordinates limited her moves and styles of play. But Acosta was a good guy, someone who deserved a chance to retire with a decent pension and live out his days on an island lanai. He wasn't disposable, dammit, not like the rest of them; not like Helena, who'd go off the rails if they ever sent her back planetside.

She was destined to die out here. Acosta deserved better.

The surge of anger that rose in her wasn't a synthetic Neon dose, but it had the same blinding effect. She fired both weapons again and again, giving in to the pain of the voltage, until her spine twisted in pain and her head pounded from the constant flow of electricity.

You've got to stop, Helena. You'll fry yourself if you keep this up. The coaxing voice at the back of her mind wasn't hers. It sounded like her mother: soft but sensible. It had been years since she'd heard that voice.

When she finally lowered her arms and let the current recede, Grady was laughing.

"You gotta be *kidding me,* Hellcat!" He pumped his arms in the air. "That was amazing."

The nearest Tiān Zhuānjiā hadn't just been shot; the corpse

emitted a grey curl of smoke, as if the body had been charred inside its suit.

You're lucky that wasn't you, the voice said.

Helena shook her head and turned back to Acosta. She was prepared to find him limp and lifeless, but he was still breathing. He lay on his back, his teeth gritted in pain, both hands pressed over a dark patch on one of his thighs.

"Let me see," Helena said. "Grady, cover us."

"Yes, ma'am!" the private called, and immediately assumed a defensive posture over them.

In order to examine him, Helena had to disentangle herself from her weapons and drop them to one side. When she moved to push Acosta's hands away, a massive spark popped between them, causing them both to yelp.

There was a terrific amount of blood. Helena had seen her share of laser injuries over the years, but as she examined the wound, her stomach still lurched. The laser blast had cut a clean, perfectly circular hole through Acosta's thigh, just grazing the bone. She could see the floor through the far side of the wound.

"Mostly cauterized," she said thickly, fighting back the urge to retch. "How does it feel?"

"Great." Acosta's voice was higher than usual, almost whiny. It must be incredibly painful. But he was alive, so that was something.

"You're going to have to leave me," he said. "I can't walk on this thing."

Helena shook her head and prodded the edges of the wound. It had almost stopped bleeding; that was the one good thing about laser wounds. They were ugly, and they'd sear a hole clean through a man, but most people didn't die from bleeding out.

"Grady, think you can carry him on your back?" she asked.

"Sure thing, boss." Grady immediately dropped his guns, then squatted. It took a little maneuvering to get Acosta in place, but he had no trouble lifting the wounded man.

Helena handed Acosta one of the rifles. "Think of this as a trust exercise. Or of Grady as a really ugly horse."

Grady cackled.

"Yes, ma'am." Acosta lifted his rifle into position and smiled despite his obvious agony. "Giddyup, pony."

Helena snatched up the other gun, and they continued their march toward the bridge. Injury or not, Acosta's aim hadn't suffered, and although Helena couldn't help noticing his greenish hue and the nervous sheen of sweat across his brow, he managed to take out two more Tiān Zhuānjiā soldiers that they crossed in the corridor before Helena even had a chance to aim.

They could hear fighting in the distance, but as they rounded the last corner, they found the Cell corralling the last of the enemy soldiers.

"You made it," Chandran said, smiling lopsidedly at them.

"And you didn't run off," Helena observed. "Are you ready to finish this?"

Their little army might be made up of castaways and leftovers, but as Helena stood shoulder-to-shoulder with Chandran Bhatt and prepared to storm the bridge of an enemy ship, it occurred to Helena that she'd never been so proud to fight beside anyone else.

Careful, said a little voice in her head that was her and hers alone, *or you're going to turn traitor to your own cause.*

You don't want to end up like Lowell.

40

LOWELL TURNED to look at Peter in shock. "What are you talking about, Chang?"

Peter took a few tottering steps forward and completely ignored him. "Dad, what are you *doing* here?"

The third figure swept forward, all but tossing his gun to the ground, and pulled Peter into a hug. "Peter! You're alive! How did you get all the way out here? Never mind that, how did you get away? They told me you were dead—I saw the pictures from Ur-An—but you're here!"

Lowell couldn't see Peter's face from this angle, but his body language was less than enthusiastic. He'd gone rigid in the other man's arms, his arms stiff at his sides. There was blood spattered across his glass visor; Lowell wasn't sure how the kid had managed to activate that mechanism on the helmet, but he was taking notes.

He also wasn't sure if Peter's reluctance to hug his father stemmed from the complete shock of encountering him on an alien moon, or if Peter's dad messed with the kid's head the way

Lowell's father messed with his. Family could be complicated, and having to deal with those emotions in the midst of a war zone, right after learning that your whole concept of reality was based on a lie, well, Lowell didn't envy that particular emotional cocktail.

But then Peter lifted his arms and returned the man's embrace. "Dad. You came all the way out here for me?"

That hit Lowell like a punch in the gut. His own father couldn't be bothered to make eye contact with him when they were in the same room, much less chase him halfway across the galaxy just to make sure he was safe.

"What's the trick here?" Lowell asked Collins.

His old brother-in-arms shrugged. "No trick, man. We're on your side. Believe it or not, we were actually worried about you."

"I hear you finally gave that dipstick Munroe what he deserved," Vasko added. "*Noice.*"

Slowly, not at all convinced that he was doing the right thing, Lowell lowered his weapon. After a moment's consideration, he held out a hand and pulled Vasko to his feet. "Not exactly. I like to think I helped, but someone else got to do the honors."

"Too bad," Vasko said. "I'd have liked a chance to spit in his eye before the end." In lieu of that, he made a rude gesture in the general direction of the sky. "Goodbye and good riddance, you traitorous jerk."

It was nice, in a way, to know that time had had no effect on Vasko. The question of whether or not they really were on Enceladus to help remained to be seen, but arguing wouldn't get him any closer to an answer. Lowell didn't relish the idea of throwing down with his old messmates, and his reticence didn't stem from purely sentimental reasons... in a fair fight, two against one, Lowell wasn't sure that he could take them. Peter was, well, *Peter*, and Muul was down for the count.

I'll go along with it for now. See how this plays out. After all, although they hadn't exactly been friends before Munroe's killing spree on Mars, both men had stuck their necks out for him during his court-martial. Even if he couldn't fully trust them, it would be nice to have them back on his side for the time being.

Lowell jerked one thumb toward Peter's dad. "How did you guys meet up?"

"Eh." Vasko shrugged. "Long story short, the guy was trying to hop the border to pull some kind of vigilante justice crap, and we saved him the trouble. Small world, am I right?" His lopsided grin made him look feral, even through the helmet.

"So he was being a reckless fool while playing hero?" Lowell snorted. "Must run in the family."

Peter could hear them perfectly well, but he was doing an admirable job of ignoring their banter. "I can't believe you're out here. Isn't this incredible? I've thought of you this whole time—you've missed so much. Just think about how this could change *everything!* Your lectures, your texts... Dad, everything we know about the universe is wrong."

Peter's father was still standing with his hands on his son's shoulders, staring at him in wonder.

So much for their relationship being a mess, Lowell thought bitterly. Not that he'd ever wish for Peter's personal relationship to be as messed up as his own. *Yeah, that's definitely not what you're doing.*

Lowell had almost gotten used to the high, clicking whine of Muul's distress call. He figured that she'd sort herself out now that the scrambler was destroyed, but she was still keening, as though it had never gone away.

Collins didn't seem in any rush to shoot him in the back, and Vasko was the sort of man who wouldn't wait until your back was turned, if that was his intent. Lowell left them to their own devices and approached the collapsed alien. She was trembling, and had yet to move from what was probably her species' equivalent of the fetal position.

"Hey," he said gently, crouching down beside her. "You okay?"

Muul's whining subsided, and she tilted her head to the side to get a better look at him. "Your species is horrible," she said weakly. "Who would invent something like that?"

"Our species?" Vasko laughed as he swaggered over. "You make it sound like you— *Hell in a handbasket!*" One look at Muul's face sent the soldier reeling. "Good God, what happened to you?"

"'*Hell in a handbasket?*'" Collins snickered. "What are you, my Nona?"

"Get over here and see how you feel." Vasko pointed an accusing finger at the prone alien. "This chick isn't right, Vasko. Something's messed up here."

"There's nothing wrong with her." Peter caught his father's arm and dragged him forward. "Dad, this is Muul."

Muul forced herself up onto her knees, and when Lowell offered a hand to help right her, she reluctantly took it. "Thank you," she said grudgingly. Her voice still quavered, and her eyes had gone strangely dull, but at least she could support herself.

Peter's dad gaped at her. "What—*who...?*"

"Muul-yeet-Jaan-yeet-Piim." The alien cocked her head. "Oh,

just wonderful. More humans. I suppose I should learn your names as well."

"Dr. Fai Chang." The man made a gesture as though he was about to adjust his glasses, and then seemed to remember where he was all at once. "It's magnificent to meet you. Truly an honor. I've imagined this moment all my life."

Muul didn't even bother to pretend that she was similarly pleased. Instead, she peered down the tunnel in the direction that their invisible attackers had retreated. "What happened to the ones who attacked us?"

"We sent 'em packing," Vasko said proudly.

Muul swung her head to glare at him, but as she moved her head, she swayed alarmingly on her feet. She might even have fallen, if Fai Chang hadn't darted forward to catch her.

"Thank you," she said with an obvious air of surprise, before refocusing on Vasko. "Now, if you don't mind, please explain how you know that they're *gone* and not just biding their time? Unless you can see them, and I can't?"

Vasko frowned. "Well…"

"We don't know," Lowell interrupted. "But you didn't just drop out of the sky, boys. I'm guessing we have even more company waiting topside for us?"

Collins and Vasko hesitated, but Fai didn't. "The ship we arrived on is in the atmosphere even as we speak. Well, they *were*." He looked up at Muul with even more reverence than his son did. "Captain Sanz told us to come down while she dealt with the matter of the UFO."

Muul stiffened. "So Goii came after us—no surprise there. If he decides to act now, your crew is as good as dead. He wants the key."

"Key?" Fai echoed.

Muul opened her mouth, then frowned. "I'm not certain I should tell you."

Lowell expected Peter to blurt out the truth to his father, but to his surprise, the kid restrained himself. "What do you think, Lowell? Should we?"

Lowell didn't have strong opinions on telling Dr. Chang the truth, but when it came to Collins and Vasko, he had to think it over. They'd acted like allies in the past, but when it came to something this big, Lowell wasn't sure that *anyone* in any position of authority should be trusted. There was too much at stake, and loyalties could always change.

"If you don't tell us," Collins said, "we'll be flying blind."

"Doesn't matter to me," Vasko put in. "As long as I know who to shoot, I'm good to go."

It would be safer, Lowell reasoned, to keep them in the dark, but that was what Munroe would have done. If he couldn't even trust these two, then maybe the human race was beyond redemption, and there was no point in going through all of this trouble.

If you can trust Muul for the moment, you can damn well trust these guys.

"Fine," Lowell said heavily, "I'll explain it. But Muul and Chang... or rather, *Peter*, need to figure out where we're going from here."

Their enemies were closing in, and if they couldn't trust each other, there was no one else. It wasn't as if more allies were going to pop up out of the darkness to save the day.

They were on their own.

41

MAJOR GENERAL ILIN was heavier than he looked, and dragging him took more effort than He Ming could have predicted. She wasn't entirely sure which part of him she was holding. His endless scream didn't help as she dragged him back across the smooth stone floor, toward the mouth of an unfamiliar tunnel. The moment that their mics popped and crackled, signaling that they'd left the radius of their connection to the shared channel, Ming dropped to her knees by the man's side. The effort of finding and disconnecting his personal cloaking device only took a few seconds, but it was seconds they didn't have if the man was going to have any chance of surviving.

"Listen," she said firmly, "I don't care how much you want to scream, but I need to see your arm." Blood loss would be bad enough, but given the extreme cold on the surface of Enceladus, frostbite could set in within seconds, and the compromised portion of his suit could easily lead to suffocation.

Ilin held up his arm. His screaming had stopped, but when

Ming looked into his terrified face, she quickly realized that it had nothing to do with reduced pain. Every time Ilin breathed out, a fresh layer of frost coated the interior of his helmet. His eyes had begun to turn black, and the dark blue blood vessels in his face stood out sharply against his increasingly pale skin.

Ming fumbled at her belt. She had a patch somewhere. It wasn't meant for sealing holes the size of a man's wrist, but as long as she could establish a proper seal, it *should* work, unless he was too far gone already.

She had the SuitSeal in her hands and was still working out how to apply it when Ilin spasmed suddenly and then went still. Blood seeped from a new hole just beneath his chin. Ming froze.

"It's for the best." General Wu's voice was soft and smooth in her ear. "He would have been dead weight anyway."

Ming swallowed hard and looked down at the dead man before her. "Yes, sir," she said.

She had known with relative certainty that one of these days, Major General Ilin would end up dead, and that he would most likely perish by their hands.

"It's a mercy." General Wu laid an invisible hand on her shoulder; she could feel the weight of that touch only as a pressure against her suit, but Ming fought the urge to recoil from it. *This is war*, she reminded herself. *It is not always clean or honorable.*

Still, Ilin made for a pitiful sight. *Another thirty seconds and he would have been dead anyway, so it shouldn't matter*, the rational part of her brain reminded her. But if he'd only waited those thirty seconds, the general's hands would have been that much cleaner. It was one thing to shoot a man in combat, but this...

They hadn't yet moved when the speaker popped again. Ming braced for another attack from Lowell and his friends, but instead of English, what came through the mic instead was a whistling, clicking language like nothing spoken on Earth.

There was no time to convey instructions, not when these newcomers might overhear. Ming had no chance to explain. All she could do was reach out for the hand that still clutched her shoulder and tug. General Wu must have understood enough to remain silent, because he stumbled after her without a word until they were well away from Ilin's corpse. When they were well out of the way, Ming pulled the general into a crouch and, at the last second, reset his cloaking device so that the blood splatter left from their fight with the Americans was no longer visible on his suit.

Ming had studied a variety of specialized languages. On Earth, it was possible to have three or four relevant translators on hand, or to send for a specialist if needed. In space, it was much more complicated, and when she'd applied for the job, Ming had been informed that she would need to understand *every* relevant language. She'd studied hard, and earned clearances held by few others in the Tiān Zhuānjiā services. She'd even received private lessons so that she could be useful in highly specialized situations.

Like this one, for example.

"What is this?" asked a disgusted voice. "*The primates have left one of their spawnbrothers behind.*"

Ming squeezed her eyes shut, as if she could will away the reality of what was happening. She'd been top of her class in alien dialects, but the government's knowledge in that field was so closely guarded that she'd only had two classmates for competition. Rote memorization of the language had been an interesting mental exercise, but she'd never fully believed that aliens were *real*, much less that she'd ever encounter them, even when she and General Wu came here in pursuit of alien technology.

Now they were here, and unlike the vague amusement she'd felt in the classroom, Ming was suddenly frozen in terror.

"*Humans have no regard for their brethren,*" another voice observed. This pronouncement was accompanied by chirrups of what Ming could only assume was agreement.

"*Are they good to eat?*"

"*No. They are dirty.*" Ming hadn't heard this voice before; the rest sounded similar to her, especially since she didn't know the language well enough to recognize dialects, but even a novice like herself could tell that this speaker was different. His voice was deeper, and accompanied by a difference in tone that made the hair prickle on the back of her neck.

"*Is it one of ours, Captain? They all look alike to me.*"

The deeper voice replied. "*No. This one's uniform is different. And he does not have the —*" Ming had never learned the word that followed, but it must refer to the key: the one Ilin had died for, the one that could be used as a terrible tool of destruction. The one held by the Americans.

Ming only hoped they would be willing to fight the aliens as viciously as they had fought against the landing party. She wouldn't have wanted Ilin to hold the key; she wasn't sure if she would rather have it in Lowell's or General Wu's possession. But if these creatures got it?

Nothing good would come of it.

"*Come on. We know where they're headed,*" the captain said. "*Leave the dead monkey. I want Muul's head in my hands before the day is out.*"

Ming watched in silence as the figures made their way down the hall toward the American group. She hadn't realized that she was shaking until the mic crackled.

Hearing those voices was like staring up at the sky of Enceladus. The whole world seemed to tilt and shift, and when it righted herself, Ming wasn't the same woman she had been before.

"Translator He?" asked the general in a soft voice. "Did you understand them?"

"Yes," she replied. "They're after the Americans and the key."

She couldn't see the general, but a moment later something bumped her shoulder, and he settled in beside her, sitting against the wall of their cavern.

"The Russian ship is destroyed," General Wu said at last.

Ming blinked. "When?"

"I got the alert when we first confronted the Americans in the tunnels outside. I didn't think it wise to inform Ilin, given his state of mind, but..." Wu sighed. "I suppose it's better that he died not knowing."

The weight of this knowledge settled on Ming's shoulders. "And our own ship?"

"Can you hail them?" Wu asked in a weary voice that told her he'd already tried.

Just for the sake of knowing, Ming tried again, but her alert went unanswered. Their channel was dead.

"Nothing," she said at last.

"That's what I thought." Wu sighed again. "And now our allies are gone, and the most powerful object in the galaxy will be fought over by our enemies."

Ming bit her lip. "Sir? There are still a few drones on the surface of the moon, and we have a ship waiting for us, albeit a small one."

A note of amusement entered the general's voice. "Are you

giving up, Miss He? I didn't think you were the type to surrender so easily."

"Easily," she echoed, and laughed at the absurdity of it. But General Wu was right—she hated to give up, even if she wasn't sure what to fight for now. Retreating could be a tactical strategy, but if they left now, the outcome would be decided without them.

"Lowell killed my only son," General Wu said thoughtfully. "I've never forgiven him for it. But have I ever told you, Ming, that I have a daughter as well?"

"You've only mentioned her in passing, sir."

"She's alive and well. Living in Beijing. She got married a few years ago. I missed the wedding. I was too busy grieving my legacy to realize that I was cutting myself off from my family's future." Wu was silent for a moment, and Ming was certain that he was wrestling with some painful memory. After a long moment, he continued. "If we leave now, I could go back to her. Say goodbye. Let the Americans and the aliens decide who will have the honor of killing us. Or..."

"Or we help decide the future," Ming finished.

She couldn't see the general's face, but she knew him well enough that she could imagine his facial expression: flat and constrained, but with crinkled crow's feet around his eyes.

"What will it be?" he asked, even though he must already know the answer.

42

CHANDRAN BHATT HAD FOUGHT a lot of battles in his life, but this was one of the stranger skirmishes. The Cell pilots had done him proud, and the Space Corpsmen, while arguably mad, had more than kept their end of the bargain.

They swept onto the bridge of the Tiān Zhuānjiă ship with the surviving Cell soldiers in sleek flight formation, and the wounded Acosta riding on his dosed countryman's back with his rifle held high.

Chandran was braced for a fight when they entered; what they found instead was a handful of engineers huddled wide-eyed on the bridge.

"Hold your fire!" Chandran barked—in English, primarily for the benefit of their allies.

"Aw, come on!" the dosed American whined. "We might as well finish what we started, dontcha think?"

Hellcat fixed him with a glare, although she didn't fire her rifle. "And why, exactly, shouldn't we scour the ship?" she demanded.

Chandran pointed to the large display at the front of the bridge. When Hellcat swung to follow his finger, her eyes popped wide.

"Holy *sh—*"

An unfamiliar ship hovered not far from their own location, hemmed in by the erratic flight plan of a Space Corps vessel. Chandran had dedicated more than two decades of his life to becoming an expert in two things: ships, and flying them. At a glance, he could say two things for certain: first, that the American pilot was an expert in the ship's controls; and second, that the strange silver ship at the center of its flight path wasn't owned by any fleet on Earth.

That explained why the Chinese fleet had been trying to call them up for service. The Tiān Zhuānjiā didn't want them to fight the enemy; they needed help against the *unknown*.

"And why, pray tell, should that encourage us to let these soldiers off the hook?" Hellcat asked at last.

Acosta answered before Chandran could. "We're going to need all the help we can get."

Hellcat glanced back at him. "Huh. Is that your plan, Bhatt? Team up with them?"

Not one of the surviving Tiān Zhuānjiā had reached for their guns. Instead, one stepped forward and spoke up in quavering English. "They destroyed the Russian ship."

"And you *imprisoned* us," Hellcat snapped back. "We're not exactly all buddy-buddy, are we?"

"Let's kill 'em," said Grady cheerfully.

"Grady, *no*," Acosta scolded, as if he was talking to a badly-behaved stray.

Chandran could feel the situation slipping away from him, but Tuhin was at his side in an instant.

"What are you planning, Bhatt?"

The Americans might not listen, but Tuhin would, and the other Cell pilots were watching them carefully. They might have started out as the unofficial Cell representatives when they were first taken prisoner, but everyone was looking to them for answers.

"Our ships are still onboard," Chandran said. "And do you remember how many drones we saw when the Tiān Zhuānjiā pulled our ship apart? There must be more." He shifted his posture slightly to include Hellcat in the conversation. "We want to survive, don't we? So let our pilots take our ships, get your prisoners to run whatever programs they need to on the drones"—he gestured vaguely at the Tiān Zhuānjiā engineers huddled by the massive screen—"and the four—eh, five?—of us will control the ship."

Hellcat frowned, and her gaze flicked around the room, taking the measure of their situation. It could be strange for some people, Chandran knew, to pivot from one mission to the next. He'd survived out here for a long time, however, and those who couldn't adapt as the situation evolved never made it as far as those who were willing to adjust.

"It's a good idea," Tuhin reassured him. "I can give commands for our fleet, and they can coordinate with the American vessel. Between all of us, we might stand a chance."

"It's our best chance," Acosta added from his place on Grady's shoulders.

Hellcat was still frowning, but in the end, she nodded firmly. "All right, Bhatt. Let's try it your way."

THOSE IDIOTS from Washington still hadn't gotten back to her, and Captain Sanz was quietly going mad.

"How much longer can we sustain this?" she asked Boswell. "The engines...?"

His gaze lingered on the readings, and he looked as harried as she felt. *We should just give up on Washington. If they can't figure it out, that's on them.*

She was about to make an executive decision when the comms officer looked up. "Captain? We've been hailed by the Tiān Zhuānjiā ship."

Sanz stared at the junior officer. That last thing she needed was a battle on two fronts. Couldn't the Chinese commander see that they had their hands full here?

"Pull it up," she said at last. "Let's see what they have to say."

"Captain, if we keep this up, we might not have the juice to retreat later on," Boswell warned her.

"I understand," she told him. One thing at a time. If the Tiān Zhuānjiā wanted to make trouble, Sanz could always give them the finger and then carry on from there.

The incoming message, however, wasn't a taunt or a declaration of war. The woman on the screen looked somewhat familiar, and both she and the man beside her wore the sort of ill-fitting jumpsuits that Sanz usually associated with prisoners of war.

"Hello there," said the woman, offering a smile that seemed to show all of her teeth. "I don't think we've met before, but I'm Lance Corporal Helena Moore. My friend here, Mr. Bhatt, thinks he has an idea of how to solve your problem if we work together. What do you say?"

I say screw Washington. Sanz slapped her palm on the console and beamed at a thunderstruck Boswell. "I'm listening. What have you got for me?"

43

WHILE LOWELL EXPLAINED THEIR SITUATION, with the help of frequent interruptions and corrections from Muul, Peter led them deeper into the heart of Enceladus. He'd longed to explore the hall when he and Lowell had first arrived, but they'd been in the middle of a mission, and there had been no time to read. Now, Peter couldn't shake the feeling that he was still under the gun, as it were.

Reading the ancient inscriptions had lost a little of its thrill, however. Now he knew about Earth's origins, and he had a bona fide alien to explain it to him.

Besides, this was no longer an intellectual exercise. They were going to the center of an artificial world in order to retrieve a terribly powerful weapon. And then what? They weren't going to be able to just hurl it into space, or carry it around in his backpack like some homework assignment. What did they really think they were going to do with the damn thing?

He got himself before he could get too morose. *You sound like*

Lowell. Stop sulking and playing your tiny violin, okay? Dad's here now. Between the lot of us, we'll come up with something.

Dr. Chang hadn't said much, but he was listening to Lowell's story with rapt attention. "That makes a good deal of sense," he said in the end.

Lowell grunted. "If you say so."

"Contextually, I mean," Dr. Chang corrected. "We've long speculated about how life came to arrive on Earth, and that properties made it unique. I actually proposed a similar theory in my paper on cellular colonization of the Milky Way... If I ever get a chance to tell Dr. Behnam, I'll take great pleasure in informing him that I was right."

"Behnam?" Vasko repeated. "Isn't that the guy who turned you over to us?"

"Wouldn't think you'd want to be pals again after that," Collins said.

"Oh, we're not *pals*," Dr. Chang said. "He's now cemented himself as an academic rival. If I get the chance to publish on the topic, I'll make sure to mention him personally in a scathing capacity. By *name*."

"Public shaming is a staple of maintaining order in my culture as well," Muul observed.

"Academics and aliens have a lot in common," Peter murmured. "Who knew?" It still baffled him that his father had come all this way just to rescue him. They had never been very close, and Dr. Chang had shown more interest in the information about Muul's people than he had shown toward Peter. And yet, he'd come all this way to assure himself of Peter's safety.

Confusing. Then again, there was no point in dwelling on it. He could deal with all that later.

The tunnel had begun to slope downwards, and more than once, if it hadn't been for the suction of his shoes, Peter would have fallen head over heels. He even had to occasionally grab for the wall, and the suction grip of the gloves proved useful indeed.

"Aw, *dammit!*" Lowell groaned. A moment later, Peter's suit released a flood of the damp, jelly-like substance that served as dermal lubricant for Muul's people.

Muul made a soft noise deep in her throat that might have been a cough.

"Yeah, laugh it up," Lowell grumbled. "Chang—Peter—dammit, *somebody,* are we close yet?"

As they walked, Peter had been diligently reading the inscriptions as they passed, although they didn't always make sense. The messages were written out in dozens of languages, but one in particular stood out to him: a thin, fluted script that looked like a combination of calligraphy and flower blossoms.

"I think we're almost there," he murmured. "Muul, can you read this?"

Muul glanced over his shoulder. "Ah, the Photosynthian passages? No, I'm afraid I don't."

"I wish I could snap a picture," Peter murmured.

Fai Chang turned to one of the soldiers. "Collins, can these contacts record images?"

"Sure. Hold your head perfectly still and don't blink for three seconds." The soldier shrugged. "Honestly, you've probably got hundreds of photos on file by now. I can teach you how to review them later."

Fai nodded and turned back to Peter. "Which passages do you want a record of?"

Peter pointed at the wall. "If you can get these two next to each other?" He indicated a passage in Muul's language that was directly beside a Photosynthian passage.

Fai stood perfectly still for much longer than three seconds. Peter wasn't certain that the record would be helpful—after all, even if he could hack a translation of another alien tongue, he might never get a chance to use it.

But if these aliens really are responsible for creating all of this, it would help to have a cipher. Just in case.

Peter slapped one hand against his father's back. "Thanks, Dad."

Fai nodded. "Happy to help."

With that task accomplished, Peter pointed to the inscription he *could* read. "I think we're getting close. There are instructions here for how to use the core, but... oh, I like that. *The Heart of Enceladus.*"

"Sounds like some shit from a VR quest text," Vasko griped.

Peter frowned over his shoulder. Lowell might be standoffish with his old friends, but they obviously had a few things in common. "We're getting pretty close to the Heart, but I'm still not clear how we're supposed to extract it."

"Here's a thought," Lowell said. "How about we stop hanging around reading ancient graffiti and waiting to get jumped by the Invisible Man again, and just plan to figure it out when we get there?"

Vasko laughed. "I missed you, buddy."

"Yes, and how well did that work out last time?" Peter demanded. "Perhaps you'll recall that we went in blind the first time around and nearly died? For nothing!"

"Not for nothing," Lowell said. "We got the key."

"And started a war, blew up a moon, and got kidnapped by

aliens! Maybe we can just take *two seconds* to stop squabbling and try to be a little more prepared this time? We're talking about a device that's powerful enough to sustain an atmosphere. Assuming it doesn't kill us, we'll be carrying around an object that's more powerful than a neutron bomb..."

The mics crackled, and Peter froze.

"What was that?" asked Fai.

"Probably just feedback," Vasko said.

"Or someone's listening in," Muul said grimly.

The static repeated, and Peter flinched. *Just feedback? No way. Someone just came into range and then backed off.* It might just be the injured Chinese soldiers looking for a way out, but if so, they'd gotten completely turned around. More likely, someone was after them.

"We need to keep moving," he said in a low voice, although he knew full well that whispering wouldn't help; he'd be just as loud to anyone within range as he was to the men right beside him.

"That's what I'm telling you, Peter," Lowell said. "We can worry about the Heart when we get there." *If we get there.* The subtext of his meaning wasn't lost on Peter.

Time was against them at every turn. No matter how this played out, they would always be one step behind.

Without another word, Peter turned and led them deeper into the darkness.

44

LOWELL HAD GOTTEN USED to the dead, grey stone tunnels beneath the surface of the little moon. It was easy to take it for granted that all life on Enceladus had been stripped away following the activation of the Anomaly.

It was a trap that Lowell had fallen into before, when his job had entailed nothing but looping trips across the moon's frozen surface. Back then, he'd believed that the moon was nothing more than a spherical ice cube, with nothing interesting going on beneath the surface. He'd been convinced that the scientists he protected were spinning their wheels, studying microbes and molecules that wouldn't amount to anything.

He'd been wrong about that, nearly *dead* wrong, and he soon discovered that he'd misjudged Enceladus' new form as well.

They were deep, now, deeper than the geological garden Peter had toppled into. The first sign of change was the sudden uptick in temperature registered by Lowell's suit. At first, the temperature only rose by a few degrees, but the deeper they went, the more steadily the temperature climbed, until it was positively balmy by the standards of the Arctic Circle, and then of an Alberta winter, and then of an autumn in Michigan. The tunnel became foggy and humid.

"What's going on out there?" Lowell asked, wiping uselessly at the moisture.

"Careful!" Muul cried, and yanked his hand out of the way just as the helmet's artificial jaws activated.

Lowell froze, painfully aware that he might have lost fingers if she hadn't been paying attention. "Thank you," he said at last.

"You're no good to me dead," she said breezily, letting go of his wrist. "Besides, you saved me from being shot during that attack earlier. It would be rude of me to let you die by your own stupidity."

Lowell rolled his eyes. "But where is all this *coming* from?"

To his surprise, it was Fai who replied. "We're approaching the Heart of Enceladus. Are you familiar with the Miller-Urey experiment?"

Lowell bit back a sigh. "No." *But something tells me that I'm about to get a lecture.*

"More than a century ago, two scientists put forth a theory of how life developed on Earth," Fai said. "They theorized that life began in what they called a primordial soup, a mixture of moisture and gases subject to repeated lightning strikes."

"Fascinating," Vasko droned.

"Isn't it?" Like Peter, the older man seemed to be completely oblivious to anyone's disinterest in his area of study. "But according to your story, this... well, let's call it a reactor in the Heart of Enceladus provides the power for creating and sustaining life. In essence, it serves as the lightning strikes within the appropriate conditions. I expect we'll find that activating this Anomaly of yours will have reset the process, but not eradicated it entirely. We are, as it were, in the soup itself." Fai rubbed his gloved hands together gleefully. "Oh, when Dr. Behnam hears about this, he'll be a wreck. We've argued the relative merits of panspermia and endemic development more times than I care to count. Just wait until he finds out that it was both!"

Lowell watched Peter carefully as his father spoke. If it had been anyone else, Peter would have joined in, inserting his own additions to the theory; but instead, for one of the first times since Peter had met him, the kid was silent.

Maybe their relationship is more complicated than I thought. If so, it certainly didn't give Lowell any pleasure to speculate on the subject.

"Our sister worlds are quite humid," Muul informed them. "If you want to see more clearly, Lowell, just adjust your helmet settings."

"How?" Lowell asked.

With a weary sigh, Muul leaned over and fiddled with the settings herself. A moment later, the fog cleared.

"Thanks," Lowell said sincerely. "Any chance you can turn off the automatic slimer?"

Muul coughed, then prodded the back of his suit a few times. "There you go."

"You can just turn it *off?*" Peter asked indignantly. "Why didn't you say anything?"

"You didn't ask." Muul made the adjustments to his suit as well. "Also, I thought it was funny."

Now that he could see better, Lowell gaped at their surroundings. The walls of the tunnel were no longer bare. Instead, mossy growths dripped from the ceiling and coated the sides of the tunnel. Tiny red-stemmed plants with drooping leaves protruded from the walls, and miniature grey-green mushrooms sprouted along the edges. It wasn't exactly a modern jungle, but everything here was definitely alive and flourishing.

"Incredible," Lowell breathed, bending down to examine the primitive foliage. This, more than anything prior, convinced him that Muul was telling the truth. According to everything Lowell believed, nothing like this should exist out here in the depths of space, and the sea life—well, that might have been a coincidence. But even after the disaster they'd wrought on the oceans of Enceladus, life persisted down here.

There was beauty in that.

"This is sure something," Vasko observed. "And what happens to all this when we take the Heart?"

Lowell stood up abruptly. Vasko was right, of course. There was no good way to defend this place against future attackers, and the vultures were circling in the skies above.

It's not like this is the only moss in the galaxy, he reminded himself. *According to Muul, those plant-people created places like this all across the universe. No harm, no foul, if it keeps Earth from being destroyed.*

On the other hand, it would be nice not to have to kill the lone survivors of one world just to spare another. Maybe that first species had made a big mistake by spreading new life all over the universe. All it did was evolve until it got greedy, and then look for ways to kill each other.

"Come on," he said gruffly. "We've got to be almost there."

As they went, the plant life around them grew increasingly complex. Simple mosses gave way to twining ferns, then pitcher plants and large-leaved tropicals. Lowell was tempted to remove his helmet and breathe deeply. It had been years since he'd been in a place where things grew like this. Approaching the Heart of Enceladus was like coming home.

They rounded a bend in the hall, and Lowell froze. They stood on a stone cliff above what looked like a moat, while a thick, soupy liquid bubbled and steamed below. There was an island at the center of the moat, ringed by the most complex plants they'd encountered so far: huge tropical trees with ornate blossoms unlike anything Lowell had ever seen on Earth. And there, at the center of the island, was the Heart.

When Peter had translated "the Heart of Enceladus," Lowell had agreed with Vasko that the name sounded unnecessarily grandiose. He'd thought of the power source as something purely mechanical. After all, Muul had said that the Photosynthians had created it. Lowell had imagined something like one of the returned nuclear reactors, or a spaceship engine.

Instead, the Heart was very much alive.

A great, bluish sphere of crackling energy pulsed at the core of the moon. As Lowell watched, a white-hot bolt of electricity crackled through that space, striking the surface of the moat with an extraordinary spark, causing it to bubble and froth.

"So." Vasko cleared his throat. "Who's going first?"

Collins peered down at the roiling liquid beneath them. "Aw, *hell* no. That's the sort of primitive stew you were talking about before, right, Doc?"

"Primordial soup," Fai corrected.

Peter shuffled closer to the ledge, but Lowell hauled him back. "No jumping for you, kid. Remember how well that went last time?"

Peter chuckled weakly and unconsciously touched the straps of his pack. "Sure. Good point. One problem, though... even if we get closer to that thing, what do we do?"

"Didn't the walls tell you?" Lowell asked.

"No, but something must have..." Peter groaned suddenly. "Oh, crap, Lowell. The tablet. I bet the tablet would have told us what to do!"

Lowell sighed. "I don't suppose you had it memorized?"

"I didn't understand it," Peter protested. "I thought it was just a map to the Anomaly. I didn't know about all this."

Muul made a soft, contemplative noise. "So far, the instructions of the ancients have been clear. If we can approach the Heart, I expect we'll be able to find more inscriptions that may help us."

There was another bolt of lightning, and everyone jumped.

"How do you propose getting closer when we have to navigate *that?*" Lowell asked.

"It's only striking the liquid," Fai observed. He made the unconscious glasses-adjusting gesture again. "The trees aren't damaged."

"The trees aren't wearing conductive space suits," Lowell reminded him.

"They aren't grounded," Collins pointed out. "It's a crapshoot, though."

"You guys talk too much." Without warning, Vasko took a running leap off the cliff, sailing over the bubbling moat and landing on his knees on the far side. He got up, dusted himself, off, and then gave the rest of them a thumbs-up. "So far, so good!"

"It's good to know that all humans are as foolhardy as you two," Muul observed.

"Not all of us," Collin corrected. "Just the members of our species reckless enough to muck around in space." With a loud *whoop*, he threw himself after Collins.

Lowell sucked his teeth. "Think you can make it over, Fai?"

The older Chang cleared his throat, backed up, then took a running start over the edge. He didn't bend his knees enough when he landed, and he would have fallen backward into the lake if Vasko and Collins hadn't caught each of his pinwheeling arms and righted him just in time.

"You next, Peter," Muul said. Instead of letting him jump, she swept him up in her arms, bridal-style, and took the leap herself. Peter squawked indignantly as she set him back on his feet.

"I can handle myself!" he cried.

Muul chuckled. "All evidence suggests the contrary."

Lowell was about to follow them when his mic popped. Instead of rushing to the cliff, he looked back toward the mouth of the tunnel behind him. *If it's the Tiān Zhuānjiā, I don't care if I can see them, I'm going to figure out a way to trip them into that damn soup.*

But it wasn't General Wu this time. Half a dozen tall, slim figures stepped out of the tunnel. As their leader approached, he said something in a smug tone. He would probably be disappointed to learn that Lowell couldn't understand a word coming out of his mouth, since he was speaking in that annoying whistle-click language of Muul's people.

"If you're trying to threaten me," Lowell growled, "it's not working."

The leader laughed. There was no doubt in Lowell's mind that he was facing Captain Goii, whose head Lowell had caved in before jumping ship. Too bad it hadn't taken.

"Lowell, get down here!" Peter barked.

Lowell ignored his friend. "Hey, Muul, I know that you weren't thrilled about telling me this before, but any chance you'd be willing to spill the beans on how I kill you people?"

"I'll do you one better. I'll show you." Muul grunted, and Peter wailed. A moment later, the alien was back at Lowell's side.

"Stop being idiots!" Peter cried. "Come on, we can outrun them."

"Of course we can't," Lowell told him. "Someone needs to translate those inscriptions, remember? We're just going to buy you some time."

Lowell drew his gun, and Goii lowered into a crouch; his cronies behind them did the same.

"You're wasting time," Muul said. "We'll hold them off as long as we can. Oh, and Peter? If the other monkeys try to hurt you? Kill them. This isn't a game."

Peter made a miserable noise, but Lowell felt more at ease than he had in hours. Peter was always going to be the egghead, and now he had his lecture-loving father to help him.

Meanwhile, Lowell was doing the thing that he was best at: fighting.

Too bad he couldn't taunt Goii, since they didn't speak the same language. He'd have to settle for firing the first shot.

45

GOII SHOULDN'T HAVE BEEN SURPRISED that the human was back on his feet, but the indignity of having to fight a man who had already tried to crush his skull—with a moderate if impermanent level of success, at that—was beyond the pale.

"I see that you kept him alive," he observed with disgust. "I must say, Muul, I thought better of you."

She fluttered her throat flap at him in response, but said nothing more. He expected nothing less from a cowardly spawn-traitor like her. Still, it was a shame that they had to be wearing suits to do this; body language was such a satisfying part of combat, and he wanted to see the fear in her eyes before he ended her.

There was an art to battle that some of Goii's subordinates didn't appreciate. Ground Leader Paak, for example, had never been patient, and now was no exception. "For the Council!" she crowed, leaping forward.

Unfortunately, Muul was ready.

Paak swiped at her, but Muul dodged, sweeping Paak's feet

out from under her. As Paak fell, Muul slapped her gloves onto either side of Paak's helmet, avoiding the external maxillary shears, gripped tight, and twisted. The sound of Paak's spine popping echoed through the speakers, but Muul wasn't done. She drove her boot into Paak's back, engaging the suction to hold her more firmly in place. She continued to twist until, with a roar, she was able to pull Paak's helmet entirely free.

Even after years of combat experience, the sight of Paak's face exposed to the atmosphere of the Heart was enough to make Goii gag. The mossy growths on the walls bore a strong resemblance to the lush quarters on their ship, but whatever chemical processes allowed these plants to flourish did not provide a hospitable environment for Goii's people. The smooth, tender skin of Paak's head bubbled and blistered; within moments, she was an unrecognizable wreck, disfigured by hideous pustules.

She was still writhing in horror and agony, screaming but unheard, when Muul kicked her toward the edge of the cliff. She released her boot's suction, and Paak fell into the gelatinous soup below, which frothed and bubbled as it pulled her under.

"How dare you," Goii hissed, advancing on Muul. "How *dare* you murder one of your spawnsisters. For what? To save the life of a human?"

Muul tossed the empty helmet after Paak's body. "To whom should my loyalty belong? To *you?*" She scoffed. "Nobody should have the kind of power you're after. Not them, not me, but *especially* not the Council."

Goii gestured sharply to his remaining ground crew. "Kill them."

Muul sank into a crouch. "I'd like to see you try."

So he gave her what she wanted.

46

PETER CRASHED THROUGH AN ALIEN JUNGLE, clutching the straps of his pack as he ran. Every time the Heart sent out a lightning bolt above him, he ducked and winced.

"This is incredible," Fai observed, somehow managing to keep pace with Peter. "Look at all these species of flora! So many of them have parallels on Earth, it's really remarkable..."

Now I know how Lowell feels, Peter thought. He could appreciate his father's enthusiasm, but this wasn't the time.

The vegetation at the edge of the lake was thick and lush; the only weapon he had—while perfectly suited to long-distance, precision combat—was useless when it came to cutting through the jungle.

As Peter elbowed his way through the tropical thicket, he heard a scream through the mic that was cut short. He paused, turning back toward the ledge where they'd left Lowell and Muul, only to see a body tumble over the cliffside.

"Muul?" he breathed.

Goii's voice said, "Kill them."

To Peter's immense relief, Muul replied, "I'd like to see you try."

Someone grabbed Peter's arm and dragged him forward; a moment later, the mic popped as they stepped out of range.

"You've got to focus," Collins said. "If you let yourself get distracted, you risk getting hurt."

"But Lowell..." Peter protested.

"Hey," said Vasko sharply, "Lowell's protecting you. You're the one with this key thing, right? So if you get killed, we're *all* screwed."

The reminder probably should have frightened him, but instead, it gave him clarity. Vasko was right. Lowell was risking his life not just for them, but for everyone else whose safety hung in the balance.

Besides, this was what they'd been suited for from the very beginning. It was why Munroe had dragged Peter out to Enceladus in the first place: to translate what nobody else on their team could read.

Peter drew in a deep breath and looked up at the Heart. Enceladus had tried to kill him more times than he could count.

Time to return the favor.

Their progress seemed to take ages, and Peter swiped and clawed at the vines around him in annoyance. Even when he tugged at the greenery, it frequently sprang back undamaged; the stems and twining foliage were supple but tough, and when he grabbed them too hard, the fingers of his gloves suctioned onto them.

What would Lowell do? he wondered.

Simple. Lowell would figure out how to make the limitations of the environment work for him, not against him.

Peter tugged a vine thoughtfully. His gloves might help him climb, but the surrounding plant life would simply give under his weight, even in the low gravity. There was another option, though.

With a self-satisfied smile, Peter dropped to the ground.

"Peter!" Fai cried. "Are you hurt?"

"Not at all." From ground level, the way through the alien jungle was much clearer: without all the leaves blocking his way, he could see a plain path forward. There was no danger of losing their way, either. The light from the Heart was too bright to miss. Peter began to army-crawl through the mossy bed. It was tough work, and slow going, but not as slow as elbowing through the leaves had been.

"Nice." Vasko dropped down beside him and began to crawl at a much faster rate. Collins followed suit, and Fai came last. He seemed to be struggling with the rifle, and he grunted softly as he scrambled forward.

"Tough on the joints, old man?" Vasko asked cheerfully.

"I told you, I'm not that old," Fai grumbled. "And this isn't my forte. The next time someone asks *you* to calculate the distance between two nebulas, I'd like to see you try."

"Fair enough, Doc," Vasko chuckled. "I'll stick to my lane."

Despite his superior strength and training, Collins had fallen back to bring up the rear, while Vasko pressed forward. *They're protecting us,* Peter thought with relief. Objectively, there wasn't much either of them could do if something went sideways, but it was nice to know that the two men actually were on their side.

Peter had his doubts about their intentions, but there was already too much to worry about; no point in adding to the list of concerns when it wasn't necessary.

Besides, there was already plenty to distract him. Peter had been counting on Muul's help when it came to deciding what to do once they reached the Heart. She knew more than he did, and that included translation as much as mechanics. He shouldn't have wasted time trying to translate the inscriptions back in the tunnel. They should have moved as fast as possible, Lowell had *told* him so, and any old fool should have known that Goii would be on their trail, that the Tiān Zhuānjiā would be the *least* of their problems.

Vasko's knee scraped through the moss, revealing the stone floor of the cavern, and Peter paused. A series of marks was visible beneath. With a sinking feeling, Peter dug his fingers beneath the moss and peeled it back, revealing a spiderweb of Photosynthian inscriptions.

"Dammit." He let his head roll forward until his forehead knocked against the moss.

"What is it?" Collins asked.

"Muul was right when she said that there would be instructions near the Heart." Peter sighed. "But they're overgrown. We're crawling right over them, but we can't *see*…"

"Oh, for God's sake," Vasko complained. "Can't anything be *simple* for once?"

Fai spoke calmly but incredulously. "Are you complaining that the aliens who seeded all other life in the universe, using a technology so far beyond ours that it might as well be magic, made the instruction manual too complicated?"

Vasko didn't miss a bear. "Damn right, that's what I'm saying.

When Collins gave you those contacts, he didn't walk you through the coding and hardware. He just told you how to make 'em go."

Fai hummed thoughtfully. "That is, I admit, a surprisingly cogent argument, but it does little to help our current circumstances."

"Although..." Peter tapped his finger on the stone. "It is a good point. When Collins handed you the contacts, he was there to tell you what they were, why you might want them, and how to use them. Once you had them in, that's when he gave you the specific instructions." The tablet he'd found in Ur-An had been a map to the Anomaly; the carvings in the halls had been an explanation of the moon's purpose, telling them what they would find at the end of the hall. The closer they got to the Heart, the more specific the instructions would be.

Which left Peter in a bit of a quandary. "Time's running out," he murmured. "But if we mess this up, we could destroy everything. Literally *everything*." He nibbled his lip, then looked around at his companions. "I think we need to figure out what it says."

He expected the soldiers to complain the way Lowell often did, but Collins nodded. "I agree. The Space Corps always wants us to follow orders and keep moving, but this is too important."

Vasko sighed. "Unfortunately, so do I. Tell us what to do."

Peter pointed to the swath of moss. "Help me pull this up."

It took all of them working together, and they kept getting tangled in the plant life, but after a minute of struggling, they were able to peel back the mossy turf until more writing was visible.

"Here!" Peter cried, diving toward the recognizable Akkadian. "One second..." He traced his fingers beneath the words, painfully aware that every second he stalled, Lowell was fighting for his life.

Don't think about him. You know this. "Okay, it says that whoever is struck by the Heart will be altered..."

"Don't get zapped by the deadly lights," Vasko deadpanned. "Useful."

"Shut up," Collins grumbled.

"... and that the Heart must be contained." Peter scowled. "Great, but *how?*"

"This is not my area of expertise," Fai said softly, "but the instructions presume that we must have whatever we need."

"You ever put together prefab furniture?" Vasko asked. "Because those instructions always assume you've got, like, ten Allen wrenches and an electric drill just lying around. Who knows what plant aliens think people will automatically have on hand?"

"They know one thing we'd need to get this far." Peter tugged on the straps of his pack. "They know we have the stellar key. The Anomaly had instructions on it, so maybe the key will activate whatever needs to hold the Heart?"

His speculation was cut short by a crackle of static, and Peter automatically dropped to his belly. His companions did the same, pressing their chests to the ground and holding their collective breath as the familiar clicks and whistles of Muul's people cut through the silence.

"This way. They must be headed toward the Heart."

"Can you imagine if those filthy monkeys get their hands on it?" The second voice made a noise of utter disgust. *"What could be more wretched than one of those hairy beasts rubbing their stubby paws all over a device of such power?"*

There were only two voices, and neither of them was Goii's, but that didn't put Peter at ease. If even two of them had gotten past Lowell and Muul, that meant they were outmatched, at the very least.

A movement at the corner of Peter's vision caught his eye. Collins was waving frantically at the group. When all four of them were looking, he made a series of hand gestures, pointing first at Vasko and himself, then at Peter and Fai. Peter perked up when Collins began to gesture in ASL. *You two, go on toward the Heart. We'll handle the enemies.*

Peter nodded, then nudged his father forward. He signed to Collins, *Take care,* then wiggled through the moss. This time, he father didn't grunt as they crawled along.

Just before they passed out of the range of the mics, they heard Vasko cackle gleefully, and one of the aliens howling, "*Shoot him! SHOOT HIM!*" and then the audio cut out again, and Peter let out a sigh of relief.

"Has it been like this the whole time?" Fai asked in a strained voice.

"Yes and no," Peter admitted. "Someone's always trying to kill us, but it's not always the same people."

Fai laughed weakly. "Comforting. You seem surprisingly calm with all of this."

Peter glanced up at the otherworldly life above him just as the Heart let off another bolt of brilliant light. "It's surprising how normal this all starts to feel after a while." He paused to peel back a layer of moss and found the same inscription beneath it, this time in Muul's language. *Whoever is struck by the Heart will be altered, and the Heart must be contained.* On one hand, it was good to know that they weren't missing all sorts of pertinent information. On the other, just a teensy bit more detail would have gone a long way to explaining what the hell Peter was supposed to do if he even *made* it to the Heart in one piece.

Within a few more feet, the greenery gave way to a large blank space. Even the moss didn't grow here, and a whole new set of inscriptions marked the floor. Despite the promise of the information Peter craved, his eye was drawn upwards from the stone carvings toward the sphere of energy above him.

They had reached the Heart of Enceladus.

47

LOWELL KNEW a thing or two about how turning on your old brothers-in-arms could mess with your head. For the first time, he was fairly sure that he knew what was going on in Muul's mind, and he didn't envy her the cognitive dissonance she must be feeling.

Then again, as she squared off against Goii, she didn't *look* terribly conflicted. As a matter of fact, she seemed like she'd been waiting for this for a long time.

Wanting to kill a shit boss who'd turned everyone against you? Yeah, Lowell knew the feeling.

Two of Goii's men fired on him at once, and Lowell feinted to the side just in time, running through his options. The electric shock of his borrowed gun might not be enough to kill them, but one thing was clear; if he could compromise their suits, they'd be in a world of hurt.

Sticky gloves. Suction boots. Helmet shears. Lowell ran through the list of available tools as he launched himself forward. Why hadn't the Space Corps thought of any of this stuff?

The aliens were obviously prepared for Lowell to attack them head-on, but instead he aimed high, using the lower gravity of Enceladus to propel him higher than he would have managed otherwise. The Muulians—as Lowell had come to think of them, in honor of the only member of their species who was merely a *partial* pain in his ass—prepared to spring up to meet him as Lowell executed a flip in midair, driving his heels into the stone ceiling. The blood rushed to his head, but he didn't plan to stay up there long. Instead, he glanced down at his attackers, gauging his trajectory.

Muul was grappling with Goii, and two of the landing party were focused on Lowell; he'd assumed that the remaining two would join the fight against Muul, but to his chagrin they were already leaping over the moat in the direction Peter and the rest of them had gone. Not great news, but Lowell had his hands full at the moment. He drove his toes against the stone, releasing the suction, and tumbled toward the first of his attackers. He folded his knees toward his chest, driving the alien to the ground and yanking at the latch of his helmet.

Muul had made it look almost easy, but she'd also given away Lowell's strategy for facing the aliens, inasmuch as he *had* a strategy. When he tried to displace one alien's helmet, it twisted around out of his grasp, snarling as it went. The other one fired on him, and Lowell was barely able to roll out of the way in time.

"I could use some backup," he grumbled.

"I'm a bit—*guh*—busy," Muul complained.

Lowell reached for his gun, but they were fighting in close quarters, and he had to keep an eye on two enemies at once. When one of them whistled, Lowell had no way of knowing if they were taunting him or planning their next attack.

There was very little that Lowell detested more than feeling helpless, and yet this whole endeavor had been one long series of being thrust into various situations he had no control over. At a certain point, he would just have to accept that he'd tipped sideways into some sort of alternate reality where nothing made sense anymore.

Thinking like a man wasn't much help. Maybe it was time to start thinking like one of *them*.

Every soldier, even the savviest of fighters, eventually fell into a rut with their thinking, and if they weren't careful, they'd get stuck in it. Lowell had been guilty of it himself at times. He'd come to rely on certain senses, or on the force of gravity, or on the notion that he could trust his superiors to act in his best interests. When those things were stripped away, he was forced to recalibrate. All he had to do was think of something that an alien might take for granted and capitalize on that.

Right. That was doable.

As soon as the thought crystallized, Lowell sprang back toward the ceiling. He experienced another wave of vertigo, but he didn't let himself falter; that would give his enemies time to take aim. He sprinted across the ceiling until he stood above the viscous moat.

Then he let himself fall.

"Lowell!" Muul exclaimed.

He didn't have time to reassure her; he had to time the drop just right and aim perfectly, all while flailing his arms to make it look like an accident. He caught a quick glimpse of Muul and Goii before he fell out of their line of sight. Then, with a tremendous effort, he drove his heels against the face of the cliff.

It was enough to arrest his fall, but he hadn't counted on how much harder it would be to cling to the wall than to dangle upside down. Even when his feet were suctioned in place, Lowell tipped backward. Standing parallel to the force of gravity was tough on the joints, and Lowell could feel the toll of his idle days on Goii's ship.

Silently cursing the effort it took to hold himself upright, relatively speaking, Lowell drew the alien pistol from its holster at his belt and waited.

If I were them, I'd want to check. I'd make extra-certain that I'm dead. Call it completionism, call it morbid curiosity, but I'd take a gander.

He practically held his breath until two alien faces appeared over the edge of the cliff. They probably expected to see his body floating in the bubbling moat below. Lowell waved up at them with one hand and fired with the other.

His first shot struck one of them in the helmet; Lowell couldn't have said for certain how badly his opponent was harmed, but they tumbled forward rather than back, and Lowell had to swing himself in toward the rock face to avoid being hit by the body as it fell. The other one fell backwards out of sight.

Did I hit them both? Either way, having to fight one enemy rather than two was a win in his book.

Only then did it occur to Lowell that he wasn't sure how to get back up. He'd slid too far past the edge of the cliff to easily jump back, and his position would make it difficult to clear the moat if he leapt toward the island.

Nice going, Carp. Out of the frying pan, huh? He tried to shuffle upwards, but stopped after the second attempt. If he slipped now, he'd have no way to catch himself.

His mic popped at the same time that Muul screamed.

"Muul?" he asked. "What's wrong?"

Her only response didn't come in any language Lowell knew, although it sounded like swearing. He stood there, frozen with indecision. The muscles in his legs were reaching their limits, and he had no idea how to extricate himself from his current predicament.

He couldn't see, he couldn't move, and he was growing weaker by the second.

If I make it out of this one, he thought wearily, *it's going to be a miracle.*

48

WILLIAM COLLINS HAD BEEN HANKERING for a stick of gum ever since they'd left the ship in orbit. He chewed gum with the same borderline religious fervor that other men smoked. A few hours without food and water? He could handle that. But he hadn't thought to stuff a stick of gum in his mouth before they left, and now he was paying the price.

Gum helped him calm his nerves. Helped him think clearly. Right now, he couldn't think for shit, and it made him want to fight someone.

The good news was, he knew exactly who to target first.

Now that Dr. Chang and his kid were officially on their own, Collins surrendered his protective instincts and allowed himself to go fully on the offensive. These aliens were going to rue the day they'd messed with him—not humans in general, but Collins *personally*.

Their pursuers were crashing around through the underbrush. Collins couldn't hear their movements, of course, but they were making no effort to disguise their passing, and it was easy enough to pinpoint their location as they traversed the jungle.

Collins paused when Vasko tapped his shoulder. His friend winked at him, then hollered, "Ca-CAW, ca-CAW!"

You immature dick, Collins signed.

Vasko shrugged, smiling serenely as their enemies broke out into a frenzied series of exclamations. A few stray bolts from their guns fizzled through the foliage at about chest height; well above their heads a few shredded leaves sifted down onto them, but they were completely unharmed.

Watch this, Vasko signed. Then he pulled his rifle into position and aimed at the boots stomping through the moss a dozen yards away.

His shot was flawless, and the alien dropped, screaming in pain as it fell. Their words meant nothing to Collins, but it was obvious that they were panicked. As he watched, some sort of yellow foam bubbled out of the hole that Vasko's laser had seared through the suit.

Mr. Alien didn't go down right away. Instead, it staggered toward them, clutching its foaming ankle while it screamed in pain. Collins felt almost sorry for it, but Vasko grinned and gave him a huge thumbs-up. Then he began crawling forward again.

He'd only made it another foot before the uninjured alien dropped to all fours. It let out a blood-curdling screech of rage before firing its electrical gun at Collins. He rolled to the side, but ended up tangled in some kind of vine, and by the time he got free, Vasko was returning fire.

The screaming hadn't stopped, and when Collins looked back toward where the injured alien was thrashing about on the ground, he realized that it was trying to take its helmet off. *Must have lost its mind,* he thought.

That, or was trying to kill itself to stop the pain.

Either way, Collins swung his rifle around and fired once, burning a perfect hole right through its temple. The thrashing stopped abruptly.

"Nice," Vasko said.

"Where's the other one?" Collins asked.

Vasko looked around, and Collins did the same, but there was no sign of the second combatant.

"Think it went after Doc and the kid?" Vasko asked.

"No." Collins rolled onto his back, looking up toward the cavern's ceiling. "I think it went high."

Something sailed down from above them and burst apart, sending pellets flying. Collins instinctively covered his eyes with one arm, but after a few seconds, he had the happy revelation that he had not, in fact, been blown to smithereens, which was a rather nice feeling. He shifted onto his side and dragged his fingers through the white residue left behind.

"What the crap," Vasko muttered. "Is this *salt?*"

The explosion hadn't been meant to hurt them, but it had served its purpose as a distraction. They were both still staring in bafflement at the salt pellets when their opponent dropped down on them from above. Vasko swore and tried to roll over in time to fire, but neither he nor Collins was fast enough. The alien landed on Collins' chest, driving one knee into his torso, crushing the whole breastplate into his ribs and knocking the breath out of him. One of his arms was pinned to his side by his leg, and the long rifle was no good for this sort of close combat. Collins fumbled uselessly with it until the alien wrenched it out of his hands and twisted to take aim at Vasko.

"Nope," Collins grunted. "Can't have that." He planted his heels in the moss and thrust upwards with enough force to overbalance his foe. The alien pitched to one side and managed to catch itself before it fell, but before it could take aim again, one well-placed shot from Vasko's rifle struck it in the neck, and the alien dropped like a stone.

Collins glared at his friend. "You don't always need to be a smartass, you know. It's going to get you killed one of these days."

"So everyone says," Vasko replied cheerfully. "But you gotta make your own fun, right?"

Collins sighed and rolled back onto his belly, shuffling away through the moss toward the heart of the dying moon. "Get yourself killed if you want, but don't drag me into it."

"Wouldn't dream of it," Vasko said. "But I don't plan on dying today. Too much going on, you know? No time for it."

He's mad, Collins thought. But then again, didn't you have to be just a *little* bit mad to sign up for all of this in the first place?

49

"INCREDIBLE," Fai breathed. He stared up the device that kept the jungle at the heart of Enceladus alive. All of his life, ever since he was a small boy, he'd stared up at the stars and wondered what awaited humankind out there. He'd pored over novels and academic papers with equal fervor. He'd teased out every theory of life on other worlds, no matter how thoroughly debunked. He'd thirsted for the sort of knowledge that would confirm what he'd always believed.

Humanity was not alone. Every lonely hour he spent staring through the telescope, or struggling and failing to connect to other people on even a superficial level, wasn't a personal failing. He hadn't been chasing fantasies, as Susan had accused him during the divorce. He'd been chasing the *truth*.

And here it was. An answer. Fai had become one of only a handful of people who knew the truth of their origins.

"What does this mean?" Peter muttered. He was staring down at the ground, running his fingers over the etchings in the rock, deliberately ignoring the wonder in front of him as he pondered the text left by their progenitors.

Fai had never understood why people insisted on looking down when they could look up, and it pained him that his son saw fit to do so along with everyone else. How could he be blind to the wonder of it all? No words in any language could come close to encapsulating the complexity of chemical interaction that must be taking place inside the Heart. Certainly, no experiments on Earth had come close to reliably replicating this phenomenon.

"What I don't understand," Peter was saying, "is how it's supposed to be contained. I mean, logically, if the Photosynthians were sailing all over the universe like Muul said, they must have had some way to transport these things. Some way to make them less volatile, you know?"

"Some way to contain it," Fai murmured. "One of the old theories on space seeding was that life was brought to Earth on meteorites. Ultra-hardy microbes, encased in stone...there are still bacteria like that on Earth, you know."

"I know," Peter said stiffly. He drummed his fingers on the rock. "Geeze, this is driving me crazy. I bet the tablet would have said something useful."

Fai turned his face toward Peter, although his eyes still drifted up toward the brilliant light above them. "What does it say here?"

"It's utter nonsense," Peter complained. "It looks like it says *the key is the key*, but they've used two different words for key. Why leave a riddle here, right when proper *clarity* would be the most helpful?" He sat back on his heels and swung off his little pack to retrieve the key.

Fai had heard an awful lot about it, but he'd yet to see this infamous object that everyone wanted so desperately to get their hands on. Compared to the Heart, it was a plain thing, almost perfectly spherical, with a series of inlaid symbols on the outside.

"What are these?" Fai asked, pointing to the marks on its surface.

"We needed it to help us line it up with the Anomaly when this all started," Peter said.

Fai held out one hand. "May I?"

He could sense Peter's reluctance to yield the very object he'd found so hard to keep, but his son passed the key over, and Fai inspected it more closely.

"What are you looking for?" Peter asked curiously. "Those aren't words."

Fai held the key up close to his face, examining it intently. He'd never seen anything quite like this before, but it jostled loose an old memory, one that he'd put aside long ago.

"When I was a boy, still living in Yunnan," he said thoughtfully, "my grandfather collected puzzles. Puzzle balls, puzzle boxes, tangram sets, metal and wood; even the antique ivory pieces, when he could get his hands on them. There was always a trick to them. Something you had to do to get them to line up just right…"

"But it's solid," Peter protested. "It's not like… oh, shoot, what was that old toy your officemate always kept on his desk?"

Fai smiled; he hadn't realized Peter remembered that. "A Rubik's cube. But you're assuming that the key itself is the entirety of the puzzle." He gestured up to the Heart. "I know that you're better at translation than I'll ever hope to be, but is there a possibility that there's more to it than what you've said? Another meaning? Because the explanation is here, and we just can't see it yet."

Peter shook his head. "I don't know. If Muul was here…"

Fai laid his free hand on his son's shoulder. "But she's not here. So let's see what we can come up with. The key and the Heart are connected, aren't they?" To demonstrate his point, he rose to his feet, holding the key above his head. "So maybe, when they come together—"

The heart pulsed again, sending out another bolt of lightning. This time, instead of arcing over their heads, the crackle of energy reached out toward Fai directly. It seemed to happen in slow motion, and he could feel the electrostatic charge pass through him. Fai smiled; he had *known* that something like this would happen. *The key is the key. The Heart must be contained.* It was either a riddle or a poor translation, but even so, he could see how it would unfold. The spark would reach out, and in moments Fai would be holding the key to life in his hands.

He was wrong. The tension snapped through him, stiffening his spine and blurring his vision.

"Dad?" Peter cried.

Fai couldn't reply. The energy flowing through him made every muscle tense with such force that his joints popped. The key tumbled from his rigid fingers.

Then the world went dark, and Fai collapsed.

50

HE MING WATCHED in stunned silence as Lowell plunged over the edge of the cliff.

Either he is a bigger idiot than I thought, or he has some sort of plan. There were men like Munroe and Ilin, who had managed to convince themselves that nothing could ever touch them. In their minds, their egos made them invulnerable. Lowell didn't strike her as the type, though.

Sure enough, when his attackers approached, a series of shots was fired up the cliff face. One alien fell, and the other stumbled back.

Three aliens, plus who knew how many more in the jungle below. Ming had wondered at the clean, wild beauty of the most recent tunnels, but she didn't know the territory, and out here the unknown went hand-in-hand with danger. What she needed now was a way to even the scales.

There was no way to consult with General Wu without giving

away their presence or their location, so Ming took matters into her own hands. One of the aliens had sided with Lowell in the tunnels, but Ming had no way to know which of them was which; they all looked the same to her, and their uniforms were identical. Lowell probably wouldn't take kindly to them shooting his ally in front of him, but of the two grappling aliens, it was impossible to tell which one was on their side—or at least, *humanity's* side—and which one was not.

There was, however, another solution, one that Ming knew was effective. General Wu had already deployed his sonic scrambler, but Ming still had hers. She pulled the pin, then hurled it right into the midst of the little battle.

The effect was instantaneous. All three of the aliens recoiled, screeching in pain. The sound of their distress was almost as grating as that of the sonic scrambler itself. Unfortunately, this weapon was harder to direct than most others, and Ming had to bite the inside of her cheek to keep from crying out along with the rest of them.

"Dammit." Lowell's aggrieved voice cut through the din. "You've got to be *kidding* me."

One of the aliens stumbled forward and stomped on the scrambler, cutting off the sound. Ming immediately felt better, but the aliens were still reeling. One of them collapsed to their knees, while the other two sprang away across the moat into the thicket below. Ming heard them leave range.

"Muul?" Lowell's voice asked. He still hadn't reappeared over the cliff's edge. "Are you all right?"

"I've been worse," the alien replied, still gripping her head. "Where did that *come* from?"

"It came from us," General Wu said. "And I have you in my sight now. Don't move."

The alien looked around, then hissed. "Spawn's sake... this is why I hate your species, Lowell. Making yourselves *invisible?* It's irritating and cowardly."

"Don't blame me, Muul," Lowell said in a tight voice.

"I don't suppose you'll be coming up here to parlay with your friends?" the alien asked.

"Can't," Lowell grunted. "I'm stuck."

The alien shook her head. "Well, hidden humans, it sounds like that's it. Either make your demands known or kill me now. Otherwise, I have spawnbrethren to kill."

Ming strolled over to the edge of the cliff and looked down. Sure enough, Lowell was clinging to the rocks like some sort of tenacious parasite. It would be so easy to shoot him now. They might not win whatever fight was coming, but at least they could stop Lowell from winning.

She reached up to switch off her cloak, then crouched down to examine him. "I see that you're in a bit of trouble," she said casually.

"Miss He," Lowell said casually. "You stuck around for the party."

She tilted her head to one side. "I could help you up from there," she said, "but I have the unfortunate feeling that you'd try to shoot me afterwards, and I'd like to avoid that if possible."

Lowell was obviously struggling, but he managed to keep the strain out of his voice. "Is that so? Because I can't imagine why you'd think that I might stab an ally in the back. Possibly because that's what you did to me and Peter?"

"The situation has changed," Ming said. She turned to Muul. "Come help me get him back up here."

"How do I know that your friend won't shoot me?" Muul asked.

Wu appeared a few feet away and made a show of lowering his gun. "I appreciate your concerns, but time is not on our side. We know about the key."

Muul trudged over in silence and lowered herself over the edge. As she clung to the lip of the cliff, she kicked Lowell in the chest; the blow dislodged him from the wall, but to Ming's surprise, his suit seemed to cling to Muul's boots. The alien dragged them both back over the cliff, depositing Lowell in a heap.

"Couldn't think of a better way to do that?" Lowell grumbled.

"Didn't try," the alien retorted. "You deserved it." She turned to Ming and the general. "I suppose you have some sort of terms?"

"We get safe passage with you when you leave," Ming said.

"Assuming we leave alive," Wu added.

"Ridiculous," Muul grumbled. "They only want the key."

Wu held out his hand toward Lowell. "I swear," he said solemnly, "on my son's death and my daughter's life: I only want to keep the power of destruction out of enemy hands. I would not hand it over to the Space Corps, or the Russian fleet, or the Cell. But you are a man who has no more alliances, Mr. Lowell, other than the ones you choose to make."

"So you think I should get all the power in the galaxy?" Lowell snorted. "That just proves you've lost it, General." He held out a hand, and when the general shook it, Lowell yanked him in close. "But if you stab me in the back this time, I swear I'll claw my way back from hell and make you pay."

"An admirable sentiment," Wu informed him. "Shall we?"

"One moment." An idea had occurred to Ming. "You go. I'll be right behind you."

"That threat goes for you, too," Lowell informed her. Muul leapt into the jungle, and Lowell and Wu followed. Ming's message only took a few seconds to send out, and then she jumped after them, plunging feet-first into the riotous verdancy below.

51

PETER SHOOK his father's shoulder. "Dad? *Baba?*"

Fai lay in a limp heap on the stone, one arm outstretched and his head thrown awkwardly back against the stone. He was still moving, but he hadn't said a word or even focused his eyes since the bolt from the Heart had struck him.

Tears were welling up in Peter's eyes, and with the helmet in the way, he couldn't brush them off. They dripped down his cheeks and splattered against the glass of his visor.

"Dad," he repeated softly. "I can't...I can't do this alone."

Fai twitched, and Peter looked up at the light above them. He was alone, for all intents and purposes, and he had no idea what the hell he was supposed to do now.

The stellar key had rolled a little way off, and Peter crawled forward on his hands and knees to retrieve it. He couldn't help his father right now, and for all he knew, everyone else was gone. If he didn't figure this out, Goii might eventually come along and snatch up the key, and then...well, by then Peter would be dead.

Don't get ahead of yourself. You can only solve what's in front of you.

Peter scurried back out of the way, terrified of being struck down just as his father had. When he reached Fai, he lifted his father and hauled him back until they were at the edge of the circle of vegetation, right on the edge of the clearing. From here, they couldn't see the moat. They might have been in some prehistoric forest on Earth, before the first fish crawled out of the oceans. There was so much promise here. So much to be learned.

But there was no *time*.

Peter propped Fai up against one of the trees, then turned his attention to the key. *The key is the key...*

It had been a long time since Peter had really stopped to look at the key. Now he turned it over in his hands, examining the bright band of material that girdled its circumference. The sigils emblazoned on its surface didn't look like any language Peter knew. If anything, they looked like...

He sat up abruptly. They looked like a map's compass.

What if the tablet hadn't just told them how to find the Anomaly? What if it had also been the instructions for how to operate the key once they arrived?

He spun the ball round, looking for marks. What was the significance of the line around the middle of the ball? It looked like an equator...

"Lowell said that one surface of Enceladus always faces Saturn," he mumbled. "They called it the giantess's face. So one side is always bright, and one side is in shadow."

He flipped the orb to examine the points farthest from the inlaid equator. One side had a tiny shape cut into the metal.

"That's the Anomaly," Peter mumbled. "So these other marks

are the tiger stripes, the geysers near where Lowell and I entered the ocean."

What had the tablet pointed them to next? The rock garden? And then there was the deep rift where Sharkie had emerged from the depths to take a bite out of them.

Peter frowned. Something wasn't lining up, quite literally. The tiger stripes were broken into two groups, and the line marking the rift in the moon's surface didn't align correctly. The map was skewed.

The key is the key. Peter had gotten so used to thinking of the object in his hands as the stellar key that he'd forgotten his original struggle to translate the name of the object. Taken literally, the phrase had translated into something more like *otherworldly light*.

Peter looked up at the brilliant object above him. That was an otherworldly light, all right.

With shaking hands, he gripped either side of the key and lifted it, twisting it in an attempt to properly align the marks.

It didn't budge.

Peter glared at the key in consternation. "Well, that's not very helpful," he muttered. He tried again. It felt as though the key was made of two pieces, but they were stuck.

"It's a puzzle, all right," he grumbled. "What am I missing?"

He was holding the key so that the stripe down the middle stood perpendicular to the floor. Before he'd been struck down, Fai had mentioned puzzle boxes. Some of those old puzzle games relied on gravity and metal pins to hold them in place. Of course, the likelihood that advanced alien technology operated like antique puzzle boxes on Earth was a bit ludicrous, but it was worth a shot. Peter rotated the stellar key so that the marking for the

Anomaly faced the ceiling, mirroring the direction of the moon's gravitational pull.

Something shifted inside the key; Peter felt it give way. This time, when he twisted, the two halves of the orb moved freely. Peter twisted the key so that the map aligned, and the key came apart in his hands.

"I did it." Peter blinked down at the two hemispheres. He couldn't understand what had held it together, or what mechanism had allowed it to come apart, but nevertheless, he'd managed it. The inside of the sphere was coated in an unfamiliar black material, not like paint but like the night sky, velvety and absolute in its darkness.

Peter struggled to his feet, keeping the two halves of the orb close to his chest. There was nothing else inside, no further instructions to tell him what to do.

"I don't know, Dad," he said. "I think you might have been right." He'd seen the way that long blue finger of lightning had reached out for the key before. It hadn't been a random strike. The Heart and the key were connected.

Of course, if he was wrong, they were all in trouble. But Lowell would have trusted his gut, and Fai would have trusted his head, and right now, both of these things were telling Peter what he had to do.

He lifted the segments of the key above his head and braced his feet in anticipation of whatever happened next.

52

HELENA WATCHED as the American ship spun around the UFO in an ever-tightening pattern.

"Bhatt? Tuhin? Are we ready?" she asked.

The two Indian pilots nodded.

Helena leaned toward the comm. "All right, Sanz. We're ready to go."

"Roger," Sanz replied. "Abandoning formation in three... two..."

The USSC vessel veered off-course, leaving Helena's path to the UFO wide open.

"Acosta," she barked. "Make sure those engineers keep our cloaks up. I want the drones heading in first—we need to determine any weakness in their defenses before the Cell pilots get involved."

Acosta nodded, then passed her orders along. From what Helena could tell, he only knew a few words of Mandarin, but he understood the controls well enough to get her point across.

"What about me?" asked the ever-eager Grady. "What have you got for me, boss?"

Helena held up a quelling finger. "Oh, don't worry, I've got a job in mind for you. The moment we know what we're doing, you're going to be on the guns."

Grady bounced on the balls of his feet. "But what about now, boss? What about right now? What do you want me to do until then?"

The guy was still riding the Neon, and Helena knew just how much those uppers affected the nervous system. Rather than snapping at him, she gestured calmly to the doors in and out of the bridge. "For now, you're on guard duty."

Grady bounded away just as Acosta looked up. "We're sending the drones in now."

"Perfect." She leaned back in her seat and steepled her fingers. "How's that leg, by the way?"

"I can see the chair through my thigh," Acosta said. "I'd say it's not good, ma'am."

"Look on the bright side." Hellcat swiveled toward the screen before them. "If we get vaporized in the next ten minutes, you'll never have to deal with it."

"You're a ray of sunshine, as always." Acosta winced as he adjusted his posture. "Let's see how this works."

The UFO had already begun to move, following the USSC ship. As they watched, a few dozen drones sped through the night to intercept the silver ship.

"Can we get visuals on them?" Hellcat asked.

Acosta spoke to one of the Tiān Zhuānjiā engineers. A moment later, images from the drones' cameras brought up exterior images of the ship. Helena leaned forward and frowned. "What the—who made this thing?"

From the station beside her, Tuhin let out a hiss of annoyance. "I don't like it. It's all plating; there are no weak points. Whenever we target a ship, we aim for the turrets, the guns, any glass or shields or cargo doors, but this…" He crossed his arms and frowned down at the screen.

Helena drummed her fingers on the arm of her chair. Ideally, that would have been her strategy, too. "What have you got for me, Acosta?"

"There's a seam on the bottom," Acosta pointed out.

Captain Sanz's voice came through the speaker. "True, but that's also the origin point of their vaporizer. When they engaged it, we could see directly into their engines, but that's like looking down the barrel of a charged laser."

Helena bit her thumbnail. "I don't like it," she mumbled. "If we do that, we only get one shot."

"We could use the drones as bait." Chandran Bhatt pointed at the screen. His eyebrows had pulled together in an expression of intense concentration. "Encourage them to open up, then have our ships fire from an angle."

"Our pilots know what they're doing," Tuhin added. "I have every faith in them."

"No offense, but none of us know what we're doing," Helena pointed out. "Not with this. Everything's a shot in the dark."

Tuhin frowned. "Do you have a better idea?"

Unfortunately, she didn't. Helena stared intently at the screen, narrowing her eyes. She could push back and refuse to run the risk of losing what few ships they had.

A good leader knows when they're beat. You know where your strengths lie, and you saw how they commanded their troops.

Your whole crew died on Enceladus. Maybe it's time you stop throwing other people's lives in the way of bullets meant for you.

Helena got sharply to her feet. "Drones won't be enough to draw their fire. You're going to need bigger bait. Bhatt, Tuhin, you're in charge; Acosta, don't get killed. Grady, you're with me."

Everyone but Grady seemed stunned by her words, but the big man came bounding up beside her. "Are we on a mission, boss?"

"We sure are. Could be a suicide mission, though."

Grady shrugged. "Not a problem for me."

Acosta was watching her somberly. "Be careful, Hellcat."

She smiled crookedly at him. "Bye, Acosta."

"We've got your back," Tuhin said, and Chandran nodded his agreement.

It felt like she was heading to her own funeral. In fact, she might have been. But she'd rather get her hands dirty than sacrifice others to get the job done, and she had done too much of that lately.

Never thought you'd get all noble right at the end, did you?

"This is going to be exciting." Grady jogged backward down the hall ahead of her. "We're going into the eye of the storm."

"That's the right attitude." Helena broke into a sprint.

If the bastards were going to kill her, by God, she wouldn't go quietly.

53

JUAA ADJUSTED the positioning of his toes. The human vessel was still bouncing around their ship, making it impossible to target them properly. He could still taste the powder of the ancestor plant on his tongue, and he was intimately aware of everything taking place onboard his vessel.

"Should we intercept them, Captain?" asked Flee from the engine room.

"Not yet." Juaa's voice came out slow and sluggish, utterly relaxed. "The flight path will take a toll on their engines. Soon, they'll be easy targets."

"Yes, Captain."

The connection from Piin in Monitoring cut in. "Captain? We have unidentified objects across the bow. Unmanned weaponry. How shall we proceed?"

"Show me." Juaa lifted three of his toes off of the control orb long enough to glance at the screen in the captain's quarters. The ships were small, and there was little risk of them doing any significant damage to his own vessel. He returned his focus to the control orb. "There is no cause for concern. Focus on the larger ship. Their weapons are primitive; I'm under the impression that they still use *lasers,* for Spawn's sake. I'm more concerned about them running away than fighting back."

"Understood, Captain."

There were no further concerns for the moment, and Juaa drifted back to the dreamy space where he and the ship were in total harmony. The human ship was nearly in their sights, and any moment, they would be reduced to mere particles.

Juaa was so focused on their future conquest that, when the first blow to the hull came, it caught him entirely off-guard.

"What was that?" he demanded on all the channels.

"There's a small fleet along Quadrant Four," Piin informed him. "I don't know where they came from, sir, they weren't there a few moments ago—"

"What kind of artillery?" A mere laser couldn't have impacted their course; they must be using some kind of physical ammunition.

"It's a shrapnel bomb of some sort, sir. They explode on impact. It's not enough to compromise us."

Juaa considered this. "Leave them for now. We'll take out their main ship."

Another barrage of artillery peppered the hull. Juaa's sense of calm was rapidly fading. "That's enough," he growled. "We're wasting time. I want that ship destroyed. Let the little ones wear themselves out if they want to, but we're taking out the main vessel. *Now.*"

CAPTAIN SANZ DUG her nails into her palms. "Bad news, Hellcat. They're not taking the bait."

Boswell looked up from the controls. "We're losing power on the engines, too."

Sanz swore and reeled back. "What are our options?"

"Few and far between, I'm afraid." Boswell ran a hand over his close-cropped hair. "Divert all power to the main engines and see if we can make it out of range, or give everything we've got to the weaponry."

Sanz crossed her arms. "We won't be able to make a run for it. They'll just follow. I guess that answers the question for us. Have you got that, Hellcat? You're our Hail Mary."

"Never was much for praying," Hellcat drawled. "But no time like the present, I guess."

"Last stand it is, then." Sanz stiffened her spine and looked around at the crew. "It's been a pleasure serving with you all. Let's go out with a bang, shall we?"

There were plenty of reasons to hate the Space Corps, not the least of which was the leadership, but as her crew cheered the sentiment, Sanz felt the sort of contentment that she'd forgotten about. Dying for a paycheck was a damn shame, but standing her ground with a crew she loved like family?

Sanz could certainly think of worse ways to go.

54

COLLINS WASN'T sure what sparked the change, but he felt a shift in the moon's gravity even before the light of the Heart began to fade.

"What the crap?" Vasko demanded. "What's going on?"

"Hopefully the Doc and his kid have figured out what they're doing." Collins glared up at the sky. "That, or they've broken the moon."

"Or both," Vasko suggested. "I'm telling you, I always thought I was in the Space Corps for life, but after this? I'm checking out my retirement options. Fighting aliens is way above my pay grade."

In all the years they'd served together, Collins had never quite figured out whether Vasko was stupid, belligerent, or just... *coping*. Half the time, Collins wasn't sure what he was doing, either. The mission briefs never included the weird stuff, and while this one topped the list of problems he'd never thought he'd get stuck dealing with, it wasn't the only time he'd been in over his head.

They squirmed along the floor side-by-side, until they reached a clearing. Only a few feet away, a body lay propped against a tree trunk.

"Shit." Vasko scrambled to his feet and hurried to the man's side. "Doc? You okay? Aw, man, Collins, he looks rough."

Ordinarily, Collins would have joined him to assess the damage, but he was still lying on his belly, staring toward the Heart in silent wonder. The brilliant blue light was now shot through with veins of black, and it seemed to be folding in on itself, collapsing into a smaller and smaller space. The sight was both beautiful and terrifying, but Collins was more entranced by the figure standing beneath the Heart, arms raised above his head as sapphire lightning danced between his palms.

"Whoa." Vasko straightened, but kept one hand on Fai's shoulder. "Peter?"

The kid didn't respond, but it was definitely him. He looked larger than life, wreathed in blue fire, more like a mythical creature come to life than a man. Even Vasko, who always had some deadpan one-liner on standby, fell silent.

The light of the Heart still pulsed. As darkness crept in at the edges, the bright point at the center became more pronounced; it was dimming, simply condensing, retaining all of its power in the process. When the entirety of the Heart was small enough to fit into Peter's palms, he clapped his hands together and the blue light vanished entirely.

The jungle was still bathed in a surreal green glow, and Collins could see just enough to make out Peter's brilliant smile as he held something aloft, looking for all the world like Collins' little nephew showing off a firefly he'd snatched out of the New Hampshire sky.

"I got it!" he crowed. "I solved it!" He came jogging back

toward them. "We've got the Heart... the source... *ariru*... whatever you want to call it, it's here." He collapsed onto the ground beside them. "What about you? Are you two okay?"

"As good as we can get with everything that's going on." Collins hooked his thumb toward Fai. "What happened to him?"

Peter's shoulders slumped. "He went down, but he was still breathing. What about now? Is he...?"

"Not great," Vasko said. "But his vitals are okay."

Peter nodded. "Good. We can try to help him when we get out of here. I don't suppose you've heard anything from Lowell?"

"Not yet. If we're done here, we should... Wait. Did you feel that?" Collins looked around. "Like the ground moved."

Sure enough, the leaves of the surrounding trees were trembling, and the ground had begun to shake.

"Oh, no." Peter groaned deeply. "Dammit! I thought we were done with this. It's another earthquake."

"I think you mean Enceladus-quake," Vasko quipped.

Collins smacked his friend in the shoulder. "Dude, seriously? You think this is funny?"

Vasko snorted. "No, but you want to know what is? Y'all listened to that alien chick run through this whole story about how the Heart is what gives this place life, and then you took it away, and you didn't expect the sky to fall in." He pointed to Fai's prone form. "We're not going to be able to army-crawl out of here while carrying him, so if anyone had a genius idea for how to get out of here in one piece, now would be a great time to tell me."

"Um." Peter's voice came out as a squeak. "We have a bigger problem." He backed away toward the middle of the clearing, clutching the silver orb to his chest with one hand and pointing into the jungle with a shaking finger.

As far as disasters, Collins would have rated *'moon imploding while we're standing dead in the center of it'* pretty damn high on the list. When he realized what Peter was pointing at, however, he could concede that the kid had a point. Two tall, narrow figures were emerging from the forest, backlit by silvery-green light. Collins wasn't certain where the glow was coming from.

It's the moat, he realized. This immediately compounded with the further realization that when the island collapsed, the caustic fluid from the moat would likely fill in the cracks, and judging by what had happened to the dying alien Muul had tossed into it earlier, that wasn't going to be good news for anybody, including the two figures slipping toward them through the underbrush.

Peter clutched the key to his chest and stepped backwards. "No. They can't have it, Collins. You didn't feel it, but it's big, and if Goii gets his hands on it..."

"*Goii?*" Vasko repeated. "That's his name? I thought it would be something cool, like... I dunno, Shredder? Maxulon? Something rad." He lifted his laser gun to his shoulder. "Hey, Goii! Eat light!" He fired a hailstorm of shots in the aliens' general direction, but they were moving in fast.

We just took out the other two, Collins thought. *No problem, right?*

Except then they hadn't had Fai and Peter and the key to worry about. And if these two had managed to get past Lowell?

Collins raised his own rifle, but he wasn't sure he liked their odds.

55

SOMETIMES IT FELT like the whole world was falling apart, until Lowell remembered where he was: on Enceladus, which was a moon, so technically it was only the *moon* collapsing in on itself.

Close enough.

Fighting alongside the Tiān Zhuānjiā was really messing with his head. Only a couple of hours ago, Wu had been trying to peel off Lowell's helmet. Now they were all buddy-buddy?

He'd have stewed in his suspicions more if the ground wasn't literally crumbling under his feet. At one point, as he shoved through the greenery, the stone beneath him split open, and a creek of bubbling green goo rose to fill the cracks. He nearly put his foot right in it, but at the last second, Wu caught his arm and yanked him almost off of his feet. Lowell shuddered. "Thanks."

"Don't mention it," Wu said flatly, which was probably more of a sincere request than an expression of largesse.

The people who designed Enceladus might have been plants themselves, but the frondescence around them fared no better than the rest of the moon. Thick, gelatinous soup swallowed them from the roots upward, and when Lowell looked back over his shoulder, he saw the vibrant green plants turn black and wither even before they were fully submerged.

Great. So toxic soup is eroding the edges of the island, and we're running right into the middle. It's going to be fun figuring out how we escape.

Before he could plot an exit strategy, however, he needed to find Peter and the rest of the crew. Maybe it would be best for everyone if they got trapped here, leaving Goii and the key to sink into the glowing primordial swamp.

Muul had figured out a way around the difficult passage afforded by the trees. She had chosen to launch herself up above the canopy, leaping from the top of one tree to the next, leaving them behind. It was too bad that the borrowed alien suit didn't include some sort of springing enhancement, although judging by Muul's agile passage, her people didn't need it.

Other than the weird greenish glow cast by the spreading moat, it was hard to see. Lowell nearly twisted an ankle on a root, and instinctively reached back to keep Ming from making the same misstep.

"Thank you," she gasped.

He smirked. "Not a runner, I take it?"

Before she could respond, their mics popped, and Vasko's voice hollered, "Eat light!" A few bursts of laser fire illuminated the jungle.

Lowell broke into a sprint, but the aliens were already shouting, and it sounded like Muul had joined the fray. As they broke through the treeline, Muul dropped from the sky onto the shoulders of one of the enemies.

I hope it's Goii. The sooner that bastard goes down, the happier I'll be.

Vasko was still firing at relative random, and Lowell caught the butt of the rifle and aimed it toward the ceiling of the cavern. "Don't shoot us, you dolt! Careful where you aim that thing."

In the split second that Lowell turned on his back on the aliens, one of their guns went off. He couldn't see who was responsible; it might even have been Muul, given that she'd had to jerk back to avoid having her shoulder bitten by the shearing mandibles on her enemy's helmet. All he knew was that one moment, Vasko was going off like a Fourth of July firework, and the next, he was screaming. He pitched forward, letting go of the gun Lowell still held, and slapped his hands over the serrated gouge in the arm of his suit.

"Friggin' Tiān Zhuānjiā!" Collins hollered, lifting his own gun.

"No!" Lowell held up a hand. "They're with me—"

His friend bucked, howling as whatever was in the air of the cavern bubbled and foamed and overflowed between his fingers, sloughing off the flesh visible through the furrow in the metal exoskeleton.

"Hold him down," Ming said, jostling against Lowell's side.

Collins brandished his rifle. "Stay away from him!"

The aliens were out of his line of sight, Lowell had lost track of the action: all he could focus on was Vasko's suffering. In the months they'd served together, Vasko had been a pain in everyone's ass, but he'd never been one to complain about discomfort or physical pain. It had to be agonizing for him to sound like this.

"Collins?" he said, looking up at his old friend. "Shut up and cover us."

Seconds were precious; they would have been even without

the caustic atmosphere at the heart of the remote moon. Vasko could suffocate within moments in a compromised suit. Lowell didn't know what Ming had in mind, but there wasn't time to talk it out. He held Vasko as still as he could while the translator dug something out of her utility belt.

The object she produced didn't make sense to Lowell: it was black and bendy, like a scrap of fabric. She whipped it out flat, then shoved Vasko's hands aside and slapped it over the damaged area. In an instant, it molded to the contours of Vasko's suit.

"What is that?" asked Collins, glancing down from his rifle sight.

"Suit patch." Ming pressed down the edges of the little square with her fingertips. "They're in beta, so we'll have to see how it works."

Lowell watched in wonder as the little patch adhered to Vasko's suit so that the edges molded almost perfectly with the exoskeleton.

"Too bad we don't have those," Collins muttered. "How come your guys get all the toys?"

"They were deemed a low priority by our government," Ming admitted. "Most suit punctures can't be repaired in time to make a difference."

"Seems like this one's working." Vasko's voice was weak, but at least he was still alive and kicking. "What happened to the aliens? And Peter?"

And General Wu, Lowell wondered as he looked around. For the moment, it was just the five of them—unless, of course, the general had opted to go invisible for the time being, but was still hovering around somewhere.

Vasko was breathing hard, but he looked from the suit patch, then up to Ming. "Thanks. It hurts like hell, but wounded is better than dead, am I right?"

Lowell would have liked a minute to plan and regroup, but then Peter's voice echoed over the mic. "No! Let go! Get off me, you—" He said something in Muul's language, which was a fairly colorful insult, judging by his intonation.

"Shit." Lowell stood up abruptly. Fai was still slumped in the corner, and Vasko wasn't going to be able to shoot for shit. He turned to Collins and made a series of sharp hand gestures. *Get them out of here if you can. We'll meet you at the tunnel.* If the aliens could hear them, he didn't want them to know who was coming, or how to cut off the stragglers.

Ming frowned, and Lowell pointed to Collins. "Cover him. He's gonna have his hands full."

Ming nodded reluctantly.

Collins signed, *I don't like that my hands are going to be tied while the Tiān Zhuānjiā girl is armed.*

"You know what you're going to like a hell of a lot less?" Lowell asked as he turned his back on the little crew. "Drowning in goo because we spent too long arguing about what to do next."

56

FOR MOST OF the time that they'd tracked the key, Goii had needed equipment to tell him where it was at any given moment. That was no longer the case. Ever since the smaller and bonier of the humans had absorbed the Heart into the mechanism, he could feel its proximity in the depths of his chest cavity, tugging him inexorably closer along some unseen meridian.

The key is mine, he thought. Ever since the Council had dispatched his ship to retrieve it, Goii had known that the Enceladus Key was his destiny. Now it was here, fully charged, only leglengths away.

Never mind that the moon was disintegrating around them. He had every advantage: the humans were slow, incompetent, and ignorant. As the man ran away on his thick, stubby primate legs, Goii sprang. The other humans were injured, and Muul had her hands full.

His time had come.

At first, the human got lucky; a crevasse opened up right in

Goii's path, releasing a gout of steam and a geyser of that thick green ooze. He had to change course, and the little man gained a handful of paces, but it wasn't enough. The humans' shrieking chatter echoed through his ears, which was annoying in and of itself, but it kept his quarry distracted.

He was almost on top of his prey—by the First Spawning, it would be *glorious* to bite against his spine and take him out of the equation for good—but he was intercepted mid-flight by Muul, who struck him with such force that she carried him away above the treetops.

"Get off me, traitor!" Goii howled. He pinned her to the ground and drove a fist into her side, knocking the breath out of her. He could have killed her for interfering. No... he wanted to see her suffer.

But he wanted the key more.

He thrust her toward the geyser and kept moving, unwilling to waste precious seconds that would allow the human to escape his line of sight. In two more springs, he was upon him. The human chattered indignantly as he fell and lashed out at Goii, clearly trying to use his helmet's mandibles as a self-defense. His fighting style would have been awkward at best, but he kept both hands to his chest, clinging to the object held between them.

Goii didn't bother trying to grab it from him. Instead, he used the sticky pads of his gloved fingers to grab Peter's shoulder, and the other hand to grab his head, forcing the two apart until the weak seam at his throat was revealed.

Just as he was about to strike, the human lifted his arm above his head, hoisted the key on high, and threw it away from them with all of his strength.

Goii didn't hesitate. If he took his eye off of the key for even a moment, it might tumble into one of the burgeoning cracks in the island floor. He released the flailing human and dove after it, snatching up the bright silver sphere before it disappeared from view.

The humans were yelling, Muul was cursing him out, and the rest of his landing crew was dead, but that didn't matter. In the ghastly light thrown by the spreading moat, Goii held the stellar key high above his head in triumph. It had all been worth it.

Let the humans die in this miserable place: Goii had what he came for. The High Council would finally take him seriously. He sprang off in the direction he'd come, carrying the one thing that would make all of his dreams a reality.

The humans would pay—not just the ones he was leaving behind, but all their kith and kin. The Council would see to it soon enough. In fact, this whole pathetic galaxy would suffer in one way or another. It was only a matter of time.

57

PETER ROLLED ONTO HIS SIDE, trying to get to his feet. He had the distinct feeling that he was going to be sick in his helmet.

I can't believe I let him have it. When he'd thrown the key, he'd been aiming for one of the cracks in the floor so that even if he died, Goii couldn't get his sticky fingers on it; but Peter's aim had always been terrible, even when he wasn't being manhandled by a murderous frog-man. In his younger days, he'd actually been kicked off the softball team at home. That had rankled, but such a small failure was nothing compared to how it felt knowing that he'd handed over one of the most powerful objects in the universe to someone who wanted to eradicate his entire species.

And not just us, either. He wants to eliminate everything on Earth. The plethora of species on his home planet might not be as unique as he'd previously assumed, but Peter had spent a good chunk of his life conscious of his environmental impact, and now he'd inadvertently handed off a galaxy-destroying weapon to an alien race, for what? Sure, he was still alive, but not for long. Even if he'd managed to save his own life in the process, the cost was much too high.

The nearby bushes shook, and Lowell came bursting through the greenery, rifle in hand.

"Peter? What happened?"

"He's gone," Peter said. He was still on his knee; Lowell offered him a hand and dragged him to his feet. "Goii has the key. It's my fault, I shouldn't have let him take it..."

Lowell shook his head. "Save the pity party for later, Chang. He's not out of here yet. Where's Muul?"

"Here," she said, and came limping over, one hand held to her side. "He broke a few ribs, but I can feel them healing already." She looked down at Peter with unreadable eyes. "Which way did he go?"

Peter pointed back toward the tunnel through which they'd entered the huge chamber. As he did so, he realized that the island had mostly given way by now. What was left of it floated like rocky outcroppings among a sea of liquid death.

"Two birds, one stone," Lowell told him. "If we're going to make it out of here, we'll need to head that way ourselves. Are you two in any shape to run?"

Muul made an indelicate sound. "Are we in any shape to *stay?*"

Lowell bared all of his teeth in a feral smile. "Fair enough."

Peter was used to running on even ground, but even the most rocky terrain he'd encountered on Earth was nowhere near as treacherous as this. Every few paces, the ground gave way, and he had to pinwheel his arms and throw his balance off to keep from toppling into the bubbling soup.

"How are you moving so fast?" he asked Lowell, who had widened the distance between them as they went.

"Reminds me of basic training," Lowell told him. "You wouldn't believe the crazy stuff they'd made us do. Never thought it would come in handy; guess I owe my old sergeant an apology for all the shit I gave him back in the day."

The rocky outcroppings were few and far between. Peter wasn't sure if the moat was rising, or the island was sinking, or some combination of the two, but either way, keeping himself upright was nearly impossible.

Peter stumbled again, and Muul appeared at his side. "You're a mess, human. How come your species is so bad at running? For an apex predator on your world, I'd have thought you'd be faster. Lowell! Catch."

"What are you— *noooo!*" Peter wailed as she lifted him by the back of the suit and tossed him toward the spit of rock where the Space Corpsman stood. Lowell caught him by the shoulder and steadied him. Muul sprang ahead to the next islet, then turned to face them.

"Never do that again," Peter said.

"Sorry," Lowell said cheerfully, "but that's the plan." A moment later, he hauled on the back of Peter's suit, lifting him clean off his feet, and flung him toward Muul. He wasn't as strong as his alien counterpart, and Peter almost didn't make it, but Muul caught his arm and pulled him to safety.

Peter panted and wished that he could wipe the trickle of sweat from his brow. "I object to this plan. Strenuously."

"Too bad," Muul told him. "I've seen what happens when you try to jump on your own." With that, she hurled him toward Lowell's new position.

Being tossed about like a disgruntled football wasn't Peter's idea of a good time, but the memory of catching his boot on a stretch of rock as he'd done when they crossed the chasm was enough to keep him quiet.

The tunnel was in sight now, above the cliff that they'd leapt down from, but there was no island left. It was a long jump; Muul would probably make it, but Peter wasn't sure that Lowell could.

But the last spit of rock they stood on was slowly sinking; they didn't have a lot of time to stand around and argue about what to do next.

"Muul?" Lowell asked. "Can you carry him?"

Muul sank to one knee, and Lowell hoisted Peter onto her back.

"Hold on," she told him. "I'm going to need both hands."

Peter clung to her like a limpet, wrapping his legs around her waist and clasping his hands in front of her neck. The force of her takeoff left him breathless, and for a moment they were suspended in the air, sailing high above the moat. When they landed, the impact was enough to rattle Peter's teeth, even in the low gravity.

"Peter?" Collins hurried over to them. Fai lay on the floor, while Vasko and the Tiān Zhuānjiā translator crouched by the mouth of the tunnel. "Are you two okay?"

"Did Goii come through here?" Peter asked. At Collins' blank look, he pointed to Muul. "The other alien. He has the key…"

Collins swore. "Haven't seen him."

"That's weird." Peter frowned. "I'm sure he was headed this way."

"Yeah," Lowell said from below. "He was."

They all turned to look; Lowell's spur of rock was sinking, but his back was toward them now. He was watching as the tall, loping figure of Goii leapt toward him from rock to rock to rock. The alien captain was closing in on Lowell, who brought his weapon to bear.

Collins aimed his rifle at the alien, but Goii was still out of range. "Get up here, Lowell!"

"Not sure I'm gonna make it," Lowell said flatly.

"You're going to try," Peter hollered. "*Now*, Lowell!"

Lowell whirled and pushed off from the stone just before Goii reached him and sailed out over the alluvium, legs spread and arms flailing, as if he hoped that the movement would help him build momentum.

He's not going to make it, Peter thought dismally.

Goii was only a few paces behind him, the key clutched in one hand, glinting in the light of the eldritch ooze as he held it aloft.

Collins hesitated. "What's your call, Chang?" he asked. "Do I risk losing the key?"

Peter wasn't sure what would happen if the key was destroyed now, or if the primordial soup below even *could* destroy it. Would that be enough to detonate the Heart and destroy the galaxy? Or would it only kill them?

Most likely, they were dying today, one way or the other. At least this way they wouldn't give Goii the choice to do something even worse.

"Shoot him," Peter said firmly. "End it, even if it kills us."

Lowell collided chest-first with the cliff face, and barely managed to keep from falling. Even up here, the stone was crumbling away, as if the very force that had held Enceladus together was eroding altogether. Peter and Muul knelt down to help Lowell as Collins took aim.

Peter wasn't looking at first, so he didn't see what was happening until Lowell was safely lifted into the ledge. Only then did he happen to glance up and notice an odd flash of movement on the periphery of his vision. One of the stones behind Goii shifted, almost as if something had moved it on purpose. The next stone moved a moment later.

Goii crouched on the stone Lowell had just vacated, clearly prepared to leap; but before he got the chance, he jerked backward.

"*How dare you!*" he whistled.

Collins frowned into his scope. "What...?"

Goii struggled against an unseen force that seemed to be tugging at the hand that held the key. With a snarl, the alien whipped his head to the side. He didn't appear to touch anything, but the mandibles of his helmet closed on a solid object, and scarlet blood dribbled from nowhere.

He Ming was at Peter's side in an instant. "General Wu!" she cried.

Goii writhed, but the key was wrenched from his fingers. It launched into the air. A split-second later, Goii tumbled forward into the bubbling ooze. He sank quickly, along with what appeared to be the outline of a man in a spacesuit; but Peter blinked, and they both disappeared in a cloud of steam.

The stellar key, bright and untarnished, sailed through the air toward them. Without thinking, Peter lurched forward, hands outstretched.

"Careful!" Lowell barked.

This time, when Peter dug his heels against the edge of the cliff, it was on purpose. With the suction from the boots, he was able to lean out farther than he could have otherwise and catch the sphere with his fingertips.

"I can't let you out of my sight for a second," Lowell scolded, pulling him back toward safety, such as it was on the dying moon.

Peter didn't argue. He held the sphere to his chest and took a steadying breath. Goii was gone, and the key was back in his hands, right where it belonged.

58

THE ALIENS WEREN'T TAKING the bait. When Helena Moore had offered herself up as a sacrifice, she'd imagined that her final moments would end in a blaze of glory as she sailed into the heart of the alien ship.

Instead, the bastards were ignoring her.

She adjusted the headpiece she wore. There had been no time to scrounge up a full suit, but given that she wasn't planning to make it out of this in one piece, she wasn't losing sleep over it. "Tuhin, Bhatt, tell your people to hold their fire. They're wasting their burrs; the hull of the ship is completely intact, and they aren't opening for us. We need a new tactic."

"Any ideas?" asked Chandran Bhatt's voice.

"I've got one!" Grady said merrily. "Shoot 'em up, pew-pew! The hull's got to give eventually."

"We can't afford to run them down. They're closing in on Sanz." Helena drummed her fingers on the dash of their small, borrowed Tiān Zhuānjiā ship.

The line went silent for a while, although Grady was still merrily firing away at the UFO. At least they weren't going to run out of ammo, so Helena left him to it.

"I hate to say this." Sanz's soft voice filtered through the speaker. "But maybe you should withdraw. With the cloaking device on your ship, you might be able to get away in one piece."

"Stow it," Helena said firmly. "I don't want to hear that kind of defeatist talk, Captain."

"It's not defeatist," Sanz said, "it's practical. Otherwise we're just throwing more lives away. If you live to fight another day, maybe you'll have a chance to figure out another strategy."

Helena's hand clenched on the dash. "Captain..."

Helena was well aware that Larry Munroe had been a terrible leader and a terrible person, but it still bothered her that she hadn't been able to get back to him. She was fully capable of working with people she neither liked nor trusted; that was part and parcel of her military training. Leaving an ally to die, when there was even the slightest chance she could help?

"Go back to your ship, Hellcat," Sanz told her. "That's an order. Report back to those dillweeds in Washington and see if they can figure out some sort of defense. We made a solid go of it. Withdraw while they're busy destroying us and get the hell out of here."

Sure enough, her ship was limping along, still suffering from the engine damage it had sustained while they were buying time.

Helena swallowed hard. "As you say, Captain. Bhatt, pull back. You heard her."

"Aw, are we running away from a fight?" Grady asked.

Helena brought the ship around. "I'm afraid we are." She

watched on their rear screens as the UFO approached Sanz's ship and began to swing sideways so that it could take aim.

"We could try now," she murmured.

"And get us all killed?" Sanz sighed. "I think not. We need someone to report back. My order stands."

Helena clenched her hand and pounded her fist against her thigh. She wasn't one to run away from a fight, but Sanz was looking at the bigger picture.

"Hellcat?" Acosta's voice cut into her thoughts. "I have an incoming message. It looks like it's coming in from Enceladus. One of the landing party must have sent it out."

"Play it back," Helena said. Her eyes were fixed on Sanz's ship. The crew deserved a witness to their final moments. Turning her back was bad enough, but averting her eyes? That was the coward's way out.

Acosta broadcast the message; it was in Mandarin, in a woman's voice. The speaker's nerves were palpable—this wasn't one of those robotic drone-generated voices, but a real person.

"If anyone's still alive out there," she said, *"you should know that the aliens don't react well to sonic scramblers or other auditory weapons."*

Helena's eyes widened.

"I can ask one of the engineers to translate it," Acosta began.

Helena didn't need a translator. She'd worked in conjunction with a Tiān Zhuānjiā team a few years back, and she'd brushed up on her Mandarin so that she could make sure that they weren't plotting behind her back.

"Don't bother. Acosta, you know the tech—do sonic cannons work outside of an atmosphere?"

"Not well," he replied.

"Explain," she barked. "Give me the dummy version. *Fast.*"

"Technically, the sound can travel along the wave particles emitted by the cannon, although the percussive blast on impact would be reduced. In other words, it would still sound like ten billion nails on a chalkboard and reduce your innards to chutney, but it wouldn't be enough to damage the hull..."

Good enough, Helena reasoned.

The UFO had opened the hatch at its base. Any moment, that beam of light would emerge, and Sanz and her crew would be atomized. That hatch was the only way past the ship's hull, though. The aliens might be preparing to take a shot at the Space Corps ship, but they were also opening themselves up for return fire.

"Sanz," she barked, "fire the sonic cannons. Now!"

59

JUAA SMILED TO HIMSELF. The smaller human ships were retreating into the darkness, and the larger one was almost within range.

"Track the little ones," he told Piin. "I suspect they have another large ship. Probably a cloaking device, too. I have to give the primates credit, that's rather clever of them."

"Yes, Captain," Piin said.

"Flee, are we ready?"

The engineer piped up. "We're coming into position now, Captain. We'll fire on your command."

"Perfect." Juaa heightened his focus. "Firing in three... two..."

It started as a ripple, a building bass boom that reverberated through the ship, rattling Juaa to his core. It built gradually toward a crescendo, and throughout the ship, his crew began to scream in pain. Through the gifts of the ancestor plant, their suffering was Juaa's suffering. He had to peel his fingers and toes away from the control orb, and stumbled back into the moss.

Crying out, he pressed his hands to his head in a vain attempt to block out the sound. It wasn't just noise: the blast was a bone-deep vibration that burned against his skin and shredded his organs to jelly, but the worst part—far more oppressive than the physical pain—was the way it seemed to worm into his auditory canals right into his brain, until it jumbled his thoughts as thoroughly as his soft tissue.

After an untold length of time, stretched toward infinity by the totality of his anguish, Juaa collapsed against the floor of the captain's quarters and sank into merciful oblivion.

SANZ SAT BACK in her chair, watching agog as the UFO crumpled before their very eyes. Anyone left inside would be crushed by the force of its collapse. "Look at that," she breathed. "Nice work, Hellcat."

"You can thank the Tiān Zhuānjiā for saving our bacon," Hellcat said. "Never thought I'd be saying that, but today's been one damn thing after another. Guess there's no point in being surprised by anything, is there?"

The fleet of Cell ships swarmed the damaged UFO, aiding in its gradual collapse by firing burrs into the damaged hull. "I've never worked with the Tiān Zhuānjiā before," she admitted. "Nor the Cell, for that matter. Operation Cascade? They should have called it Operation Avalanche. We're either going to be buried under everything that's happened, or we're going to rise to the surface."

"I prefer the latter," Hellcat said.

"Should we rendezvous and develop a strategy for what to do

next?" *And message those bastards in Washington to tell them where they can stuff their orders.*

"You're going to need some repairs to your engines, at the very least," said Acosta. "Good thing that we happen to have some Chinese engineers on board."

"We could use the help," Boswell said.

The Cell fleet headed back toward the Tiān Zhuānjiā transport ship, their work complete. This series of questionable alliances would take some getting used to, but if it kept them alive out here, then they'd learn to adjust. This was no ordinary battlefield, and as today had shown, they couldn't always rely on their commanders to protect them. They would have to look out for one another.

Speaking of which…

"Contact Collins and Vasko," she told Boswell. "We'll rendezvous with them, too. See if they found the other landing party—"

Boswell's face went grey, and he tipped his head toward the window. "Ma'am? I don't think we'll get a chance."

What now? Sanz thought wearily. Wasn't *one* alien spaceship enough for the day? If that damn ship had suddenly figured out how to reinflate after taking so much damage…

But Boswell wasn't looking at the UFO, which was still a wreck of twisted metal floating through space. He was pointing at Enceladus, floating between them and the hazy brown bulk of Saturn beyond.

She and her crew had only narrowly escaped being reduced to their atomic components.

The frozen moon wasn't as lucky.

60

LOWELL SCRAMBLED TO HIS FEET, looking back in wonder at the spot where General Wu and Captain Goii had disappeared.

"General." Ming was trembling, and she looked like she was thinking about pitching herself over the ledge after him.

There was no time to stand around; a crack had appeared in the cavern's ceiling, and the moss around them was withering and turning black. Fai wasn't moving, and Vasko was clearly struggling to stay upright.

"We need to move," Lowell said. "Collins, can you carry the doctor?"

Collins slung his rifle over his shoulder and bent to pick up Fai. Lowell wasn't even certain that the man was still alive, but there was no way he was going to leave the man behind, not when Peter was standing right there. Lowell hurried over to Vasko and propped the other man up.

"Let's go," he said.

Peter followed Collins, and Muul stayed with him. The translator, however, remained rooted to the spot.

"Come on, Miss He," Lowell said gently.

He Ming sucked in a breath and turned her back on the cavern, stumbling after them.

"I don't suppose you have a working ship?" Lowell asked Vasko.

"Yeah." The injured soldier snorted. "Except we're so damn clever that we left it all the way on the surface… but don't worry, we can fire up the engines, assuming we make it that far!" He gave Lowell a falsely cheerful thumbs-up.

"Our ship is in the tunnels," Ming said in a strained voice.

Collins glanced over his shoulder. "Yeah, except that if we try to go back in that, Captain Sanz will shoot us on sight."

Ming scoffed. "Surely you realize that we can't go back there?"

"Why not?" Collins retorted. "Because of whatever agreement your general made with Lowell?"

"He died to make sure we had the key," Lowell said. "He was on our side at the end."

Collins made a skeptical noise.

It was Muul who answered the soldier's question. "We can't go back to your people, or mine, or hers… we can't take the key to anyone who would want to use it. Do you trust your government with that sort of power?"

This time, Collins didn't answer at all.

Lowell was glad that he couldn't hear whatever was happening behind them. Whether the lower tunnels were gradually flooding with caustic sludge, or simply collapsing into rubble, Lowell was pretty sure that the moon wasn't going to fare particularly well this time around.

Peter kept glancing up at the carvings as they ran and sighing heavily.

"Getting heartsick about all the knowledge you're missing out on?" Lowell asked.

"Only a little," Peter lied.

Vasko stumbled, and Lowell almost went down with him.

"Keep up," Muul called back. She was the farthest ahead now, in spite of whatever injuries she'd sustained to her ribs.

Vasko tried to take another step, but Lowell could feel him going down. "On your feet, soldier," he snapped.

Vasko shook his head, cradling his wounded arm against his stomach. He was sweaty and pale. "Sorry, Lowell. Maybe you should leave me."

With a tremendous force of effort, Lowell swept Vasko off his feet and kept moving.

"Aw," Vasko said weakly, "that's sweet. I've always wanted to be princess-carried."

"Christ, what have you been eating? You weigh a ton," Lowell complained.

"You must be getting weak in your old age." Vasko's head rolled back, and his eyes closed. "I'm fit as a fiddle... and the gravity's... weaker here..."

"Stick with me," Lowell said. "If you chased me down all the way out here only to die on me, I'm going to be angrier than you can imagine."

Vasko smiled, but he couldn't seem to muster the energy for another round of backtalk. That, more than anything, worried Lowell.

After what felt like an eternity, they reached the Grand

Chamber. Peter tripped over something and looked around in confusion. "What was that?"

"The corpse of one of our soldiers," Ming said. "The one you killed."

"Oh." Peter sounded sheepish. "Right."

A little ways onward, they passed the body of a one-handed Russian officer. Vasko feebly lifted one hand to flip the dead man the bird.

Lowell knew the way from here. The last time he'd encountered the rough-hewn staircase into the tunnels, they'd been underwater. Now, he had to shuffle sideways as he dismounted them, keeping his back to the wall so that he could maneuver Vasko through without smacking his head against the side of the tunnel.

"You're more trouble than you're worth," he grunted, hoping to keep Vasko cognizant of his surroundings.

"Nah." Vasko licked his lips and smiled. His veins were visible through his pale skin. "I'm too pretty to leave behind."

There was another corpse outside the Tiān Zhuānjiā ship, a Russian conscript this time. Ming didn't even look down at him as she stepped into the little vessel.

Collins hefted Fai into the cockpit, looking around. "You think that this thing will break atmo with all of us onboard?"

"There were five of us in here before," Ming informed him.

"And seven of us now." Collins shook his head. "I don't think we can make it."

Ming turned to glare at him. "Then what do you suggest?"

"Take us up to our ship," Collins said. "That way we don't have to trust in faulty Tiān Zhuānjiā engineering."

Ming scowled, but Lowell propped Vasko against the seat. "I

know you two hate each other, and I get it, but we're running on borrowed time. Miss He, do you think we can make it out of atmo in this thing? General Wu died to protect the key, and if we don't make it off this rock, then he did it in vain."

Ming pursed her lips and turned away. "We can make it. Besides, we have a cloaking device on this ship. If the aliens are waiting for us up there—or anyone, for that matter—we'll be better off if we can stay hidden."

Lowell nodded, then turned to Collins as Ming fired up the engines. "She has a point."

Collins narrowed his eyes. He obviously didn't trust Ming, and he seemed reluctant to take Lowell's advice and set their old animosity aside. One glance out the window revealed that their time was running out.

"I don't like it," he conceded, "but we have to get out of here. I'll trust her."

"Not like you have a lot of choice," Ming muttered.

The door sealed behind them, and Ming lifted off, rocketing them forward so fast that Lowell's neck popped.

"You sure you know what you're doing?" Collins asked.

"Are you concerned about *turbulence?*" Ming taunted. They sailed out over the ravine, then banked sharply upwards.

When Lowell and Peter had left the icy ocean after the Anomaly was activated, they'd almost failed to make it off-world. Lowell had no intention of repeating the incident. They were leaving Enceladus behind—for good this time.

At the back of the craft, Peter curled into a ball; Muul held onto the side of the ship with her sticky gloves, visibly startled by the g-forces associated with their departure; Fai and Vasko were both dead to the world.

In spite of all that, when they finally broke atmo, Lowell sighed with relief. They might have simply exchanged one set of problems for another, but problems meant that they were still alive. Once again, he and Peter had scraped by, and this time they'd actually come out on top.

"I told you we could make it," Ming said smugly.

"Yeah, yeah," Collins grumbled. "Lucky break."

Behind them, Enceladus vanished in a puff of dust. There was nothing but a nebula of loose particles left in its wake, floating through space in a vaguely orb-shaped cloud. It quickly dissipated, becoming one with the loess and ice that formed the rest of Saturn's rings.

In the span of only a few breaths, it was as if Enceladus had never existed at all.

61

PETER'S GRIP on the stellar key relaxed slightly. The immediate danger had faded, but he couldn't quite bring himself to relax. Now that he didn't have to worry about anyone snatching the key away from him in the immediate future, he could focus on his father.

"Is the atmosphere stable?" he asked.

In answer, Ming removed her helmet and set it aside. Peter followed suit, and Lowell did the same, then turned to Vasko. The injured man had gone completely limp.

Once Fai's helmet was removed, Peter laid his fingers on his father's throat, checking for a pulse. To Peter's immense relief, his heart was still being, albeit very slowly.

"Oh, *God*." Lowell had wrestled part of Vasko's damaged suit off to reveal a swath of pustules and open sores all along the man's arm. "It stinks. You hear me, Vasko? You smell like a raw steak that got left in the fridge for a month."

Vasko didn't move.

"Let me help." Muul moved closer to inspect the wound. After prodding it with her fingers, she spat on it.

"Hey!" Lowell wrinkled his nose. "What are you doing? Stop that."

Muul tilted her head to one side. "My secondary glottal sac contains an antihistamine. I'm not certain that it will help with the inflammation, but at the very least, it will dull the pain when he wakes up."

"That's gross," Lowell muttered.

Muul shrugged. "Perhaps. But it helped you."

"Helped me..." Realization dawned on Lowell's face. "Did you spit on me after we escaped your ship? When I was poisoned?"

"You might have recovered on your own, but I couldn't be sure how your body would respond otherwise."

Lowell turned to glare at Peter. "You knew about this?"

Peter shrugged.

"I hate both of you."

In spite of Lowell's protests, the pustules on Vasko's arm were already looking better.

"So where do we go?" Collins asked. "If we can't go back to Earth, or get help from anyone we know, what options does that leave?"

"There's an abandoned outpost on Titan," Ming said. "One of ours." She swiveled around in the pilot's seat to face them. Her eyes were puffy and red-rimmed, but her jaw was set firmly. "There should be medical supplies and equipment, and as far as I know, the equipment still works. There should be food and water, too."

"Food." Lowell's expression turned dreamy. "Not bogbugs."

"I can't remember the last time I ate," Collins said.

Peter dug through his pack and produced one of the rations Muul had packed for them. "Here. We can split what we have until we get to Titan. How far do we have to go?"

"It's less than a day's journey." Ming glanced down at her controls. "Fourteen hours and fifty-six minutes, to be exact."

"And this place is deserted?" Collins asked. "We're not going to be attacked by Tiān Zhuānjiǎ when we arrive?"

Ming shot him an exasperated look. "If you don't trust me, take me prisoner, and *you* can decide where to go."

Collins used his teeth to open the wrapper of the rations Peter had tossed him, and ignored her.

"This isn't over." Muul pulled her legs toward her chest and stared out into the night. "Goii said that the Council was on their way. Even if your people believe that the key was destroyed along with Enceladus, mine won't stop looking. They'll be able to track it; they can detect the material from light years away, and now that it's charged, it will cause notable readings, even on your scans. We'll have to come up with a tactical strategy for how to deal with anyone who comes after us."

"When we get to Titan," Lowell said. He closed his eyes and leaned back. "I'm exhausted, and we don't know what resources we'll find there. We need to rest. Regroup. Figure out our options. Something tells me that the key doesn't have an off-switch, but we don't even know how it works."

He had a point, and at any rate, Peter was exhausted in body and soul. He held onto the key with one hand, and his father with the other.

Whoever is struck by the Heart will be altered. Peter didn't know what that meant. He didn't know what *any* of it meant. But as they sailed through the darkness, illuminated only by the looming gas giant and the distant stars, he promised himself that he'd do whatever it took to find out.

62

VICE-PRESIDENT PEREZ MASSAGED his temples as he looked around the otherwise empty room. Sanz's report had come in only an hour before. It had been crisp but vague: apparently the UFO had been destroyed, but she didn't say how. Everyone else had left: dismissed by Perez to collapse face-first into their beds, he assumed, but a combination of a lingering caffeine high and indistinct suspicion left Perez on edge.

We should have been prepared for this. He drummed his fingers on the tabletop and closed his eyes, trying to organize the mess of scattered thoughts tumbling through his head. He needed a shower and a long sleep, but even with that, something was niggling at the edges of his consciousness.

How had Kelley known about the aliens?

He lurched to his feet and began to pace. That information was top-secret. Only a select few knew about the government's involvement with extraterrestrials—it had been over a century since their last direct contact, and there were countless heads of state that didn't know the truth. Hell, even Perez's knowledge was limited. Kelley didn't have the clearances.

He must have come by the information another way.

"Marc?" The President's voice came through the doorway, and Perez spun to face her.

"Madame President," he said. "What are you doing here? It's..." He checked the time, then laughed. "Three in the afternoon. Sorry, I haven't slept in—" Perez trailed off, then began counting the hours out on his fingers, and immediately confused himself. "Some time," he said at last.

President Jackson stepped through the door. "We need to talk, Marc."

Perez examined her more closely; she was dressed in a navy-blue suit and crisp white shirt, with every hair in perfect place as if she was preparing for some sort of public appearance, but her brown eyes were haunted. She stepped a little further into the room, revealing the figure of Press Secretary Kelley behind her. Perez's shoulders immediately tensed.

"*You*," he grumbled. "I thought you'd gone."

"I know you don't like me," Kelley said blithely, because even in this moment he had to prove that he knew everything. He really was the worst. "But even so, we have to work together. I know a few things that you're going to want to hear."

Perez resisted the urge to roll his eyes.

"He has information that wasn't available even to me," Jackson said softly. She reached for one of the empty chairs and sank heavily into it, looking even more exhausted than Perez felt.

"Is that so?" Perez eyed his colleague suspiciously. "And how did you come by it?"

Kelley smiled smugly and perched in the chair at the head of the long table. He clasped his hands in front of him. He could be giving a school report.

"I know that you're not one for reading, Mr. Perez, but fortunately, you have me to fill that void. I've done a fair bit of digging—*ha!* So to speak. Pardon the pun." His eyes twinkled. "I've unearthed a bit of lore that you might want to look over. Don't worry, I've translated it—rather painstakingly I might add. I didn't want to risk revealing state secrets to some unfortunate academic whose disappearance would have to be swept under the rug later." He rifled through his briefcase and produced a file, which he slid down the table to where Perez sat.

Perez waited a beat before opening the cover of the file and examining its contents. When he read the first line, he groaned. "Naram-Sin? The Akkadian Empire? Come on, this is ancient history. These were the classes I slept through at Harvard." Perez shot an exasperated look at President Jackson. He knew how she felt about Kelley.

This time, however, she was rubbing her palms together as she stared down at her hands, lost in thought. She was taking Kelley seriously.

"I understand that a busy man such as yourself might have a hard time focusing on anything so *tedious*." Kelley beamed. "But that's why I'm here: to summarize. To squeeze big concepts into tiny words for your edification."

"*Kelley.*" Jackson sighed. "Would you please get on with it?"

Kelley sat forward. "Very well, ma'am. You're aware, I suppose, that Lt. Larry Munroe had decided to focus his search for the Enceladus Tablet in the ancient city Ur-An because of a tip contained in the files from Area 51?"

"Yes." Perez's eyebrows pinched together. "And before you get smart with me, I read those files."

"But did you read the ancient texts they refer to?" Kelley waggled his finger at the file lying open on the table. "Because there's more to the story, Perez. The tablet didn't just happen to end up in a random city, and the orb Munroe found wasn't tossed onto Mars by accident. Moreover, it's not the only one of its kind."

Perez frowned down at the file. "Meaning?"

Kelley's smile widened to the point of being practically grotesque. "Have you been watching the news lately, Mr. Perez? Perhaps you'd better flip to the next page."

Perez's pounding headache had pushed him toward the edge of violence. *How do I get my hands on one of those alien vaporizer doohickeys?* He'd love to reduce Kelley to his base elements.

President Jackson was eyeing him intently, however, so Perez played nice and flipped the page. It was a printout of a marine research website, featuring a photograph of the Anomaly.

"What?" He squinted down at the picture. "How did they get their hands on this? Did someone send it out before the research station was destroyed, or..." He squinted down at the words. "Hang on. *Scientist Discovers Enchanting Mineral Deposit in Mariana Trench?*" He hadn't brought his reading glasses, and after so many hours awake, his vision was playing tricks on him. The smaller words were harder to make out, but eventually he managed. "*Captain Avery Mills, owner of the* Cadmium III *and independent deep-sea researcher, has released photos taken from his recent expedition...*" Perez blinked rapidly, wondering how this had slipped by them. "This is on Earth."

Kelley steeped his fingers. "Indeed."

Perez slumped forward. "So Earth could undergo what Enceladus just experienced."

He was too tired to deal with this right now. He couldn't think clearly, couldn't plan, could barely *move*. And now some wealthy entrepreneur was posting pictures of Earth's greatest weakness on the web? With *coordinates*?

"Do we know if the key that worked on Enceladus would work on Earth as well?" Perez asked.

"We do," Kelley said. "Or rather, *I* do. And the answer is no: there's one key per world. It's expressly stated in the ancient texts."

"So let me get this straight." Perez returned his attention to the photographs. "Not only could the key that was lost in Operation Cascade be used to wipe out the galaxy, but there's another key floating around that could be used on Earth?"

Kelley nodded. "Now you're up to speed."

Perez and Jackson stared at each other for a long moment. He wasn't entirely sure what she was thinking, but he had a guess.

Whoever held this key held, in essence, complete control over the fate of the world—and now the photos were out there where anyone on Earth could see them.

"Can we pull the plug on the site?" Perez asked. "Any chance of keeping this quiet?"

"Images have already been distributed across the web," Jackson said. "It's too late."

"Then I guess we'd better keep our fingers crossed that nobody has that damn key," Perez said.

EPILOGUE

AVERY MILLS SCROLLED through the photos of his recent discoveries once more. He had a glass of Scotch in one hand and smooth jazz playing through the feedback of his sound system. Sitting in the living room of his plush rented apartment in Osaka sometimes made him feel that his time underwater was a dream. He'd split his time between Osaka and London these last few years, but as much as he loved his lifestyle, it never quite felt real. When he was in the deeps? *That* was real. It was raw and rugged, and made him feel more connected to the world than in any mountain or forest, much less any city street.

Avery had encountered all sorts of things beneath the ocean, but the silvery mineral deposit held his attention like nothing else. It was unique. Out of place. It didn't *belong*. How had it gotten there, and what was its purpose? Avery loved a good mystery, and the mineral deposit provided a unique distraction from his general ennui.

He was still gazing thoughtfully at the photographs when the house-wide sound system stopped playing soothing music. "Mr. Mills, you have a phone call," said the polite, robotic voice he'd chosen for that of his personal secretary.

"Put them through," Avery said without looking up at the screen. This was a private line, so if someone was ringing him at this time of night, it was probably urgent, or at least interesting.

"You are now speaking to Mr. Avery Mills," the voice said. Whoever was on the other line would hear it, too. It was probably his mother; he'd tried to call her on her birthday, but she'd been in the air to Dubai when he'd reached out, and they hadn't connected since.

"Hello," he said cheerfully.

"Hello, Mr. Mills." The voice on the other line was certainly *not* his mum's. It was deep and smooth, and made the hair on the back of Avery's neck prickle in alarm. He didn't know that voice.

"Who is this? How did you get my number?" he asked, with a great deal less warmth than he had the first time.

"I do apologize. I know how important privacy can be. I'm afraid that the matter is somewhat urgent, however...you are the owner of the *Cadmium III*, aren't you? The one who made that astonishing discovery in the Trench?"

Avery was excruciatingly aware that the man hadn't yet identified himself, but a little flattery went a long way. Besides, a second mystery had fallen into his lap like manna from heaven. "Indeed I am."

"Splendid." The silky baritone featured a slight accent, one that Avery couldn't quite place. It was posh; judging by the sound alone, the owner of this voice wouldn't have been out of place at Oxford. Avery couldn't quite put his finger on it, but the man sounded *educated*. This fact alone made him relax his guard slightly.

"I'm so pleased that I was able to reach you," the stranger continued. "You see, I—like you—have an interest in Earth's mysteries. I would like to propose an exchange of knowledge. If I were to tell you what I know, would you be able to take me to the place you found?"

Avery's heart began to pound, and he sat up a little straighter. "Do you know what it is?"

"I know a great deal more than that," the voice said. "I belong to a... oh, pardon me, Mr. Mills. To call it a *brotherhood* sounds so arcane, very cloak-and-dagger. Suffice to say, I am one of a few individuals who values knowledge above all else. Does that make us sound like a cult? I assure you, this is not the case. We are people who have learned from the past, Mr. Mills, in an attempt to avoid the mistakes made by our ancestors."

The man was right: it all sounded a bit cultish, and Avery Mills was savvy enough to know that those who presented themselves as intellectuals were often after something else. Money, power, fame... the sorts of things that his family already had in spades.

But the object at the bottom of the ocean was still staring up at him from the darkening screen, and Avery had the same weightless, unmoored feeling that he often experienced in the private submarine.

"I'd like to know more," he said.

"Excellent," the voice purred. "We'll be in touch."

The line went dead, and the smooth jazz resumed. Avery sat in his silent apartment, staring out the floor-to-ceiling windows that overlooked the lights of the bustling city.

Other explorers looked to the stars, but Avery Mills had stumbled upon a real mystery, right here in the oceans, that his peers took for granted. He turned off the screen and went to the window, wondering where the call had come from, and what secrets would be revealed to him.

It might all be a hoax of some kind. Don't get too excited. Still, as he laid one hand against the cool glass, Avery couldn't help but smile.

He had stumbled into an adventure, all right, which suited him just fine. After all, wasn't that the only thing worth living for?

FIND OUT WHAT HAPPENS NEXT!

Click here to read
LINEAGE
(Saturn's Legacy Book 3)

GET FREE BOOKS!

Building a relationship with readers is my favorite thing about writing.

My regular newsletter, *The Reader Crew,* is the best way to stay up-to-date on new releases, special offers, and all kinds of cool stuff about science fiction past and present.

Just for joining the fun, I'll send you 3 free books.

Join The Reader Crew (it's free) today!

—Joshua James

ALSO BY JOSHUA JAMES

Lucky's Marines (Books 1-9)

Lucky's Mercs (Books 1-4)

The Lost Starship (Books 1-3)

Planet Hell

Gunn & Salvo (ongoing)

With Scott Bartlett:

Relentless Box Set: The Complete Fleet Ops Trilogy

With Sean D. King:

Honor in Exile (ongoing)

With Daniel Young:

Oblivion (Books 1-9)

Outcast Starship (Books 1-9)

Legacy of War (Books 1-3)

Heritage of War (ongoing)

Stars Dark (Books 1-8)

Copyright © 2022 by Joshua James

All rights reserved.

No part of this book may be reproduced in any form or by any electronic or mechanical means, including information storage and retrieval systems, without written permission from the author, except for the use of brief quotations in a book review.

Click here to read
LINEAGE
(Saturn's Legacy Book 3)

Printed in Great Britain
by Amazon